AFRICAN WRITERS SERIES

Money Galore

Money Galore

AMU DJOLETO

HEINEMANN

Heinemann is an imprint of Pearson Education Limited, a
company incorporated in England and Wales, having its registered
office at Edinburgh Gate, Harlow, Essex, CM20 2JE.
Registered company number: 872828

www.heinemann.co.uk

Heinemann is a registered trademark of Pearson Education Limited

ISBN 978 0 435 90161 5

Printed by Multivista Global Ltd.

12   11   10

16 15 14 13

To the Memory of my Father
the Reverend Frederick Augustus Badu Djoleto
1893–1969 – a Great Lover of Children

1

It was nine in the morning. The pupils of National Secondary School, Cape Coast, had had a break and were taking a fifteen-minute breakfast. The headmaster, Mr Benjy Baisi, tall, broad-shouldered and full of good looks, was chewing the end of a pencil. He had slapped a boy before this for chewing a pencil in the mathematics class. The boy had just paused from working out long additions and subtractions. He found them difficult. Mr Baisi was himself a gifted mathematician and, though now the headmaster, he still enjoyed teaching maths in the top class. Mr Baisi had a secret disrespect for boys who could not grapple with mathematics in the school, and was profoundly suspicious if those who never did well in the subject at school were reported to be doing well in life.

Mr Baisi happened to be doing additions and subtractions. This was caused by a letter which he had received from the Department of Welfare Services and Pedagogy. The last few sentences of the letter read: 'And I am directed to convey to you that no extra fees should be charged from pupils to offset any temporary deficit that may occur in the school budget as a result of this cut. It would be appreciated if headmasters would refrain from taking bank loans as this in the past has led to infringement of the Financial Rules and the Department has had to take disciplinary action against a few financial malefactors reported by the Auditor-General.' The letter ended: 'I have the honour to be, Sir, Your obedient Servant, M. K. Tawia.'

This both annoyed and amused Mr Baisi. Mr Tawia had been his senior at school and was now, in the civil service. He had always been snobbish, especially when he became Assistant Director of the Department of Welfare Services and Pedagogy. After instructing him not to raise school fees, he signed himself as an obedient servant. 'Servant to whom?' Mr Baisi asked as the letter hung limp between his fingers. 'Foolish!' he answered, and heaved a sigh.

Mr Baisi bit the pencil once again as he sat back in the headmaster's chair. He hated pencil-chewing. He read for the fourth time the letter cutting school grants. No reasons were given for issuing it and it came in the middle of the term. He looked at the additions and subtractions before him. The school budget was in trouble. He could not balance it. He had been working on it since 6.45 that morning. He continued working. After making cuts here and adjustments there, it became reasonably apparent by 9.55 that he would require around ten thousand cedis from somewhere to be able to feed the boys and pay the labourers and kitchen staff up to the end of the term. He was not very sure whether he could pay the full salaries of the bursar and typist during the school holidays.

He grew apprehensive. If the labourers did not get their pay, one of them in particular who was a school dropout might use it as an excuse to take wee (marijuana) and assault him on the school compound. If the kitchen staff were affected they might mess up the meals, and this could be used as an excuse by the pupils for a demonstration. As for the bursar, the mere possibility of a deficit might make him start tampering with the books, with the connivance of the typist who sometimes acted as the school cashier.

'Good Lord,' he said softly, 'the government hasn't got the money. They know there isn't any. And yet they want to please the public and show up headmasters. If they can't provide free education, let the damned parents pay for it. I've said this on several occasions but no one listens. They want me to be a Director of Public Debts Recovery before they'll lap up my ideas. And there's that supine press. You never talk sense until you become the Speaker of the National Parliament, or a Major-General or something. This school is not for the government. It's for the children. I've got to feed them, or they'll go home! Why weren't headmasters consulted or given enough notice? Lack of imagination? Bad administration? This is the trouble. The Department is full of stagnant minds from top to bottom. They don't even know the difference between policy and efficacy. There is neither a collective nor an individual work ethic; and ... oh ... hell!'

Baisi smiled thoughtfully and said to himself, 'Take Tawia. He's an ass. He's been like that since childhood. He confuses personal authority with management skill. He runs the Department like a secondary school. Silly. He's forgotten his maths! He posts official letters because someone asked him to write, before he thinks of what's in them. I've made this school. This school has got to make me. I won't let the civil servants ruin my career. I'm an honest, hard worker. Those first-year boys, good Lord, they look so handsome! They're bright, very bright. They came here well fed. They're supposed to live on thirty-five pesewas a day, and the bread for breakfast alone costs five pesewas. Their food is all starch and water. I've been trying to make it protein. Then this letter comes and ...' There was a sharp, careless, big knock on the door. It gave him a start. He literally jumped up and shouted, 'Come in!' As headmaster, he usually asked people to come in coolly and authoritatively, and never got up when they did.

His full length showed. He was five feet eleven, aged about forty-seven or forty-nine. There was no grey in his hair, which he wore bushy. He had a well-grown moustache; it almost completely hid his upper lip; otherwise he was cleanly-shaven. His eyes were large; the eyebrows curving, nice and shiny. He had a rich brown skin and a lot of hair on his arms and chest. A lean waist went with his broad shoulders, giving him a youthful, manly look. He wore a fashionable striped, open-neck, buttoned-down-collar, American-style shirt. His trousers were slightly bell-bottomed; he had bought them from Wilson and Waller, Southampton Row, London, to set his pupils thinking. He wore a broad belt. He knew he was being up to date and his boys would have nothing to complain about. He had a quiet modulated voice and would smile without parting his lips. 'Come in,' he said again; this time not so loudly.

It was the school bread contractor, Mr Anson Berko. Mr Berko looked prosperous. He was born in Kumasi, though his father came from Offinso. His mother was a dark, beautiful woman from Obo. Mr Berko had never finished elementary school, but he was extremely good at mental arithmetic, a talent which endeared him to Benjy Baisi. He was good at taking quick and firm decisions, especially where they affected his prosperity. Before he became a contractor, he had been happily married to a fair-coloured Cape Coast girl who couldn't finish secondary school because Anson was in a hurry and she needed his support. He was a lean man then. Now he was fat; his head was completely shaven, though the hair had grown for a week. He was of medium height, with round, somewhat small arms that were not used to manual work.

Anson Berko was wearing a cloth. He wore a pair of khaki shorts under it. His ample waist required no belt to support the shorts, which hung firmly just under an overlapping, copious stomach. He had fat, baggy cheeks, small eyes and ears and a well-shaped, pointed nose. His lips were thin and his teeth were so neatly set and white that one would think they were dentures. He had a persuasive voice and seemed always to be in a hurry. He spoke excellent Fante and interlaced it with English as the occasion demanded. His English phrases could sometimes be surprisingly apt.

He did not wait for Mr Benjy Baisi to open the door. After the one big knock and a little pause, he turned the knob and pushed in. 'Hello, Benjy, what's the trouble? You look worried. Is the matron still taking the food home?'

'No, no; no, no; not at all; not at all! I don't object if she takes a little meal home, you know. She's here with us the whole day. She has no way of preparing her own meal for her family. I don't worry about a little food for her kids' dinner. It's when she takes the yams and plantains home that I talk to her straight.'

'Yes, but you don't look too good today. What's the matter? I've come for payment for the January and February supplies. Mr Antonio says there's money.'

'Who told him?' Benjy asked rather irritably.

'Well, he is your bursar. I'll get my money anyway. I've come really to discuss a different matter – not very important.'

'What matter?'

'Business, if you like.'

'Which business?'

'It's the bread I supply.'

'What about it?'

'The loaves are too big for five pesewas each.'

'So?'

'So I've decided.'

'To?'

'To keep the size but reduce the weight.'

'But you've done that before. Wasn't it three years ago that I had flat tyres for one week running? Why provoke the boys again? Anson, I don't want any of your tricks. How much money do you really want to make in life?'

'As much as I can while the going is good.'

'So you make money and ruin my school, right?'

'Of course, I could make as much for you, if you're interested.'

'In what?'

'In making money.'

'But I don't need money.'

'True, nobody needs money.'

'Oh?'

'No. Money is only what you want to buy with it. It's not the paper or coin or the bank account. Now, Benjy, be serious. You come from Anomabo, don't you?'

'Yes.'

'And you work in Cape Coast here?'

'Yes.'

'How old are you?'

'What has my age got to do with a bread contractor?'

'Never mind! You're getting on towards fifty. The campaigns are going to start and I hear the new government will fix the retiring age at fifty-five.'

'So what?'

'How are you getting ready for it? You own no house. You've been having it good in a school bungalow. You don't even own a mattress, but you feel smug when you call me only a bread contractor. One day you'll sleep in a swish stone house in Anomabo with a bathroom a mile away.'

'But this is my personal affair.'

'Personal? Benjy, use your head. You're the headmaster of a big secondary school. What do you call it? National School, Cape Coast. You're old and you own no house. When you die there will be nowhere to lay your body in state unless you're put

5

in Anomabo Town Hall, having been carted in a deep freezer from Cape Coast. By the way, have you people got a Town Hall?'

'Anson, I'm a busy man. Stop talking rubbish. You have no right to alter the bread.'

'I have. There is no flour in the country. I had to pay a deposit of five thousand cedis to the Grain Company to guarantee a regular supply. They were compiling a list of the big buyers. Then I had to pay two hundred cedis goodwill money to the top men through some anaemic-looking sub-accountant from Leklebidafor.'

'That's bribery and corruption.'

'Yes. I bribed to get your boys fed.'

'You shouldn't have done that!'

'Why? It's not in the Ten Commandments. Have you ever seen "Thou shalt not indulge in bribery and corruption" in the Bible? I wanted flour to feed your boys. The hyenas were in my way so I threw the carcass at them. My business isn't charity, though. I've got to pass it on. Five thousand two hundred cedis isn't small money. You can't save that in five years. Benjy, be reasonable. I can't lock up my capital. By the way, there is the other idea.'

'What is it?'

'You can have a cut.'

'What cut?'

'How many boys have you?'

'One thousand and twenty-five, but call it one thousand.'

'One thousand times two pesewas, that makes twenty cedis a day. So you get ten cedis a day. That, times approximately three hundred school days, gives you three thousand cedis a year. So you get three thousand at the end of this year and start putting up a house right here in Cape Coast. I can arrange land in Adisadel area for you. It'll cost about five hundred cedis. I'll arrange for the building materials on easy terms with the manager of GTTM. So the bread will be the same size but two pesewas will be cut off. One pesewa for you, the other for me, and you get a house before you retire or get sacked. Are you aware that in this country anything can happen?'

'Anson, why do you tempt me?' Benjy Baisi asked, looking distressed and confused.

'Think straight, Benjy. It's not money you want. It's a house.

You lose nothing. I could have reduced the bread without telling you. You'll complain, I know, but I'll reduce it bit by bit until the boys get used to it. You've sacrificed so much in building up this school and what have you gained? The Church is plotting to have you removed!'

'The Church? Benjy Baisi asked, completely surprised but not completely disbelieving.

'Sure, the Church. You remember the Executive had their Semi-annual Conference here and I invited them?'

'Yes, you did. You forget I was there.'

'You saw me with Rev. Andoh, the Secretary to Conference?'

'Yes, I remember. You seemed to be talking close together and he was enjoying his whisky.'

'True. I didn't invite them for nothing, though I'm a staunch member. He thanked me for helping the school but some members of Conference felt you must go.'

'Why? Why?' Benjy Baisi asked, as if talking to himself and not to Anson.

'You dress like a fifteen-year-old boy. You come from Anomabo where there is no secondary school. You don't attend communion. You ask the boys to read African writers, and debunk Latin and Shakespeare. You tell them openly that the school is no longer for the Church but for the government. So you don't admit enough children of Church members and old boys into the school. You are undermining what took over fifty years to establish, and one of the best schools in the country at that. You must go. To whom should I give your money?'

'Why, which money?'

'I mean your cut. I'm starting right now, for your own good. I don't do this for everybody. By the way, watch that boy Kafu. He wants to take your place.'

'I have been suspecting this.'

'I'm glad you do. His father is the Rev. Kafu, the retired head of the Church. Your father was only a lay preacher and he joined the Apostolic Church before he died. I hear Kafu has more degrees than you and he belongs more to Cape Coast.'

'How does he? His father comes from Egya No. 2 and his mother comes from Elmina. I know both have made Cape Coast their home, but who really comes from Cape Coast?'

7

'Elmina is nearer Cape Coast than Anomabo. There is no secondary school in either town, so you both have to compete here. And you know the Church: every government has a quiet way of making concessions to it. The Church can unmake you, Benjy. I'll pay the cut to your wife. I went to see her before I came here. She complained you hadn't had breakfast and you talk in your sleep about school fees. You refuse to talk about your business troubles with her. I told her you need a house. She agreed. She said you've worked for twenty-six years. You've spent your money in looking after other people's children. Ten of them in all. No one helps with yours. When your father died none of those children even attended the funeral. What's your aim in life?'

'Service, Anson, service. Selfless service.'

'True, Benjy. A taxi driver provides service and is paid. You train other people's children and bastards and the Church plots to deprive you of your daily bread. I've given your wife a cheque for eight hundred cedis. We *are* starting this building.'

'Anson, I know you're a crook and I'm always afraid of you. But I know you can be kind, though I'm not too sure that it isn't all part of your crookery. The main fact, of course, is that you've offered to help me. I thank you. But please don't let us make these boys pay for my house. I love them. They're so nice and intelligent. I have eight thousand in my savings. I need about four or five thousand more to get the type of house I want. Any money my wife receives from you must be considered a loan to be paid back in full by me. I know I'm getting on in years, and I know I ought to have my own house. Thank you, Anson. But tell me, is it true they want to get rid of me and put Kafu in my place? They've done it before, you know. To Mr Okine, the former Principal of Labone Training College. In his case because he refused to be ordained a minister of religion, which the Church considered mandatory for the head of a College founded by it. He opposed the principle. He said it was irrelevant. And the Church, in collusion with the Department, threw him out!'

'Look, Benjy, it's not a question of whether it's true. I've told you what I know. Watch that boy. I don't know, but he may be your ruin. That big degree he has, MA or something, what did he take it in?'

'The Production of Mulattoes by British Convict Soldiers and African Slave Girls in the Castle Towns of the Gold Coast with Special Reference to Cape Coast and James Town, Accra.'

'Nonsense.'

'Why?'

There were a few brisk knocks on the door.

'Go and see who it is,' Anson Berko whispered.

Mr Benjy Baisi went softly and opened the door gently. It was Mr Abraham Kafu, the Senior History Master. 'Oh, it's you,' Mr Benjy Baisi said. 'I'll see you in a moment.' He closed the door and went back.

'Who is it?' Anson asked, almost in a whisper.

'It's Kafu,' Benjy Baisi whispered back.

'You see!' Anson whispered. Then he said loudly, 'The flour is expensive and difficult to get, Mr Baisi, but I'll do my best. The most important thing is constant supplies. Goodbye!'

'Goodbye, Mr Anson Berko. Keep the school informed of any difficulties, will you?'

'Yes, indeed, I will.' And he went out. He saw Mr Abraham Kafu and said, 'Oh, it's you, Kafu. How is life treating you?'

'Badly,' Kafu said curtly.

'You'd better fight it like a man, but make sure you don't break your neck!'

'Me? Never!' Kafu said, and looked contemptuously at Anson Berko.

'Mr Benjy Baisi is waiting for you. Goodbye,' Anson said with a derisive smile, and shambled away.

Kafu entered the office. He was thirty-two and of medium height, rather on the hefty side. He was extremely dark. He had a big head and kinky hair which always looked dirty. His face was round and handsome but not charming. His voice was deep and rough. His legs were slightly bowed, though shapely. His gait, however, was imprecise and careless. Kafu hated two things most: the Department of Welfare Services and Pedagogy, and headmasters. He loved two things most: politics and himself. This was how Mr Benjy Baisi rated him in his confidential reports to the Department. Of course no one there bothered to read them.

'Morning, sir,' Kafu said.

'Good morning, Kafu. Any problems?'

'Just one.'

'And it is?'

'My promotion to the grade of Assistant Headmaster of this school.'

'But you've one more year to do.'

'Why?'

'That's the rule.'

'What about the MA I've got now?'

'Of course, you've been compensated: you received four incremental credits soon after the good news.'

'But can't you persuade the Department to take my MA into account and upgrade me right now? My market value is increased. I can move into any University any time now.'

'I know. But your degree is not in school administration. Even, if it were, you still need the experience. A year is not much time.'

'Can't you petition on my behalf?'

'I can't. I've nothing to base a petition on.'

'You mean you aren't interested in my future?'

'My interest and loyalty are given to the work. Not to individuals.'

'So individuals and staff should owe no loyalty to you?'

'It depends.'

'I see. I give you three months to fight my case and win. If you don't I'll let you know where I stand with the school. And as far as you are concerned, you'll regret this kind of utterance in future.'

'But what's all this? What have I done to you, Kafu?'

'Nothing. You have no loyalty to individuals. You neither love nor hate them, so you can't do them any harm!' He left, banging the door.

2

Some weeks later, Mr Benjy Baisi was sitting at leisure in his office. It was late afternoon. The day's session was over. He looked fairly contented. He had been to Accra and had been assured that if in spite of economies his school ran into a deficit, the Department might step in to bail it out. On certain conditions, of course. He was expected to introduce some stringent economies. The boys must do some practice farming, so that they could supply their own vegetable requirements. They must raise poultry for eggs and meat. They could do some fishing. They must lay the tables and generally do the menial work. It sounded all very well: both in principle and as a form of instruction. The boys approved of the idea and clapped when it was announced to the morning assembly. A third-year boy was so aroused that he involuntarily shouted: 'Hip, hip, hip!' and both the pupils and some of the staff roared 'Hurrah!' the first-year boys prolonging it for a matter of a full minute.

Mr Baisi found this enthusiastic welcome of the new measures heart-warming. He knew, though, that implementing them would not be easy, because of the teachers. Experience had taught him that teachers could be counted among the most conservative creatures on earth. He thought perhaps it was in the very nature of their job to be so. Perhaps it was because the young were usually avant-garde so teachers preferred to anchor them in the certainty of the old before they let them loose on the uncertainty of the new. He had observed that teachers, above all, deeply resented the Department of Welfare Services and Pedagogy. Their resentment was such that they would grumble against any directive at all that came from the Department, even before they considered its merits. He had often been told that the Department had no interest in the welfare of teachers, and teachers quietly refused as far as possible to cooperate with it. He knew that the teachers of National Secondary School were no exception to this rule, but they never grudged their service to him or the school, perhaps because their confidence in him was so strong.

Kafu found this unsatisfactory. He spent most of his free periods in the staff room where he either read a novel or talked. He found a close companion there in Rev. Dan Opia Sese. Rev. Sese was the chaplain of the school. He had several diplomas in divinity but no degree. He also taught religion, Fante and world history to the lower classes. He was sixty-one but did not want to retire from the service of the school. He had retired, in fact, when he was sixty, the mandatory age, but he did so much subtle lobbying that Mr Benjy Baisi had to write a strongly worded letter to the Department pleading for a year's extension. The Department allowed him to stay on, with the stipulation that a second year's extension would not be considered since there was no shortage of qualified younger people to take his place. Rev. Sese felt the one-year extension was not enough and it was all the fault of Mr Benjy Baisi. When he told Kafu how Benjy Baisi had let him down, Kafu said he was not surprised. 'That man never helps anybody,' he said.

Of course, Rev. Sese looked vigorous. He was tall and lanky and very nimble on his feet. He was bald and fair-coloured and always wore trendy and expensive shirts and ties, but he found it difficult to discard old coats and trousers. He was not fond of clerical garb. He had a clear voice which when excited became a little shrill. He always wore dark glasses, having lost one eye in a fight with his first wife, who was now dead. He had had no child by her. His present wife was thirty years old. He had married her at the age of seventeen in her first year at Labone Training College. He had wanted to evade the marriage, but the girl's parents stood firm. They were powerful members of his pastoral circuit and he capitulated. The Church had had to intervene vigorously, and he was posted to National Secondary School to avoid an open scandal. The Church also demanded that the government should pay his salary, so he was technically employed as a teacher of religion, Fante and history. When he told Kafu this story, Kafu thought the Church had done well.

Rev. Opia Dan Sese neither drank nor smoked in public. He was always smiling and never missed a funeral service. He appeared incapable of doing harm to both those he loved and those he hated. One of his biggest boasts was that he was a pure born-and-bred Fante. He had very refined manners and his English was impeccable. Kafu found him a sympathetic listener and a top-rate gentleman.

It must be said in passing that Rev. Sese had three children, a girl and two boys. The twelve-year-old girl, Lucy, had just entered Wesley Girls' High School, Cape Coast. The boys were eight and four. His wife was expecting a fourth child. 'The last one,' he confided in Kafu, who replied amiably. 'Good try!' Then after a pause Kafu said, intentionally showing disrespect to the headmaster: 'Baisi must help you get another contract or you'll be in financial trouble.'

'Precisely!' Rev. Sese said, with a smile that was very near to looking silly.

'But have you told him your problems?'

'I've told him that I'll face financial embarrassment if I retire now.'

'Did you give him any details?'

'Oh, well, you know, a minister must know how far he should make his private life public.' He said this with impressive dignity.

'You mean it would be in bad taste to tell him you're still producing children? You suspect he might take advantage of it and lecture you on family planning?'

'Exactly. As a minister I must maintain a certain dignity. I appreciate your understanding.' He flashed another charming smile.

'And you expect Baisi to have enough common sense to appreciate this?'

'Yes, indeed. But he doesn't seem to have a subtle enough imagination for my case.'

'Have you ever come across a headmaster who had a subtle imagination? They're either giving orders or taking instructions from the Department.'

'True. I know one or two who are different, though. Do you know Mr Kwabla of Awutu Secondary School?'

'No, I don't. But Baisi certainly has no imagination. Do you think the Department seriously wants the boys to do farming and menial work?'

'I'm sure the government means business. I suppose as far as the Department is concerned, someone was told to write.'

'To write that farming should be done in Cape Coast?' Kafu asked in disgust.

'They write to the whole country. Then when you complain, they wait for two months and make an exception in deliberately ambiguous language.' Rev. Sese explained this as if he had made a special study of the behaviour of civil servants.

'I've been telling the graduate staff not to help with the projects. The non-graduates are so servile they will probably do so. We shall soon get a letter from the Department neither confirming nor denying that we should do farming in Cape Coast. We should be able to frustrate the whole business.'

'Well, as a minister of religion I don't do farming. . . . Of course in the civil service they work according to a well-established technique. You get these bland letters – no responsibility, no commitment.'

'I have got to change all that!' Kafu said slowly but with passion.

'How can you change the civil service from a secondary school in Cape Coast?' Rev. Sese asked, rather amused.

'Politics, politics is the answer. With politics you can change anything!'

'Who told you so?'

'I'm a historian, and I know. I'm re-reading Niccolo Machiavelli's *The Prince*. Politics is the answer.'

'Politics can change anything? Perhaps; but in this country even politics can't tamper with the civil service, the medical service or the Church and get away with it.' Rev. Sese spoke with great cocksureness. He ran his right palm over his bald head and then gently tapped the hair on the sides.

'Why?'

'If you meddled with the civil service they would quietly dump you before you were aware you had been dumped. Politicians need medical attention, so I suppose they spare doctors without even knowing they're sparing them. The churches are better organised than political parties and can sow disaffection more effectively than any other group.'

Kafu looked a little disconcerted by this brief analysis. But he mustered courage and said, 'Damn it, it's the soldiers and police I fear most. They organise a coup as if it were an ordinary bush parade. They brush off the political life of a man as if it were all a farce.'

'I know what you mean.' Rev. Sese stretched his legs out and lolled his head on the back-rest cushion. 'The soldiers and police are disruptive, but essentially they're organisers. In business you would call them executives. The real governors' power is diffuse and subtle, and it lies elsewhere. I would watch the public services and the church, Kafu, *I* would watch them, especially the civil service. That service is like Johnnie Walker, you know. It can make you lose your head and slip but someone else will quickly come around and try it once again.'

'Osofo,' – Kafu addressed Rev. Sese intimately for the first time – 'don't worry about the civil service. If ever I become a minister, I'll purge it. We will trim it and make it work like the private sector. No nonsense! Tcha-a-a! No nonsense! It's clear in my mind where to begin, and, in the name of the Lord, I won't let the country down.'

'I wish you well Kafu, I wish you well. Man must live, man must strive. I seem to have spent my time just fighting to live, but you're young yet. Yes, young. I can foretell your achieving more than fighting to live.'

'Osofo, thank you. Thank you. If only Baisi would wish me well, as you do.'

'I'm sure he does. He loves people.'

'Are you sure?'

'Yes, I am.'

'But he told me he wasn't interested in anybody. He wouldn't therefore press for my promotion.'

'Maybe. The trouble is, he doesn't know how to break rules unless he is mesmerised to do it. You know that urchin, Adzankunu, in class three? Baisi caught him once at midnight in the lavatory smoking wee. The rule is that the boy should be dismissed. So Baisi was going to dismiss him. But, you see, he was the only one who knew of the offence. He could have given the boy a serious warning and hushed it up, but he was going strictly by the rules. So I had to step in when Adzankunu appealed to me. He's very bright and he's been doing well. He confessed to me later that he wanted to know what wee smoking was all about and I told him not to be a stupid fool. It could be the beginning of the end for him. Baisi doesn't like to deviate from the rules. He runs this school well, but otherwise he is a useless fellow! Forgive me, Kafu, I never use strong language, heh?'

'Osofo, tomorrow I'm going to confront Baisi. It's serious. There's no money in teaching, and if you want a promotion just to earn a little more, you have to appeal and appeal to some devil either here or in the Department. It makes me angry. The job carries no respect. I must get out of this rat hole, Osofo.'

'Where to?'

'Things are taking shape. I'll tell you some day. You know the elections will be held in July?'

'So I hear.'

'The country needs intellectuals in parliament. Men like myself who know their books, to reconstruct the country.'

'But, I beg your pardon,' Rev. Sese said with a smile, 'there is nothing to reconstruct in this country. How can you reconstruct something you have not constructed?'

'Osofo!'

'Yes?'

'You know nothing about politics! We are the intellectuals, and we are going to reconstruct the country. Money is what I need to fight the elections, and Baisi is in my way. I'm going to confront him!' Kafu started thinking deeply.

They sat quietly saying nothing for about five minutes. Kafu began to doze, and in a few minutes he was snoring heavily. Rev. Sese found this a little embarrassing, so he shook him and asked him to go home. He had some exercises to correct before leaving.

Mr Baisi was still in his office. A top-form boy, Osei Kwame, who had a pointed head, a thin face and a flat bottom, knocked and was asked to come in. Osei had throughout his four academic years collected prizes in history. He was a good athlete and his compositions often won high marks. He always grinned ingratiatingly whenever he saw a master and delighted in talking to them about other masters. He would approach a master and ask casually for an explanation of a problem. When this had been given he would smile toothily and ask the master, feigning innocence, what he thought about a certain practice in the school, or the performance of another master, especially a new one. If the master was not on his guard and gave an opinion which went against the school administration or a member of staff, Osei would go to the senior housemaster and tell him. If it was something against the administration, the senior housemaster would tell it to Mr Baisi as if he had heard it first. If it was against a member of staff he would ask Osei Kwame to go and tell Mr Baisi. The senior housemaster liked Osei Kwame and gave him good terminal reports. Mr Baisi had an aversion to both.

When Mr Baisi saw Osei Kwame and his facile grin, his strong dislike of the boy welled up in him. But he kept cool and asked, deliberately sternly, 'What is it, Osei Kwame?'

'Sir, Mr Kafu has not been teaching us well.'

'How is that?' Mr Baisi asked, with a frown to frighten Osei Kwame.

'He talks politics all the time and then cracks jokes.'

'Who takes you in current affairs?'

'Mr Kafu, sir.'

'Do you know the difference between current affairs and politics?' Mr Baisi asked, hoping to discourage Osei Kwame.

'They overlap, sir,' Osei Kwame said with a broad grin which infuriated Mr Baisi, 'but the trouble, sir, is that Mr Kafu doesn't go by the history syllabus. It's current affairs ... er ... politics all the time. And the final exams are due in June, sir.'

'Anything else?' Mr Baisi asked.

'Yes, sir, Mr Kafu sometimes comes to class drunk.'

'What!'

'Yes, sir. The class can confirm this, sir.'

'Are you very sure? This is a serious matter.'

'Yes, sir. Sometimes he comes in fifteen minutes late. During the last two weeks he has cut two periods, sir.'

'Is that all?' Mr Baisi asked Osei Kwame, in a voice to warn him that enough was enough.

'No, sir. Last week, several people who were being mentioned in the press as candidates for the elections visited his flat. A lady Peace-Corps teacher stayed in his flat up to midnight last Saturday. His wife had gone ...'

'Shut up! You foul-mouthed, wretched, little snake! I've a good mind to give you twelve lashes and throw you out of this school. Get out!'

Osei Kwame's face fell, more out of shock than genuine regret.

17

He quickly ran out of the office and, in two seconds, his steps had died out along the corridor.

Mr Benjy Baisi turned over carefully in his mind what he had been told. He knew every bit of it was true, except the Peace-Corps story, which was probably nothing but a juvenile mis-interpretation of a social visit. He despised Osei Kwame. 'That boy is absolute dirt. He must have been born out of wedlock. The parents don't live together. Such boys are a complete nuisance in boarding schools. They lie, steal, fight and never wash. Here is this boy. He knows it's the Senior Prefect's job to tell me, not his. It's this underhand business I hate most. Kafu is an open trouble-maker. But this boy, Osei Kwame, what do I do with him? Lord, what do I do with him? Can I change him? Can I succeed?' He heaved a sigh and stared at the photograph of the first head-master of the school which hung high up in front of him.

There was a knock on the door. It was Kafu. He was in crumpled, very short white shorts, a colourful Joromi shirt and foam-rubber sandals. He was smoking Tusker cigarettes. He held the packet of cigarettes and a box of matches in his left hand. There was a copy of the latest issue of the *Legon Observer* under his left armpit. He held an evening paper which he had folded thrice in his right hand. He smelt and looked like someone who had just taken a lot of beer. He was a little unsteady on his feet. He was smiling defiantly. Mr Baisi spoke first. He forgot to let Kafu tell him what he wanted to see him about. He said, 'Kafu, what is this I hear about you?'

'Look, Baisi, why not let me tell you why I'm here?'

'Fair enough, Kafu.'

'Have you written the petition?'

'No.'

'Why not?'

'You don't deserve it.'

'Why?'

'Apart from the seven years required for the post, you haven't demonstrated you can be an efficient assistant headmaster. In my view your problem is not inability but wilful neglect and black-mail. Kafu, why can't you take interest in your work and in the school?'

'Baisi, you're speaking generally. If you'd had the discipline of taking a master's degree, you wouldn't have talked loosely like this. What are the specifics? What's the evidence against me?'

'Right now you're drunk.'

'So what? Shouldn't a teacher drink?'

'You go to classes drunk, Kafu.'

'When? And what did you do about it, Mr Benjy Baisi?'

'You confide a lot in Rev. Sese.'

'How do you know?'

'You don't mark exercises.'

'But Baisi, for a whole term you yourself haven't checked whether or not I've marked exercises, have you?'

'You have been telling other staff not to help with the farming and poultry.'

'This is slanderous.'

'You talk politics in class and crack unnecessary jokes.'

'Have you visited my class recently to check on the truth of what you're saying? Baisi, let me tell you this. You know I'm going to stand in the elections and you hate the idea. You hate me. I know you hate me. You don't like the Liberation Party because you can't match the intellectual excellence of the top crop of its members. But I can advise you, Baisi. No matter what people say, only the educated can save this country.'

'And only the educated can ruin this country, Kafu.'

'And only the unrefined intellect cannot appreciate the potential of the educated, Baisi. One thing is clear, though. You hate the Liberation Party and you'd like to get rid of me. You want to see me sacked from this school. You want to stand between me and my ambition, wealth, everything. But none of your stratagems will work. I haven't finished with you yet!' Before Mr Baisi could utter a word, Kafu banged the door and laughed loudly as he hurried away along the corridor.

3

It was the third week of April. The boys had been on holiday and were back to finish off the academic year. It was the third term and a period of hectic academic and social life for the school. There would be the promotion examinations and the external examination for the top class. Everybody was busy in National Secondary School. Kafu, too, was busy. He had not resigned yet.

Kafu had been nominated by the National Executive of the Liberation Party to stand in Accra Central. This surprised everybody and annoyed quite a few. Nobody had heard before of Abraham Kofi Kafu, MA, Dip. Ed., 32, Senior History Master, National Secondary School, Cape Coast. The party press, *The Liberator*, described him as 'a young, energetic intellectual, hardworking, frugal, and a champion of the masses who wants to rid Accra Central of poverty, unemployment, congestion and the hoarding of smuggled goods. Above all,' the *Liberator* continued, 'Mr Kafu is the man to shake up the bloated, privileged and reactionary civil service and cleanse the public services once and for all of bribery and corruption. That he has been chosen to stand in Accra Central is in itself a unique achievement of the Liberation Party. It shows that tribalism and parochialism no longer have a place in the conduct of national affairs. The nation-wreckers must note. This was in the Friday, April 19 issue. His portrait took up a quarter of the front page.

On Monday at about eleven in the morning, Nee Otu Lartey was sipping beer at the Hotel Ogua. He was going once again through the Friday, April 19 copy of the *Liberator*. He was sitting on a stool at the counter of the hotel bar. The bar was practically empty of customers except for an elderly fisherman in an almost tattered cloth, his head shiny and completely shaven. He was taking a late breakfast of eggs, bacon, butter, sausage, bread and tea. He seemed to be used to this kind of breakfast and was taking it as a matter of course. Otu Lartey wondered whether this was the normal feeding style of the people of the place. He looked at the man's cloth and head and smiled.

There was a gap in Nee Otu Lartey's teeth, not in front but on the left side. He was a short man, thickset and very compact. His skin was dark brown and coarse. He kept his hair very short. Looking at his chest, neck, face and head, one might have taken him for a very seasoned farmer from the remote backwoods of the Afram Plains.

In fact Nee Otu Lartey was a real Accra Central man. His father, Nee James Hutchison Lartey, had been a clerk of the Colonial Secretariat. He never went on transfer and he reached the maximum of £205 per annum before he retired. He was born at Akoto Lante, he lived at Akoto Lante and he died there. So Nee Otu Lartey was a genuine Akoto Lante man. His mother came from James Town, but her marriage to Hutchison Lartey was in the best tradition of the constant intermarriage that goes on between the two close, teeming and decaying quarters.

Nee Otu Lartey went to Accra Royal School. He managed to complete his elementary school there only after several repeats, for two things interfered with his schooling: truancy and casual labour. Naturally the latter flowed from the first, but the real motivating factor was an impulsive and innocent desire for coins. This began when he was seven at the fishing grounds of Mensah Guinea, where boys who helped the fishermen were given fish which they sold to the women for cash. When on his father's death he dropped out from National Secondary School, Cape Coast, where he had been sent as an insurance against his wayward tendencies, he decided to become a mason and joined the Public Works Department. His goal was to become a building contractor as soon as possible. A shrewd move; for he soon became a foreman, not so much through his skill as through a great sense of leadership and an extraordinary verbal ability.

As supervisor, he displayed tremendous resourcefulness. He was responsible for the maintenance of government quarters and bungalows and began to divert large quantities of materials into his private depot in Nima, Accra. All he had to do was to over-requisition stores, or, instead of replacement, he would order repairs and again divert the stores. Those under him soon learnt the art and he pretended he did not know.

He was in the supervisory post for five years, during which time he put up a three-story block of flats to let and a comfortable six-room, one-story house to live in himself. With a capital of two thousand cedis, and after the necessary contacts with engineers, architects, quantity surveyors and permanent secretaries, he set up shop as a full-fledged contractor. He was so enterprising that he managed to become a ·Category B contractor in no time, his contracts spreading across the country.

He took a vow neither to drink nor smoke for, as he told it, his first wife, a university graduate and a lawyer, was unfaithful to him and he was so hurt by this that he decided to become a Moslem. So he now had wives in four regional capitals, one each in Accra, Kumasi, Tamale and Sekondi, with nineteen children all told. He had just turned thirty-six. He had been a classmate of Kafu at National Secondary School, Cape Coast, and he felt the political rise of Kafu was a great honour to his classmates and another opening for himself. He gave Kafu a call on Saturday from Accra, congratulated him and told him that he would be visiting Cape Coast on Monday to inspect a dormitory block he was constructing for the technical institute. He asked Kafu to meet him at the Hotel Ogua at 11.15 where they could 'at least' swap reminiscences.

At 11.15 sharp Kafu appeared. 'Hello, Kofi Kafu, how great to see you! How many years now? Sixteen, yes, sixteen long years. Except that you haven't changed a bit. I knew you'd be great, Kafu! I said so! You've proved Mr John Eduban wrong. You remember his abuse in the arithmetic class? That you were a bushy-headed rascal who'd wind up deceiving himself? What nonsense! How can a man deceive himself? It's not natural, you know. It's so good to see you. Sit down. Barman, one beer, one glass, please. Why, Kafu, no classes? I was wondering whether you could make it. Free period? Barman, hurry up! Big man is here.'

'I knew,' Kafu replied with cool self-assurance, 'that the time wouldn't be ideal. It would conflict with a history lesson I'm supposed to have with the fourth class, but I never like to disappoint old schoolmates, especially classmates. The boys can look after themselves. I can't be everywhere. I'm starting the campaign in Accra in a week or two. I'm doing the groundwork. It takes a lot of time. Mr Baisi is standing in for me.'

'Good old Baisi, has he abandoned his maths?'

'He can't. He's been brushing up his history, he says. That is, by

22

teaching the boys. Of course, he's more interested in the facts than in the interpretation. The boys seem to like that sort of teaching, or perhaps it's what they've been offered all along. Teaching styles die hard, don't they? What have you been doing with yourself all these years, Otu Lartey?' Kafu was deliberately skirting the real topic.

'I've a lot of children, but it's not my business to think about teaching styles,' Otu Lartey said, smiling. 'That's for teachers like you to worry about. As for what I've been doing with myself, I construct buildings and get paid.'

'Is it profitable?'

'If there was no profit whatever, I wouldn't be in it. I manage somehow. As a rule, I don't carry all my eggs in one polythene bag. I have a beer shop for my "chop money". When you're in business, you must find other investment avenues, especially these days when one unexpected government announcement can ruin your business for good.'

'When we come into power, this sort of thing won't continue. By the way, are you with us?' Kafu came to the point now.

'You mean the Liberation Party?'

'Yes.'

'Of course I am. I've read your manifesto. It makes sense. You will liberate national businessmen from all these restrictions. What I don't understand is, when you make profits fast, government says you're cheating. When you make profits slowly, the same government says you lack business know-how and must go to the "School of Productivity" to be lectured at.'

'Why not make it slow, slow; quick, quick; slow?' Kafu asked playfully.

'It's not natural to see money for the picking and go slow!'

'Do you have a party card?'

'Oh, yes. Here it is.' Otu Lartey gave it to Kafu, who examined it very slowly and then sipped his beer. In fact he was thinking. Otu Lartey patiently watched him. He was trying to read his mind. Kafu said, 'Otu, you know what? I'm in this campaign and I must win. But it's not easy. No matter how good our organisational plans, we need money to carry them out. We need real hard cash.' He lowered his voice so that he wouldn't be heard by the bar attendant, held Otu Lartey's hand and continued, 'My

23

complaint against my countrymen is that everybody says he is for you but nobody gives you the money. The ordinary fellow never gives you a pesewa, yet he's the same person who expects you to win and run the country according to some big morality and ideals. Without cash, I might as well forget it. But I won't give up if good old friends like you are interested.'

'Surely, we are! Do you think I'd go to the lengths of ringing you and coming all the way to this place for nothing? I mean to help you and the Party. If we need stability in this country, we must pay for it. That's my philosophy. But I don't wish to be misunderstood either. If I come out with a fanfare pledging my support for the Party, tongues will wag and my motive will be misrepresented. I want to do my best for this great country, I want to help. As it is said: "They also help who do their little bit." I'm sorry, I don't know whether my quotation is correct. I never finished school. But you see what I mean?' He smiled so broadly that the side gap in his teeth showed.

'Perfectly!' Kafu said with the great feeling that he was getting somewhere. He squeezed Otu Lartey's hand and asked, 'How do you mean to help?'

'Well, I am a true Accra Central man. I know every inch of the ground and everybody worth knowing. I can give you a detailed history of Bukom Square from 1947, when it became a great political spot, to about a few months ago, when it became the favourite haunt of common criminals who snatched wristwatches when people went there to buy kenkey and fried fish. The police and army have succeeded in flushing the rats out of there.'

'Ahaa, this is what I want the police and army to do!' Kafu exploded. 'Not meddling in politics!'

'Power, Kafu, power. It's a prize to be won. The problem is how to get it and how to use it. Some find it fascinating, and so at thirty-two Abraham Kofi Kafu is fascinated by it; and we, the masses, who sometimes queue up to buy milk for our babies – I don't drink milk myself – have to cheer whoever comes to the power scene. Power is so boring.'

'Hear! hear! From building contractor to political philosophy!' Kafu said with an ill-concealed sneer, clapping. He guffawed and then said, 'I've always told my pupils that insight into the human predicament is not the monopoly of the universities. It is always with us in our ordinary conversations. Otu Lartey,' Kafu called looking dead serious, 'you say that you know every inch of my constituency. I'll need your help in two ways. I'll tell you bluntly what they are. The first is money and the second, contacts. What do you say?'

'Kafu, I really came to renew acquaintanceship and pledge support for you and the Liberation Party. I didn't know you would get me fully involved. There are risks, you realise that?'

'I know.'

'What's the insurance?'

'How do you mean?'

'In this modern world, when you're going to take a risk you insure yourself, don't you? The money I'll give you and raise for you is not yours. How do we get our money back and how will it be increased? You want me to organise in Accra Central for you. Apart from the party van, you'll need a car for the constituency organisers. You have to think of petrol and maintenance. Accra Central is a tough place. It is a place of the unexpected. You'll need your own private bodyguards. It's a long list. What's the total amount you want to raise?'

Kafu pulled out a thick bunch of sheets of paper from his Joromi pocket. He was in Joromi, tight trousers and well-polished shoes. His hair was uncombed. On the last sheet was a summary of estimates. He went carefully over this sheet and told Otu Lartey, 'Thirty thousand cedis.'

'What? Thirty thousand cedis?'

'Yes, thirty thousand to cover everything.'

'How much are you going to contribute yourself?'

'Two hundred.'

'I beg your pardon?'

'I said two hundred cedis,' Kafu repeated, sweating.

Otu Lartey gave a long, loud laugh. 'You must be crazy, Kofi Kafu. You want to stand elections in Accra and all the money you have is two hundred cedis. You're wasting your time. Count me out!'

Kafu suddenly felt that the bar was stuffy. The sweat ran down his chubby cheeks like tears. He grabbed the glass and took a long swig. His fingers were unsteady. He said, 'Nee Otu Lartey, I can

25

understand your reaction, but it's too late now. What would the public and the Party think if I pulled out at this stage? You have seen the *Liberator* of the 19th. There is no turning back. Fate has brought you here, I'm sure, for the good of both of us. Keep cool, Otu. Work it out, Otu. That's how to go about things. How much can you give? Work it out!'

'All right, Kafu, I'll work it out, and the insurance, too, is part of it. You must also work it out. Politics is not like church service where you go and display your wealth and return home smiling endlessly on the way. You'll have to give guarantees. Altogether, I'll give you fifteen thousand. I'll raise eight thousand from Madam Odofo Lamptey and seven thousand from Auntie Salamatu. They are both in Accra. One is at Labone and the other is at Kaneshie. I live in the Labone residential area myself. You must come on Friday and stay the weekend with me, is that clear?'

'Yes.'

'Good. You must leave Cape Coast on Friday afternoon. We will start planning in the evening. We will see the two ladies on Saturday at Makola. Odofo is a big textile retailer and Salamatu deals in sundry goods. Each owns about three houses. They are in the posh areas of Accra: Roman Ridge, Airport, and the like. I won't tell you what sort of persons they are. You're a politician and must find out for yourself. Anything else?'

'Nothing I can think of now. Thank you very much, Nee Otu. It's so wonderful. You need lunch now. We must go to my flat and have something.'

'Thank you, Kafu. Is that Anson Berko coming in?' Nee Otu asked, looking over to the doorway.

'Yes. It's Berko all right. He's our school bread contractor and a great friend of Benjy Baisi.'

'I see. I know Anson well. He's a member of the National Contractors Association and represents the Central Region on the Executive. I like him.'

'He doesn't seem to like me. I don't know why. I had better leave and tell Grace to prepare lunch for us. Anson Berko can tell you where my flat is. It's not difficult to find.'

Kafu finished his glass quickly. He would have preferred not to have a conversation with Anson Berko. But this proved difficult.

26

Anson Berko strode in and, halfway to the bar, saw Kafu. He gave him an apparently friendly pat on the shoulder and asked, 'No classes?'

'What's wrong with classes?' Kafu grunted, his eyes showing hostility.

'Never mind, Kafu. I mean no trouble. You're going to be a minister, so you can afford not to teach the boys. Not so?'

'Is that what you've been spreading around about me, Anson? Did Baisi tell you this?'

'Don't drag in Baisi. I have no time to spread rumours about you! Hello, Nee Otu Lartey! I haven't seen you for ages. What wind blows you here?'

Kafu looked at Anson Berko up and down. Berko had now reached the counter and had proffered his hand to Mr Lartey for a shake. He looked back and saw Kafu transfixed, his right hand in his pocket, looking him up and down in cold anger. 'Goodbye, Kafu!' Anson Berko said cheerfully. Kafu hurried out without a word.

'What are you doing with that boy, Nee Otu?'

'I want to help him. I really believe in the Liberation Party. The country needs stability. The people must decide at any time who should rule them. This boy was bright at school. I hear he's a fine scholar and teacher. We must give people like him a chance.'

'To ruin the country?'

'He says you don't like him.'

'How should I? He's lazy and reckless. That's all. He can't be a contractor, how much more a politician? I hear he knows more about the half-breed girls of James Town than about why the people of James Town and Akoto Lante refused to be resettled at Korlegonno and Link Road! Now they must move to near the cemetery at mile eleven, Winneba Road!'

'I hear! I hear! This is the trouble! You're prejudiced against him.'

'I don't know. I wouldn't help such a man to run the country.'

'Who would you put in his place?'

'I don't know. Those I think could do the job well don't like politics.'

'Anson, you can't do a job well if you don't like it or try it or take risks. I'm going to help Kafu!'

27

'I don't know. Go ahead! Barman, cool beer, please!'

'I must be leaving. Can you tell me where Kafu lives?'

'Just drive to the National Secondary School. As you enter the compound, you'll find a block of flats on your right. He's in No. 3 on the first floor. Cheerio, and take good care of yourself. I would prefer to help a man like Benji Baisi and not Kafu. Cheerio, Nee Lartey.'

'Cheerio, and good luck to you, Anson Berko!'

Nee Otu Lartey had no difficulty in finding the flat. Lunch was ready. Kafu and his wife, Grace, were waiting for him. He was struck by the beauty and charm of Grace. She was about the same height as her husband. She was neither slim nor fat and was well curved. Her skin was extremely light. She wore no wig, and her natural hair looked better than a wig. She seemed to be conscious of this because she was always softly tapping her hair to keep it in shape, though this was not necessary. Her legs were shapely and her face displayed an attractive nose. Her eyes were big and her lips looked rather voluptuous. She was expecting a baby. A two-year-old boy, called Abraham Kofi Kafu, Junior, was playing with a decrepit toy lorry on an old tattered carpet. He seemed very alert.

After the lunch, Nee Otu Lartey belched loudly and said, 'Mrs Kafu!'

'You can call me Grace.'

'Well, Grace, the lunch was excellent!' Nee Otu Lartey said stretching out his short legs, which did not reach the floor from the chair, and caressing the bare belly under the loose shirt he wore over very tight trousers.

'It's a pleasure,' Grace said. 'I'm glad you liked it. I had very short notice!'

'I must be leaving for Accra. Of course, I'll take a quick look at a project I have in Cape Coast here before I go. Your husband spoke to me and I've decided to help him as much as I can. He's got to be pretty smart. That's what he's got to be! Well, I must be going. Thank you, Grace.'

'Thank you and goodbye,' Grace said with great charm.

'Kafu, don't forget Friday.',

'No, I won't. Till then!'

On Friday, Kafu missed the last two periods. He left Cape

Coast at three-thirty. He broke the journey at Winneba Junction. He was in his Peugeot 404 car which he had used for four years but which was in fact ten years old. He had bought it second-hand. It had been well kept before he acquired it, but he did not look after it properly and the acceleration was erratic.

He ordered beer and a stick of barbecue at the Junction restaurant. As he was drinking the second bottle, he noticed a young woman of about twenty-one who had just come in and was sitting by herself taking a soft drink. She looked attractive, in fact irresistible. She was in a two-piece Ghanian dress. Her hair was plaited. She looked very gentle. He looked hard at her. The girl noticed it, turned away her head and finished off her Coca-Cola. She rose and went to the roadside. He watched as she stood there: brown smooth skin, slim waist, a full bosom, a full bottom – very good! 'You marry and get on in years, and you find all the time that more beautiful girls emerge each day. Each new batch is an improvement on the previous one. Good show for the country! That sweet little thing must be a student. She's probably going home to collect her fees. I'll give her a drive. It'll be good company. I nearly slept on my way here. Too little sleep. Too much thinking. The beering. She'll keep me awake. Let me go and pick her up before some packed bus comes along to take her. She'll have no comfort in it.'

Kafu quickly finished off the refreshment, went up to her and offered a drive. She was grateful. Kafu felt good and launched into conversation with her. The car picked up speed.

She was the daughter of Dr Ghartey of Korle Bu Hospital. Her name was Essi Mansima. After finishing at Achimota School, she had done her post-secondary teacher training at Komenda Training College. She taught for two years and was now at the Advanced Teacher Training College, Winneba. Her field was the teaching of English in primary school. The conversation waxed and both time and car flew.

'And you say you're not interested in politics?' Kafu asked.

'I don't mean that,' she replied. 'I think there has been too much of it and I feel a little tired of it.'

'Can you pinpoint what you're tired of? As a politician I may find your observations useful.'

'I'm not too sure. It seems to me there is so much to do and yet there is so much talk. Not a day passes without someone in the government reading pages and pages of typed notes to an audience that is clearly not listening. It's interesting.'

'What's interesting?'

'Oh, the speech-makers must know that no one is listening! It's the same thing: promise, promise; in future, in future.... I suppose it's simply everyone playing it on everybody. Of course I know it's such fun to be alive and be deceived. Don't you think so? I believe the future may ... Look, there is a taxi coming! You can't overtake ... the ... bus! Oh, God!'

Kafu's car somersaulted into the open country at mile fourteen, near the Brigade Camp at Omankope. It landed wheels up. The taxi ran into the hedge of the camp. The passengers of the bus came to help. Essi Mansima was flung clear of the car — dead.

4

The news of Kafu's accident was a front page story in the *Liberator* of the following day. The owner of the taxi was identified as Mr Mensah Quartey, the national propaganda secretary of the National Union Party, the only party that was contesting the elections with the Liberation Party. The National Union Party had a countrywide following but it did not have its own press, though it found powerful backing in the *Morning Herald* of Kumasi and the *Evening Echo* of Accra. These two papers supported and spread the socialist ideology of the NUP, but they were so shrill with their doctrinaire brand of it that Akpeteshie distillers, Kwawu storekeepers, cocoa farmers, private doctors and lawyers, moneylenders and other self-employed people began to speculate that if the NUP formed a government and captured the commanding heights of the economy, they might descend on them and dispossess them. In fact, it was the Liberation Party that turned the speculation into a nation-wide rumour.

The NUP had dedicated supporters in the town and cities, and most of its functionaries were recruited from the National Tenants' Association and the Bus Drivers' Union. The National Landlords' Association and Makola Women's Union offered their services, free of charge, to the Liberation Party, so increasing the vast support which the Party already enjoyed in the rural areas, including the Gomoa and Efutu constituencies.

The NUP national executive and supporters were not surprised when the *Liberator* said the following morning, among the other things in its opinion columns, that

'It is noted with interest that a taxi owned by a person who does not believe in capitalist enterprise was in the right lane of the road but would not bother to slow down to avoid the fatal accident. Dr Paul Ghartey is no politician but his brother, Akwesi Ghartey, is the organising secretary of the NUP for the Efutu constituency. The loss of Essi Mansima is as cruel and wicked as it is untimely. By the grace of God, Mr Abraham Kofi Kafu has been spared to serve the country and show the NUP where it has gone wrong. The struggle continues!'

A two-man delegation of the national executive of the NUP was dispatched to the editor of the *Evening Echo* to counter the *Liberator* publication and by six in the evening a long editorial, sprawled in huge columns in heavy type on both the front and back pages, was being read all over the country. The last paragraph declared:

'Mr Mensah Quartey is neither a dishonourable socialist nor a heartless capitalist exploiting the masses in the frightening manner of the Western imperialist countries and South Africa. Socialism does not mean going naked or starvation. Man must live. Until the suffering masses give the NUP the mandate to rule the country and stamp out for ever from this dear country of ours the exploitation of man by man, individuals cannot but control their own small means of production to keep body and soul intact. It must be emphasised that Mr Mensah Quartey is not, repeat, not a capitalist tycoon growing fat on the cheap labour of others. Our detractors must know that accidents are no respecters of persons and those who desire to exploit the working class must not confuse their political rise with the hazards of the road. We shall overcome!'

The positions of these papers had some effect on Essi Mansima's funeral. It became a subject of discussion all over the country, so that Kafu, too, received unprecedented attention. Essi Mansima was buried at Winneba the following Saturday. The lapse of a week was enough for the elaborate preparations that were made. She was laid in state in front of the altar; for her father, though a medical doctor, was very devout, a phenomenon that was not common among his colleagues. His daughter had followed in his footsteps and sang regularly with the choir on Sundays. In addition, her death was of national interest, and the church had to play a fitting role so as not to be caught napping.

Above all, the national executive of the Liberation Party decided that Kafu must be helped to the hilt. The family of Essi Mansima must be saved all expense, condoled with fully and made to feel that their daughter's death was nothing but one more example of the vexatious, inexplicable but continual tragedies that frustrate human existence. As a demonstration of their sorrow and their desire to lessen the impact of the misfortune, Winneba must be saturated with people, drink and anything else that money could provide for the occasion. In concluding his address on the subject, the president of the executive said:

'Ladies and gentlemen, could we make the occasion one of expiation for our comrade, Kofi? I need not remind you that very often it is through such tragedies that great things are accomplished. God has not spared Kafu for nothing. He is one of the great hopes of the Party and we must rally our resources to help him in his hour of need.'

The grave was tiled blue and white. The coffin was custom-made by A. Lang Ltd, Accra. It had a glass top and Essi Mansima, embalmed and as beautiful as ever, could be seen for the last time under the glass.

The funeral procession was a mile long. The asafo companies were in full attendance with their flags, ancient cap guns and drums, lustily singing their war songs. They gave no trouble, as they explained later, not so much because of the ubiquitous presence of the police but because they all supported the Liberation Party and were in no mood to let it down. Even when a scuffle broke out between two hunchbacked supporters of the NUP and the Liberation Party, it was some of the asafo young men who turned the scene into a good-natured joke, requested the police to leave it to them, invited the embattled hunchbacks to the nearest beer shop, where beer had been laid on free for all by the Liberation Party, and asked them to cool it off. After they had taken a bottle each, the hunchbacks shook hands, began to sing asafo songs together, and danced out of the bar, arm in arm.

The funeral was fully reported by the *Liberator* and the other papers, and copies were taken to Kafu at Korle Bu Hospital by Nee Otu Lartey. Grace, Kafu's wife, went along with him; she had come over and was staying with him. Kafu was sitting on the edge of the bed in a side ward. His hospital dress was a little oversized but comfortable. He did not have his own morning gown. The hospital one was wine-in colour and faded. He was alone there and was being well cared for. His plastered left arm was in a sling. It was not a bad fracture and was coming along beautifully. After a few exchanges, Kafu went straight to what was on his mind. 'Nee Otu, the doctor says I've got one more week to do here. I don't understand why. I feel all right. I'd like to go and see Essi Mansima's family and apologise. It was all my fault. I didn't know, I didn't know ...!' And he wiped a tear.

'Easy, Kafu, easy! Everybody understands. You have to get over it quickly. The campaigns must start as soon as you're discharged. As I've told you, the party took full responsibility for the funeral. Dr and Mrs Ghartey are generous souls. I don't think there will be any legal action. Can you guess what Dr Ghartey said? "There may well have been careless driving but I don't suppose he intended to kill my daughter." I found your car was not insured for the year. Had you renewed your driving licence?'

'No, Nee Otu,' Kafu said, still tearful and morose.

'Too bad,' Nee Otu said quietly and thoughtfully. 'It means more money will have to be put in the slot. The whole process is time-consuming. Anyway, I've got Inspector Yebribia working on this accident. I think we can be pretty sure that the whole affair will soon be filed away in a closed docket. This is a time for the essentials, Kafu. The first is that you've got to relax here for another week so that you can take the full plunge into things when you get out. We appealed to your doctors and they've been very kind. Mind you, you were brought here unconscious; there must be no hurry. Politically, it's wise to have you here for some time. Our propaganda machinery is using it to whip up sympathy for you. It's working marvellously. Donations are pouring in, particularly from the Makola Women's Union. We've got five thousand from it alone. These market women are generous but we've got to watch them; they can make a man with their money, but they can undo him with their tongues. It's their tongues we should watch. But we have their five thousand, plus three thousand from other sources. I'll tell you later. Grace is surprised at the amounts being mentioned, heh?'

'I didn't know it would take so much money,' she said charmingly. The day was hot and she was in a thin, loose-fitting dress. One could partly see through it. The strands of hair on her legs were very noticeable under the fluorescent lights that were kept burning. Kafu asked her to sit by him. She expertly wiped the drying tears and sweat off his face.

'Oh yes, it takes a lot,' Nee Otu replied. 'We have eight thousand so far. That brings the thirty thousand we need down to twenty-two. I've rescheduled the thirty thousand. I'll give ten thousand and the two ladies will give six thousand each. You will now operate two bank accounts in Accra, a political one and a personal one, but both in your name. You'll start with two thousand cedis in each. You'll also need a house. We've rented one for you at Labone. It has a big lounge with wall-to-wall carpeting, three bathrooms, four air-conditioned bedrooms, a modern kitchen with a deep-freeze. The rent is four hundred cedis a month. We've made a down-payment of two thousand four hundred. That gives you six months.'

'But Nee Otu, suppose Kofi doesn't win?' Grace asked, frightened by the figures.

'Grace, get this straight and don't ask again: if Kafu wasn't going to win, we wouldn't back him. Soldiers seize power; we pay for it. As for the people, so long as their stomachs are full and life is not too expensive, they don't very much care what happens.'

'Hear, hear!' Kafu said, and clapped. His arm hurt.

'Be careful, Kofi,' Grace cautioned him.

Nee Otu said, 'Ah, ah; Kafu, watch it. To continue, now. You'll need a new car. The old one is beyond repair. We'll get you a second-hand Peugeot 204. The people like a show of modesty. They would rejoice at your downfall if you had lived at all well as a politician. There has to be a Party hierarchy in the constituency. This has been arranged. Mr Mills Blankson is the constituency chairman. He's sixty and a real-estate man with thousands and thousands of cedis invested in government stock. He's a powerful church elder and patron of the Accra Central Women's Fellowship. He can wheel and deal if it comes to it. He lives in Accra Central itself. When you meet him, you'll find that some part of his dress is always torn, but don't look down on him. He likes scholars in particular to respect him. Then there is the constituency secretary, Odoi Hammond. As you know, he's an ex-national-heavyweight champion. He's forty-seven and the darling of the middle-aged widows in the area. He's a good organiser and has a devastating tongue. Once in a while he may have to dispense unexpected punches here and there when the Party propaganda van-drivers start a brawl over free "molasses". Kafu, you'll find that the people you'll be dealing with are prepared to help and you've got to display a flexible response. I'll be back here in a day or two to report on what progress I've made with the two ladies. I'll come and collect you on your discharge. You'll have to stay in Accra for some time before you go to Cape Coast; but you'll soon find you have to stay more often in Accra. Grace can stay behind. I have to go and look after constituency matters.' He gave Grace money to take a taxi with and left.

'What a man!' Grace said with a sigh.

'What a man, as you say. I feel like he's a brother, Grace. He's been so helpful.' Kafu slumped back on the bed, lying on his back. He held his wife's hand, felt its warmth and said, 'Darling, I never dreamt it was as dispiriting as this, you know.'

'What is?'

'This place. I have no doubt at all that it has some of the finest

35

doctors in the country. Perhaps they do more than the country really wants to pay for.'

'You've always said the same about teachers.'

'Yes, but I'm talking about this hospital. I've seen very good doctors here, but there is so much degradation.'

'How?'

'This place is just like Makola. Ill-arranged buildings all over the place, no landscaping to soothe the mind, teaming with people, mostly women, as if only the women were sick. Then no privacy, no privacy at all. You come here and everybody knows you're a sick man. I was wheeled to the X-ray department. The place was narrow, dingy and crowded. It was a congestion of the rag-tag of humanity – hefty students looking for medical reports and sporting God's gift of health, frightening tuberculosis patients, cardiac patients whose breathing scares you, all sorts of cases both strong and dying – you feel you're trapped – all your ego goes.'

'It's good for you, Kofi. Your ego must be deflated once in a while. I think Cape Coast, too, is congested. Why pick on Korle Bu?'

'True, Cape Coast is congested but you never feel you're lost in a crowd of unfortunates. I don't remember this country ever decorating any of its architects. We could begin with those who drew up all this mass of buildings.'

'People with any money don't come here. They go to 37 General Hospital.'

'Look at the O.P.D. here. The corridors in front of the consulting rooms are six feet wide and lined on both sides with concrete slabs and hardwood benches for seats. Everybody stares into everybody else's face, wondering, thinking, helpless, for hours. Nurses, doctors, patients move up and down, non-stop, and you have to turn sideways each time on the bare concrete or wood to let them pass. You know, I was taken over there once on a stretcher. Any ablebodied busybody who passed by peered into my face as if to ask, "Why the hell did you get involved in an accident?" '

'Why didn't you tell them to mind their own business?'

'Tell them? You don't seem to understand. You're sick. You're dumb. It's as if you're in a prison vault of the faceless sick. It's

36

when you're one of them that you feel sorry for yourself and for what people can do to their own people. Grace, I prayed, "Don't let me ever come here again. Never!" But is it possible? Can one always escape it? I wish I could do something about it.'

'Maybe you can. That's why you're in politics. You must try.'

'I suppose so, but can I? This hospital is in fact in my constituency. The trouble is, though, that it's easier to handle a crowd of fishermen than a sophisticated organisation of doctors. They will tell me to set up this and that committee which will produce sheafs and sheafs of readable reports, but apart from me, how many will be really committed to change? I will try. By the way, dear, do you think you'd like to live in Accra?' he asked, caressing her hand.

'I don't know. If only the whole of Accra is not like Korle Bu. Kofi, so far it's been very exciting but I think it's so unreal. I feel as if I'm being treated like Cinderella taken back to the palace. It's all very generous and comfortable and, as I've said, exciting but, Kofi, I think what we should do is to have our own house here. If you win the elections, you may never go back to teaching. At least not at Cape Coast. Your own house can make a world of difference. I'm thinking of a two-story building, each story self-contained. If the worst comes, we could let out one floor and live on the other. The rent would keep us going.'

'That's a good idea, Grace. I'll take it up at once with Nee Otu.'

'Right. And about Nee Otu. Don't you think he'll meddle with us if we settle here?'

'Well, darling, a politician's life is not his own. You've got to learn this, too.'

'To what extent, Kofi? Isn't it possible to do politics and have privacy? We've been poor and we've never had friends. Can't we do business with whoever comes along, but live our own lives? Kofi, I think we could keep ourselves to ourselves and yet be sociable enough?'

'Politics, privacy, sociability ... These are not the real things in my mind now. Do you know what are?'

She shook her head.

'My own house, yes. The country owes me one. My father lives in rented rooms after forty years' service to this nasty country.

His pension is ten cedis a month. I have to give him forty each month. I can't save. This is just because he was a teacher. He was one. I am one. A teacher. The tradition continues. Your whole family have been labourers. In a national camp. Exploited, in the land of their birth, by a country that does not know how to say thank you. In a country where everybody smiles. Trust no one! Bullshit!'

'And so?' Grace asked. She had heard this from her husband almost every day at night, in bed.

'So you have to do something about it. Nothing is free. If you are a public man and you want privacy, you have to buy it. Nee Otu is a conduit right into your bedchamber. Don't touch him. Leave him to me and learn to keep yourself to yourself. You'll probably need to learn that as the wife of your darling husband, Kofi.'

'I see!'

'Seriously, though,' Kafu said, adjusting his plastered arm in the sling, 'I'm going to take up this building project. We need a house pretty soon. It shouldn't take more than six months. Then I will have a home for the first time! I'll be a minister! I'll be rich! Oh, gorgeous!'

They were beginning to kiss when a doctor strode in.

Meanwhile Nee Otu Lartey was at Makola, talking to Madam Odofo Lamptey. Her stall was eight feet by twelve. It was right in the thick and filth of the market. There was a small drain eight inches deep running in front of it. It had been cleaned the evening before but had now filled up again with dead mice, rotting vegetables, fish and urine. Opposite her stall were the palm oil, dried fish and grain stalls. Dirt reigned over all and the awful smell of dried fish permeated the whole area. The Gaos who sold the grains had not washed for a week. They lay idly on the bags of grains, picking their noses and scratching their arses. Once in a while they would scratch their legs and thighs, too, making white perpendicular lines all over their exposed parts.

However, Madam Odofo's stall was very neat indeed and heavily scented with air-freshener. She had two assistants, and there were several women customers who had come to buy pieces of textile print. All the walls were lined from top to bottom with the textile pieces. As she spoke to Nee Otu, she kept an eye on the transactions. She was thirty-six. Five feet seven. Light brown skin. Well put together. A beautiful round face, full breast and a slightly bulging stomach. Her thighs were large and tended to make her knock-kneed when she walked. Her forearms were fat like yams. She always looked cheerful, almost gay and fetching. She asked Nee Otu,

'This man Kafu, how old is he?'

'Didn't you read it in the *Liberator*?'

'You know I have no time to read. Just tell me?'

'Thirty-two.'

'Oh he's a young man! Is he circumcised?'

'I don't know. Aren't the Fantes circumcised?'

'I've never had a Fanteman before. Did you say he's handsome?'

'He's not bad at all. He's strong. As good as myself!'

'You? Tcha-a-a! You couldn't do much and you ran away. You took a university woman. They're poor weaklings, but she too ran away. No, no, my shorty!'

'You never used to complain of my being short, my dear!'

'Go on, you naughty fellow! You tricked Araba, the pig-trotter dealer. Then you took my money. You still owe me two thousand. Don't forget that. All my love for you is finished!'

'Oh, you liar!'

'Oh, you runaway rascal! Do you think Kafu will be nice? How much does he want?'

'Six thousand.'

'Can he pay it back? Any guarantees? I'm on the alert this time. No man can come around again and fool me as you did. It's my turn now.'

'He might not be able to pay cash, but he will arrange an import licence for you. Just as I did. I mean for the wax print. If you mention that two thousand cedis again, I'll tell Kafu to throw you out of the Party.'

'Come on, little dear. Bring Kafu here some day. Now, about this money, why not give me ... oh ... let's see ... a week?'

'I don't think a week is too bad. I'll be around, but get some good lunch ready for me, you hear? I'm going to talk to Salamatu.'

'Salamatu! She's as thin as a stick. You talk to her still, you?

You silly man. She looks at me with funny eyes. Maybe because of you and the honest business I do. I'll box her ears one of these days and her blood pressure will sky-rocket. You go away! A short man like you!'

'Damn it, you mustn't touch her. Make sure the lunch is good. She's thin but ... er ... you know!'

'Aha-a-a,' Odofo exclaimed, laughing and clapping her beauti-fully manicured hands, 'never mind, you'll come back all right, pleading hard! You know you will. You little rascal!'

'Make the lunch a good one or you're sacked, you hear?' Nee Otu said, pleasantly grinning and as he hurried away to Auntie Salamatu's stall.

Her stall was some fifty feet away from that of Odofo Lamp-tey, and was opposite to it. She sold all sorts of goods including wines and spirits, which she never displayed. Actually she had no licence to to sell them but her clientele was varied and ran through the entire range of social strata. Her stall was the same size as Odofo's and a lot of her wares were displayed in front of it. They were things like wigs, ladies' and men's underwear, per-fumery, toilet items, beverages and canned provisions. The inside served more as a warehouse than anything else.

Auntie Salamatu watched intently as Nee Otu Lartey came along. He looked very cheerful but she was frowning; and of course when she frowned, she looked extremely attractive. She was not only tall and lightly built but lithe and seductive. Her supple waist was supported by shapely thighs. Her arms were long and well-shaped, and so were her fingers. Her face was slightly narrow and her nose as straight as if it had been chiselled by a sculptor. Her eyes were large and sleepy. She was always well dressed and scented. She was a good twenty-eight years old. As soon as Nee Otu was within earshot, while he was still draw-ing near to take her hand, she asked, 'What were you doing with Fat-Thighs?'

'Nothing in particular. I went to see if I could buy a piece of cloth.'

'And you spent so long about it?'

'I was trying to choose.'

'And you talked so much?'

'To beat down the price. How are you, my dear?'

'Did you say "my dear" to Odofo?'

'Of course not. You know she no longer wants me. Besides she's a Christian. Don't you trust me?'

'Why didn't you come last night?'

'I went to visit my friend, Kafu. I've told him all about you.'

'Does he have a troublesome wife?'

'No, you will get along with him splendidly. Can you give him the six thousand? If he can get you an import licence for a hundred thouand cedis' worth of turkey tails and another one for twenty thousand cedis' worth of black hair dye, you'll easily write off the six thousand, won't you?'

'Definitely. I'll make a clean twelve thousand, but you won't get a cut, mind you!'

'Oh, come on. You know I love you the most. You know I do!'

'Me!' she exclaimed putting her hand gently on her breast.

'You! I swear!' Nee Otu said, pointing his forefinger to the heavens and looking grave.

'Ataa Otu, how soon is the money wanted?'

'What about tonight?'

'Will you come for it, and will you bring Kafu?'

'He hasn't been discharged yet.'

'I see. Does he drink?'

'Yes, he does.'

'What kind?'

'Beer.'

'Beer drinkers sleep too much. I'll try him. I like it when you take whisky. Come tonight, darling!'

5

Mr Benjy Baisi looked as youthful, erect and fresh as ever as he strode along the long linking corridors at Korle Bu. Rev. Opia Dan Sese, who had virtually become assistant headmaster during the absence of Kafu, was in step with him. When they entered Kafu's side ward, he was reading *The Prince*.

'Are you still reading Machiavelli?' Opia asked, happy to see Kafu in excellent health.

'The prose is very Augustan,' Benjy Baisi interjected with a smile.

'It's very good reading for a sick man,' Kafu said, raising himself unenthusiastically to sit up on the bed. The presence of Baisi made him uncomfortable. He had an impulsive aversion to the man and had always striven without success to rationalise it and exorcise it. He said, 'I'm sorry, Mr Baisi, I couldn't ask permission before I left the school. I thought I could make it over the weekend and return before Monday morning.'

'It's nice to see you well, Kafu. Are your nomination papers filed?'

'Yes.'

'That means you'll definitely enter politics and quit the school?'

'I'm on my way out. I'll write formally very shortly.'

'I hope you've considered the full implications for your teaching career, or, shall I say, to your career, generally?'

'Why not? I'm on my way out. You refused to help me. What else could you expect me to do?'

'It's never been a question of helping you. No, it never has been.'

'How is Grace doing, Abraham?' Opia Sese asked Kafu, soothingly.

'She's very well, thank you.'

'The school farm is doing well, Kafu. We've cleared the ground and planted it. Opia Sese is supervising the whole farming project. He's doing a wonderful job,' Mr Baisi informed Kafu, making every effort to sound as amicable as possible. He

42

added, 'When we harvest, I'm sure we will send you some of the produce, won't we, Opia?'

'Yes, yes; we will. In fact, I've started a backyard garden of banana, coco-yam, pepper, onion and pineapple. You'll get a surprise load from me some day, Abraham. And what a lovely bunch of roses you've got here!'

'Oh, these? They were brought in by the cleaner this morning,' Kafu said casually.

'I see,' said Opia Sese. 'This cleaner must have a very good taste. I love roses. They make me feel good. I'll bring you some when we come next.'

'Thank you. Don't bother. I'm getting out of here today or tomorrow. I must round off the campaign. All the groundwork has been done for me.'

'You're lucky,' Benjy Baisi said.

'Oh yes, in Accra they help others! I thought you knew?'

'I've never been a close political observer. The point is noted,' Benjy Baisi said as he dabbed his face with a neat handkerchief, not amused.

'Of course, Abraham, some people get help at the right time for the right job. We feel proud to be here with you when you're on the threshold of greatness. We're very proud of you,' Rev. Opia Dan Sese said with a highly civilised smile.

'Thank you Osofo. You see not everybody ... Hello! Nee Otu, you're welcome. This is Mr Baisi, headmaster of my school, and Rev. Sese, his assistant. Gentlemen, this is a friend.'

'I thought you said the assistant post was vacant?' Nee Otu said as he studied the two gentlemen closely.

'It's true the post is vacant, Mr ...?' Opia Sese modulated his voice to ask Nee Otu's name.

'Otu Lartey,' Nee Otu obliged.

'I've retired, Mr Otu Lartey. I'm only trying to help the country in whatever capacity I'm needed. Mr Baisi asked me to act since our brother is not well and is likely to leave the school soon.'

'Very good,' Nee Otu replied, 'this is the kind of selflessness that is needed in this country. To serve the country hard until you grow old and drop dead.'

'Thank you! Thank you, sir!' Opia Sese said gravely and with a bow. 'I've been telling the younger generation in the classroom

43

and from the pulpit that to serve without reward is the basis of true national greatness.'

'I'm glad to hear this, Reverend Sese. I understand the young boys and girls say they're working out their own philosophies. They find the old philosophies hollow.'

'Oh yes! Oh yes! Let them try, while the republic totters and the military and the police, too, work out everlasting philosophies,' Rev. Sese said with a smile. 'We, too, are trying to survive, coup or no coup, with the old philosophies, aren't we?'

'Correct!' Kafu shouted.

'Well, Kafu, we must leave. We're going back to Cape Coast right now. Don't forget to give my love to your wife. And take good care of yourself,' Mr Baisi said.

Hands were shaken, goodbyes were said and the two gentlemen left.

'Kafu, I think that reverend minister is great!'

'He is. I trust him. Now Nee Otu, before you say anything else, there is something I want you to do for me.'

'Name it.'

'I want a house.'

'But we've hired one for you.'

'No, no; Nee Otu, I mean my own house on my own plot of land right here in Accra.'

'Why not in Cape Coast?'

'In Cape Coast? You must be joking. My relations would decide that the house was too big for me and they'd come and occupy half of it and ask me to feed them on top of it. In Accra you live in anonymity. I want a two-story building, four bedrooms and baths and a study on each floor. Both floors should be self-contained.'

'In which part of Accra?'

'I don't know Accra very well. You choose.'

'There are four possible areas, I think. They are swank and are being developed fast. They're Labone, Roman Ridge, Airport and Asylum Down. Personally, I like a place where I can see the sea, so I would choose Labone.'

'How about the land?'

'We will have to apply to the Lands Department, but they won't give you any.'

'Why not?

'You have nothing. Two hundred cedis in your savings account? Kafu, you have nothing. You will be ignored.'

'So what do we do. Nee Otu?'

'The solution is at our fingertips. We will divert the money from Salamatu and Odofo into your personal bank account. That gives you twelve thousand. Add the two thousand and you get fourteen thousand. It's not a bad figure. Fourteen thousand plus your political standing – this is what the civil servant wants to hear most. His reasoning is impeccable. Your house will cost thirty-six thousand, you have more than one-third of the amount. If you win the elections you may become a minister, and who knows what would happen if you hadn't had a service you were entitled to – at least according to the regulations. So the plot you shall get. Tomorrow! The building starts in eight days. I have a plan which answers your specifications. We will start the building before the plan is approved by the authorities! Leave them to me!'

'Nee Otu, whoever says life is not beautiful is an ass, you know?'

'True, Kafu. You cannot dig life on a school compound. I am not surprised at the large number of teachers seeking election.'

'And do you see these roses, Nee Otu? I was with Grace here when a doctor hurried in. We were kissing somewhat, when he came in. I thought it was my doctor but it wasn't. He was going to admonish me, but I told him it was my own wife and it was about as far as we could go. He was rather tall and handsome and soft-spoken. He told me he had been asked by Salamatu to come and say hello to me. He brought me these roses from her this morning. Do you know him?'

'I suppose so.'

'Who is he?'

'Dr Mills Blankson. He's the son of your constituency chairman. He's a young man of twenty-seven. We all went to Accra Royal School, he and Salamatu and I, though I was far ahead of him. He was fond of Salamatu, but his love was either calf or platonic, I couldn't care. I've been down-to-earth from childhood. He has never forgotten her nor forgiven me. And he says Salamatu sent you these roses?'

'Yes, it was a sort of pleasant surprise but I didn't understand it very well. Grace, too, was a little puzzled, but she thought it was probably all political.'

'It's all right as far as it goes,' Nee Otu said, weighing up the situation. 'Salamatu has a way of playing on the instincts of men so as to squeeze money from them all the time. That doctor chap is in her firm grip, Kafu. We don't want to antagonise him or his father. They're a very rich family. Kafu, you'll have to play your cards well with Salamatu, you know. We will see her some time. Haven't you been discharged yet?'

'Yes, I have been.'

'Why didn't you say so?'

'I didn't want Mr Baisi to know.'

'Then let's pack up and go home. We've a lot to do.'

Some days later, Kafu and Nee Otu Lartey visited Odofo at her stall. Trade was brisk and money was pouring in. Kafu was amazed at the large amounts of money carried by the women dealers in textiles. Odofo was operating passbooks with G. B. Ollivant, UAC, GNTC, UTC, SCOA and CFAO. She had virtually all the brands and everyone was anxious to clear as much stock as possible. What struck Kafu most about the women was their air of self-assurance and independence, apart from the fact that they looked well-fed, and, in many cases, overfed.

Many of them recognised Kafu and rushed on him. Shouts of 'our darling!', 'my sweetheart!', 'my husband!', 'my boyfriend!', 'my handsome young man!', 'the redeemer of Makola from filth!', 'the provider of new lavatories and bathrooms!', 'the one who will make the Gaos wash and stop seducing schoolgirls!', 'vote Liberation Party, the NUP are cowards!', 'Accra Central is all for you, Kafu!' filled the air. They embraced him, some removed their cover-cloth to fan him like a chief, some sprayed him with lavender and a daring eighteen-year-old girl poured white powder on his head and tied a white calico strip round his neck to signify victory. A nine-year-old girl lit a firecracker and others of her age responded here and there. It was all noise and hilarity interspersed with the protestations of the Gaos, who, when they heard the women's insults, stopped scratching themselves and started booing. One of them said he had enough money to marry any of them, any time; except that they were all too fat and he would be cuckolded anyway. This sparked off a low exchange of words in which all were deeply interested and entertained, but some pretended it was only the Gaos who were being coarse. Eventually, so much attention was diverted by the verbal interlude that the pressure on Kafu eased off. Odofo grabbed him by the cuff and led him to a place like a little room at the back of her stall, behind the displayed cloths. There Nee Otu, Odofo and Kafu heaved a sigh.

'What a reception!' Kafu said, overwhelmed but happy.

'Don't be inept, dear,' Odofo told him. 'Go back and thank the crowd. Tell them when you get into power the gutters will be swept twice, lavatories will be provided and street lamps installed all over the market. Don't talk about the Gaos. We can easily raise money from them. Just say if they don't keep their stalls clean, their licences might be reviewed. Get out and speak with authority!'

Kafu stood on a table in front of Odofo's stall and delivered a speech which made the crowd clap again and again. He spoke in measured tones when he reached this portion of his speech:

'This country has given me an expensive, long and brilliant education. It has done so at the expense of many others. Today there are many clever children who do not get my opportunity because of their background. The country has never asked me to pay back, but I have decided to help in any way I can. I stand here as your servant dedicated to seeking your basic needs for you. Without you, Accra will starve. And yet you work in surroundings which are absolutely deplorable. You have been deceived by successive administrations. The Liberation Party will liberate you for ever from their deceit. We shall form a government of scholars whose capacity for turning this country into a paradise no other administration can match. We shall never, never disappoint you. Vote for Kafu: the man who knows more about the history of your neglect than any other person!'

Kafu was once again mobbed, but once again Odofo rescued him and took him to the back of the stall. There was a deep-freeze and a fridge there. In a twinkle of an eye a slim, young girl of about seventeen had spread a little table with salad, small chops, beer and soft drinks. The beer was as cool as ever. Odofo struck Kafu as a woman careful of detail, for she supervised very closely every bit the refreshment. 'Kafu,' she called, 'I've whisky, Dimple Haig, would you care for some?'

'No, thank you. I relax with whisky. It's too early yet.'

'Ataa Otu, you hear? Here's a gentleman. You drink whisky any time, and you call yourself a Moslem.'

'Shut up. You do the same.'

'Come on, I'm not a Moslem, am I?'

'Odofo,' Kafu said.

'My dear,' she replied.

'I have to thank you very much for the money. It's been paid into my bank account. I do not come from a family that handles much money. I appreciate your help.'

'Don't mention it, my dear. I'm in business. At the moment business is good. It's a trend we pray will continue. We don't know books, but we know that we get governments which without notice change the whole trend of business through a radio announcement. People get ruined overnight. You see, there are hardly any rich people in this country. The businessmen people think are rich are really overdraft millionaires like Nee Otu.'

'Oh, you shut up,' Nee Otu said, as he began to drink whisky with the left hand and caress his bare belly with the right. He wore a loose shirt, and on this hot day he had not put on an undervest.

'It's true, Kafu. When a so-called rich businessman dies in this country, he never leaves behind as much as he made people expect.'

'How about you?' Nee Otu asked her, winking at Kafu.

'Me? When my mother died, I was the only surviving child. She left me this business with a capital of one thousand cedis, and three plots of land, on one of which she had a three-room house where we lived. I have improved that house and still live in it. I have now got buildings on the two other plots. To tell the truth, I'm making money but I don't consider myself rich. I've had two husbands but they deserted me. Ataa Otu came along to try but he ran away before he could made an impression. I have no child, Kafu. Maybe I pamper the men. Nee Otu simply ran away. He wanted money every day and there were too many women. So Kafu, here I am. The whole of me. Take this two hundred cedis and use it as pocket-money for a day or two. You'll need it for the rally at Bukom Square.'

'How about me?' Nee Otu said.

'Nothing.'

'Come on, Odofo, don't pretend you don't know me today. Do something!'

'Kafu, you see what a rascal he is? All right, you take this twenty-five and don't ask me for any more till the end of the year. Now, Kafu, the Makola Women's Union has been fully organised for the big rally. Mr Mills Blankson says it's going to be the biggest and the greatest. We hear the NUP are organising another one at Post Office Square to undercut ours. I feel so sorry for your opponent, what do they call him?'

'Adjin Yeboah,' Kafu and Nee Otu said almost at the same time.

'Yes, Adjin. He's such a handsome young man.'

'Is he? Do you like him too?' Nee Otu asked.

'No of course not. But he's entitled to try.'

'Really?' Nee Otu was upset by Odofo's admission.

'Why not? I keep it open. I feel so sorry for him. He simply hasn't got the money.'

'But he's a lawyer,' Nee Otu contended.

'That's the trouble. Everybody thinks because he's a lawyer he must have money. We in trade know how fast things are changing in this country. In Makola we know that not all the lawyers who go to court nowadays have money, as was the case when I was a schoolgirl. We hear some of them are as broke as stranded Lebanese. Adjin Yeboah is one of them. I suppose he expects to make money in politics. If so, he's a fool. He's chosen the wrong party. Kafu, he's a real Ga and a distant relation of mine, but in Accra we give everybody a chance. I don't care about him. I can't help him. He says no one should trade and that only government should sell goods. Does he expect us here in Makola to live on sand? We are prepared to compete with the government in trade, but instead of opening its own stores everywhere in the city, including Nima, Nungua and Apenkwa, they want to wreck what has taken me and my mother years to build up. Fools! We will teach them. Kafu, show them that you didn't go to school for nothing!'

'How old is Adjin Yeboah?' Kafu asked.

'He's twenty-six,' Odofo replied.

'Did he go to university?'

'No, he never did. He read his law here behind Makola, and instead of helping us to work in better surroundings he talks about depriving us of our daily bread. And, after all, he's entering politics to make money himself. He'll get the shock of his life. People think we Makola women cannot think for ourselves, so they try to meddle with us.'

'What sort of person is he?' Kafu asked. He wanted to know more about his rival.

'As I've said, he's handsome. . . .'

'For you every man is handsome,' Nee Otu cut in.

'At least he's taller than you! Some five feet ten, and lanky. He looks like someone who is either hungry or sick. He doesn't seem to have much energy in him. But he has a handsome face. He comes from Atukpai, from poor parents, went to Accra High School and did brilliantly there. He would have gone to the university but the allowance was too little, and besides, his father, a fisherman, died the very year he would have gone. So he had to work. He went to work in the Supreme Court as a clerk, became interested in law, and studied hard just across the road from here. He's a young barrister now. He could go and work with the State Insurance Corporation, take a loan, put up a house and let it to get extra income. Now he wants to do politics so that his name will be heard every day on the radio doing this or that – a great man. The same radio will announce his downfall with glee, if I know my countrymen. Look, Kafu, we mean business. I will stand on your right at the rally. We will give the NUP hell. Our stand is simple : man must work to eat. He must create work for himself. The government cannot employ and feed all of us. We women are trying to work and feed ourselves and not depend on rascals like Nee Otu. Why should the NUP destroy us? Ask them for us. Poor Adjin Yeboah, I feel sorry for him personally. He's up to the neck in debt. The NUP has no funds.'

'Odofo, be careful. You don't feed my wives,' Nee Otu protested.

'Oh my darling, you're right!' and she gave Nee Otu a nice warm kiss. Nee Otu grinned. She grabbed Kafu by the shoulders and gave him a buss. Aroused, Kafu embraced her firmly and gave her a long passionate kiss. Nee Otu looked on, blinking.

Odofo was right. The rally at Bukom was the largest ever. Both the National Landlords' Association and the Makola Women's Union displayed extraordinary organising ability. They had wonderful support from the Taxi Drivers' Union. Members of that Union feared that if the NUP won they would first ban private taxi business and then fail to provide the people with state buses and taxis. The NUP must be forestalled before it did any mischief. So they carted people from all parts of Accra to Bukom Square free of charge. All sorts of people wanted to ride taxis free for the first and perhaps the last time in their lives. They flocked to the place.

At Bukom Square itself the bunting was flying. The following bands were present: Baya, Kpanlogo, Kolomashi, The Superstar Zoundz and Bukom Brass Band, popularly known as BBB. These bands were playing in different sections for those of different tastes. The public address system was brand new, supplied free by Mr Doku Lamptey, the well-known electrical contractor of Kokomlemle, who swore that if the NUP won he would commit suicide.

On the dais were the constituency stalwarts, with Mr Mills Blankson and Odoi Hammond very much in evidence. Mr Mills Blankson's bald head was particularly well scrubbed on this afternoon, and was shining brightly. He was dressed in a jumper and rich kente. Odoi Hammond wore shorts and Joromi: excellent attire for any trouble. Salamatu and Dr Mills Blankson were there, so was Nee Otu. He was in charge of operations. Odofo was as militant as ever. She wore a Liberation Party cloth.

Kafu was carried from the Bombay Bazaar roundabout like a chief. He was also in rich kente. Talking drums preceded and followed him. The crowd was so thick that newspapermen, cameramen, TV crews and amateur photographers had to beg their way into two-story buildings or stand on the roofs of cars to take pictures. There was singing and shouting of slogans. It was both a solemn and an enthusiastic mass movement to Bukom Square.

Barely half a mile from Bukom Square at Post Office Square, in front of Ghana House, the NUP rally was well under way. The police had wanted to refuse the NUP a licence to hold the rally so close to that of the Liberation Party. It was feared that if a misunderstanding broke out between supporters there would be ugly scenes. But when the subject was given further thought, both parties were given an equal opportunity to make their final appeals.

No doubt the NUP had its zealous followers, mostly messengers, tenants, labourers, members of the Bus Drivers' Union, some university lecturers who had become apostles of social justice, sanitary labourers, industrial workers, commercial workers, railway workers, mine workers, mortuary attendants and teachers who had not been promoted in ten years. It was a serious-minded group with a compelling theme: they must get on as well as anybody else. The state must be an instrument for achieving this. Without state intervention, man would exploit man – a condition of social injustice. It happened that the NUP were more expert at words than at mobilisation, so the count of their rally was under five thousand while the Bukom Square rally commanded eighty thousand, some of whom spilled over to the Sraha, Atukpai and Akoto Lante areas.

Adjin Yeboah was, however, not perturbed by the poor attendance. He had been assured by a survey and opinion polls conducted by university lecturers that the NUP would definitely win in Accra Central. Besides, Adjin Yeboah had a deep-seated feeling that his own people would never let him down by voting for someone who had come all the way from Cape Coast to represent their interests. He was sure that Kafu did not know the problems of the constituency as well as he did, since he was born and bred there. The constituents were his own kith and kin.

This was a strong platform theme for him, and he played it up vigorously as he spoke that day. He insisted that Accra Central had been neglected for too long and that areas like Atukpai, Gbese, James Town, Akoto Lante, Asre and Ogbamenaa formed one vast dishonourable slum. 'Anybody from these places who makes money runs away to build elsewhere, never to return. So, go to Korlegonno, Link Road, Kaneshie, Ringway Estate and Labone, just to mention a few, and you'll find our own people who have abandoned their place of birth, leaving it to old men and women to rot in!'

Then he shouted into the microphone: 'I have a vision of Accra Central transformed into a showpiece of this country, with its apartment buildings, supermarkets, first-class elementary and secondary schools, a hospital and supporting clinics, where our children will have beautiful homes to which they will feel proud to belong. It is not for my glory that I seek these things. "He who is down, need fear no fall." It is for you, ladies and gentlemen, that I'm sacrificing all that I have so that you, too, shall enjoy the abundance of our country. You don't betray me if you don't vote for me; you betray your own welfare. Away with exploitation! I will win! I will strive for the good life for you till I die! Long live social justice!'

The crowd began to sing *Yen Ara Asase Ni.* Those who didn't know the words hummed it courageously.

Meanwhile Kafu, too, was blasting away at Bukom. Salamatu was talking to Dr Mills Blankson. Nee Otu would have very much liked to know what on earth they were talking so intimately about, but there were two rows between them. Their conversation was, however, merely political. Dr Mills Blankson was unhappy about the health of Adjin Yeboah. As children, they had played football in the streets together, from gutter to gutter, to the annoyance of motorists. They had also had several juvenile escapades, such as stealing plantains from lorries that had parked in front of Sraha. Adjin Yeboah had complained of tiredness and sleeplessness and he had given him sedatives. Kafu, too, knew this. He said, after pausing for effect: 'Ladies and gentlemen, the man who is standing against me is a true product of Accra Central. Everybody knows this. Indeed, his very energy and health have vanished, though he has not even started serving you! We want someone who is strong and healthy, kith or no kith, who will fight for you and see his schemes through; not someone who will collapse on the way. I have the energy. I have the knowledge. Yes, I have had the guts to sacrifice all I have and come over to Accra Central to ensure that those who have shall have more and those who have not shall begin to have. I say, you do not vote only for Kafu when you vote for me. You vote for your own welfare when you vote for Kafu!' The applause erupted and the BBB at the instigation of Odoi Hammond broke into a Bo, bo; bo, boo, bo!

So Kafu shuttled between Accra and Cape Coast. He and his family had more or less taken residence in the rented house at

Labone. He had not resigned yet but missed a lot of classes. Mr Benjy Baisi bore it all without complaint. When the elections were held, Kafu won.

Adjin Yeboah was aghast. He had stayed by the TV up to 3 am at Party Headquarters in Kimberley Avenue. Soon after the news, he rose painfully from an old couch and said feebly that he needed sleep and could be expected back at Headquarters by ten in the morning. He would make a press statement and congratulate Kafu. Before going to bed, however, he took an overdose of barbiturates.

6

Accra Central was important to the Liberation Party. Of the 21,868 votes cast there, Kafu garnered 18,562. Grace was so excited by the news that she gave birth to a baby girl the following morning. Nee Otu Lartey was jubilant. He drank half a bottle of whisky at Odofo's house at Labone. On his way back home he ran into the rear of a brand new Toyota taxi. The driver called him a bastard and wanted to thrash him, but was restrained by a group of young men who realised that Nee Otu was drunk. Nee Otu pulled out his wallet and counted a hundred cedis in rustling, new, denominations of ten. The taxi driver's eyes began to pop out of their sockets. Nee Otu waved the notes in his face and asked, 'Are you keen on getting the police?'

'What do you think, sir?' replied the taxi driver, removing his cap and holding it in his hand.

'I'm not very keen myself,' Nee Otu said.

'Nor me, sir!' the driver said quickly.

'All right. Take this and don't be foolish next time.'

Nee Otu handed him the hundred cedis. There was hardly any damage done to the taxi, as the impact had been on the bumper.

'Yes, sir. Thank you very much, sir. I will behave next time, sir,' the man said hurriedly, anxious to leave the place with the money.

'Wait, man! Won't you count the money?' Nee Otu asked him.

'Yes, sir. Yes, sir,' the man answered and counted the money with trembling fingers. As he got into his car, Nee Otu went over to him and asked, 'Who's the owner of this taxi?'

'Her name is Auntie Salamatu, sir. She is a Moslem and doesn't tolerate drunken men, sir.'

'I see. Goodbye, idiot!' Nee Otu dismissed him.

'Yes, sir,' he replied adjusting his cap.

He drove off wondering. Nee Otu drove straight to Salamatu, who put him to bed. When he woke up, Kafu was sitting close to her on a sofa. Salamatu was taking brandy and was smoking a filtered king-size cigarette. Kafu was on beer. He was in new, extremely well-tailored, slightly bell-bottomed trousers, with a broad belt, a new pair of trendy black shoes and an expensive Joromi. His Peugeot 204 was chauffeur-driven now and the driver was fast asleep in it outside the house, dead tired.

Salamatu was in a lace dress, custom-sewn. It had cost two hundred and fifty cedis. It was a beautiful Hausa robe and she looked like a great Fulani-Hausa queen. She was dignified but not supercilious, saying little but implying much with her motions and looks, graceful but deliberate and very much in control of herself.

Kafu was relaxed. He looked like a man of authority. His hair was on this occasion well combed. When Nee Otu woke from his slumbers, he asked, 'Ata Otu, what happened?'

'H-mm! I went to the Hotel President to celebrate on my own, between me and Allah. It's your great victory. I sometimes like to celebrate all on my own, and collect my thoughts. When I had finished and was driving home, I had a flat tyre at the bus stop near the Holy Spirit Cathedral. Some young men came to help me fix it. I think they suspected I was tight, and they picked my wallet of one hundred cedis. I must go to your building site tomorrow morning before I go to the bank.'

'Ata Otu,' Salamatu said with an amused smile, 'you want money, all right?'

'Of course!'

'You'll get it,' she said, 'but let's talk business, Kafu has been assigned the Ministry of Internal Welfare. I'm disappointed. I would have liked the Ministry of Trade. That's where he can help us directly. Over ten thousand cedis of mine has gone into these elections. By the way, Kafu, what did you do with the six thousand? I know I contributed two thousand for the Bukom rally, one thousand for the maintenance of the constituency office and one thousand for the running and maintenance of the constituency propaganda van. What was the six thousand used for?'

'Salamatu,' Nee Otu replied, 'don't be so simple. The six thousand was used for canvassing.'

'But Kafu, you said it was used in buying your car?'

'Look here, girl,' Nee Otu said, 'it comes to the same thing. If you don't have a car, you can't canvass. Salamatu, you want a licence for turkey tails, right?'

'Right,' she agreed.

'Then why not say so instead of looking into the accounts?' He spoke in a no-nonsense manner. 'Girl, you've got to give Kafu time to settle down. You'll get your licence. Where's my money? And serve me some ginger ale, please.'

The drink was served. The money was given to Nee Otu and they had an excellent dinner together. All along, Kafu was admiring Salamatu without intermission or inhibition. It was her eyes and waist that charmed him most. He could not take his eyes off them. Nee Otu was wondering what was new about them that so attracted him. He thought, 'Here's the son of a minister of religion. He was born on a church compound. Raised under strict discipline. Went to boarding school. Attended University. Came out. Taught in a boys' boarding school. Married a girl whose parents are highly educated, disciplined and religious. Now he meets a real woman and can't stop looking at her. What a frog!'

Kafu said, 'Nee Otu, what are you thinking about? I'll be going to the Ministry tomorrow to see what the place is like. I'll start business in a week. There are some constituency matters to sort out. I'm making up my mind on several issues. I'll take good care of Salamatu. She shouldn't worry. She will be rewarded. I feel so sorry for Adjin Yeboah. He died for nothing.'

'I agree,' said Nee Otu. 'He never properly understood money.

Where there are free elections, no one gets power by sheer moral appeal.'

Kafu asked for a cigarette and two fingers of whisky which he took neat and straight. He had never done this before. He felt Adjin Yeboah's death was all wrong. 'There is nothing he should have sacrificed his life for,' he said almost to himself. Nee Otu sighed. Salamatu was not interested.

Kafu arrived at the Ministry of Internal Welfare at nine-fifteen. A police orderly sat by his driver while he sat majestically behind. He was in the 204. An official car was being arranged for him. When his car pulled up in front of the ministry, the orderly jumped out, opened the door with unnecessary haste and saluted with a flourish. The word went round the ministry building in a flash that the new minister had arrived. The entire ministry was hushed and work went on like clockwork.

Kafu was received by Mr Nutor Vuga, who had long before been up-graded to the rank of permanent secretary and transferred from the Department of Welfare Services and Pedagogy to the Ministry of Internal Welfare. He was a cadaverous man. His hair was always cut short and there was a lot of grey in it. He wore huge bifocal glasses which seemed to swallow most of his big, broad nose. He always wore expensive, old-fashioned shirts with stiff cuffs and highly priced links. His trousers were conventional, so also were his shoes which were usually over-polished. He had spoken so often softly to his superiors that he seemed by nature to be soft-spoken. He had worked in the civil service for thirty years and knew by heart the numbers of hundreds of files.

Mr Vuga had no political philosophy. For thirty years, his life had been so conditioned by rules and regulations that he had no great convictions beyond apearing to be honest with his work and being seen to be hard-working. He equated real or hard work with putting in long hours, from six in the morning to seven or eight in the evening. He spent them toiling away at heaps and heaps of files, each marked for either urgent or immediate action. Even when he had not much file work to do, he would hold interviews and start more file work after six in the evening.

He never went on leave because he had worked for so long both in the office and at home that he no longer knew how to relax, at home or elsewhere. He tried once to go on leave but changed his mind because he felt strongly that his deputy, an ambitious young man, was unequal to the task. By the same token, he was convinced that none of his top officers should go on leave, and if any of them succeeded in doing so he manoeuvered to have him recalled on the grounds of emergency work. When an officer enjoyed his full leave, he was terribly disappointed. He devised subtle ways to harass him after his return, preferably psychologically. Of course, he would often explain quietly in harmless tones, that the regulations stated that the entire time of an officer was at the disposal of the government, and all he had to do was to let the government have value for money.

Of the three hundred people working under him in the ministry, Mr Vuga knew only eight well. These were the most senior ones. He never called them by their first names and never smiled at them, particularly if he saw them outside the ministry. He hardly ever held meetings, unless he wanted to check up on those who were not on the premises. He communicated with his top staff through minuting. He had an unshaken belief in recording everything. 'One never knows,' he once said.

Mr Vuga had no reason to believe in delegation of authority. He tried it once, but the same ambitious deputy, W. W. Mensah, displayed so much resourcefulness that he felt it was nothing but a one-man conspiracy to perform better than himself.

Indeed, Mr Nutor Vuga was so dedicated, so hard-working and efficient that he had no time to read, think or relax.

He had a profound disrespect for politicians. He saw them as adventurers from whom he had to take dutiful instructions in order to keep his family and himself going, and to consolidate the substantial gratuity and the pension he would collect when he retired in the not-too-distant future.

He was married with six children. One was an undergraduate at the University of Science and Technology, Kumasi; four were in secondary boarding schools and the last was in kindergarten. His wife, called Beauty, was functionally literate, fat, middle-aged and afraid to have any more children. She had no income beyond what her husband gave her. She was frugal with his food and extravagant with her dress.

Because of the oath of secrecy, Mr Vuga never discussed with her anything whatsoever that took place at the ministry, whether official or unofficial. Virtually all the conversation he could afford to have with Beauty centred around the management of the house. Mr Vuga had an entertainment allowance which he was supposed to use to bring his staff together, but since he was not anxious to betray his wife, who had never attended nor organised a party for executives, he used the money to buy socks for himself and underwear for his children.

Mr Nutor Vuga was well known through the entire ministry for one great personal code: no one should lose his job through him and no one should rise to his level or earn as big a salary as himself if he could help it. He observed this code so meticulously that the one thing he came to detest most was recommending people for promotion or for any form of advancement in other careers. He hated deeply anyone who left the ministry for a better job. In his judgement, each year produced more incompetent or sick officers not worthy of advancement. On the day Kafu arrived at the ministry, there were over one hundred unfilled vacancies. No one in the whole country questioned him. The more his staff grumbled, the happier he became inwardly, feeling they were nothing but a bunch of incompetent, complaining lazybones. He was adept at giving ministers this impression. They relied on him absolutely.

'Hello, Mr Nutor Vuga,' Kafu said without condescension. 'I understand you're the permanent secretary around here.'

'Yes, sir.'

'Where do you come from, incidentally?'

'From Keta, sir.'

'I hear your people catch shrimps and sell them to France. Why don't they eat them? Shrimps are very good.'

'They eat some and sell some, sir. It's good for their bodies and the body politic, sir,' Mr Vuga replied, concealing his anger.

'And what do they do with the shrimp money? Use it to stop the sea from swallowing the place up, or buy contraband goods from Lome?'

'To stop the sea if they can, but I don't know about contraband goods, sir.'

'Of course, you wouldn't. I hear a good civil servant never knows anything until he sees it on a file. Well, now, where is my office?'

59

'This way, sir,' Mr Vuga said dryly. He was wondering what sort of man he had got on his hands. He had worked with many different types of politicians and he knew there was one thing common to all of them: they enter with a bang and vanish in a whiff. Would Kafu fit the pattern? Could he work with him or would Kafu, with these unusual introductory questions, have him removed and dumped in a ministry where he would have to begin to learn and adapt all over again?

As they moved along the long verandah, Kafu asked, 'Where do you expect to spend your retirement – Ho, Denu or Keta?'

'I haven't decided yet, sir,' Mr Vuga answered. He was not used to talking about his personal affairs in the ministry.

'You haven't decided yet?' Kafu asked smiling. 'I hear that when a Ketaman of your standing retires, he settles either at Ho or Denu; or is it Ho, really?'

Mr Vuga decided to ignore the question. He said, 'This way, sir. Here's your office, sir.'

'Good,' Kafu said. 'It's a big room all right. Who chose the carpet?'

'I did, sir.'

'You like blue?'

'Not altogether, sir,' Mr Vuga replied. Actually Mr Vuga's favourite colour was blue. The year before he was prepared to wait for eight months in order to buy a blue Ford Cortina.

'If you don't, why is it here? Have it removed at once, you understand? I want something that matches the colour of the walls and furniture, all right?'

'Yes, sir.'

'I want a better writing-desk.'

'Yes, sir.'

'Remove those pictures of past politicians from the walls. You should have done this long ago.'

'Yes, sir.'

'I want a refrigerator.'

'Yes, sir.'

'It should be stocked with cider, beer and soft drinks. And you must keep a stock of whisky, gin and two or three bottles of champagne, right?'

'We have no vote for strong drinks, sir,' Mr Vuga replied. He thought, 'None of the people I've worked with started like this!'

'I beg your pardon, Mr Vuga?' Kafu asked impatiently.

'I said we have no vote for strong drinks, sir.'

'What do you expect to do, then?'

'I'll apply to the Treasury for permission, sir.'

'You'd better do that. What's that big file on my table for?' Kafu asked, looking at a thick solitary file on his desk.

'It sets out for you, sir, the duties, responsibilities, scope, manpower, policies, estimates, development and progress in connection with this ministry.'

'Can't you summarise all that in one page?'

'This is a big ministry, sir.'

'I didn't ask you the size of the ministry. Can you or can you not summarise all that in at most two pages, to give me an overview before I go into details?'

'I'll try, sir.'

'It's not a question of trying, Mr Vuga. I want it ready today week, you understand?'

'Yes, sir.'

'Very good. Now, Mr Vuga, please sit down,' Kafu commanded as he settled confidently behind his desk. Mr Vuga sat in front of him with a ubiquitous little notebook that never parted from him. His ballpoint pen was ready. He was first-class at taking down instructions.

Kafu began as if he was dictating a letter to a secretary. 'Write to the headmaster of National Secondary School, Mr Benjy Baisi, and inform him that he has been relieved of his post as headmaster of the school with immediate effect. He should hand over the administration of the school to Rev. Opia Dan Sese. He must vacate the school bungalow within thirty-six hours and should not thereafter be seen on or near the school compound.'

'This is absolutely irregular, sir.' Mr Vuga protested. He had never opposed a minister directly in such language before.

'What's irregular about it?' Kafu asked coolly, lolling back and forth in his ministerial chair and once in a while wheeling round for the sheer enjoyment of the seat.

'It is not the responsibility of this ministry to sack headmasters, sir.'

'So?'

'The procedure is most irregular, sir.'

'I see,' Kafu said with forensic detachment. 'What's the name of this ministry, Mr Vuga?'

'The Ministry of Internal Welfare, sir.'

'Is this ministry responsible or not for the social, physical, moral and spiritual welfare of all citizens irrespective of age, sex, occupation or religion?'

'It is, sir.'

'Has this ministry the right to restrain the activities of any citizen whose conduct is not conducive to the public good?'

'It has discretionary powers, sir.'

'What do you mean by discretionary powers? You realise you're talking to your minister?'

'I do, sir.' Mr Vuga was beginning to feel helpless. He had never had an experience quite like this and had been taken unawares.

'Now listen, Mr Vuga,' Kafu began with determination. 'This is a land of uniformity or, if you like, the wearing of uniform right from the nursery to the university. At the university, if you don't wear a gown you don't eat your dinner. Go to the churches, they have uniform. Makola women groups have uniform, free benevolent societies have uniform, sanitary inspectors and labourers have uniform. Families wear the same dress material to memorial service. I know a society whose members wear black woollen dress with aprons to the cemetery despite the hot sun, as uniform. As you move up in this society, you wear sashes and other accoutrements in grand style. To be photographed in such paraphernalia is the proudest achievement of its members. Teachers have been put in uniform to connect the past with the present and link the present with the future. It's a neat chain that must be preserved. You may wonder what I'm leading up to?'

'Exactly, sir.'

'Benjy Baisi is determined to corrupt the boys under his care. He wears bell-bottomed trousers, a broad belt and a bushy moustache. He can't do that in a school founded by the Church or in a town like Cape Coast where there are several schools. The state must ensure, even if it means the use of force, that all, everybody, shall dress like adults and not like teenagers looking for kicks and mischief.'

'Sir, he has not yet been officially warned,' Mr Vuga explained.

Kafu ignored the point and continued, 'He forces boys to read African writers and has made Shakespeare optional. Nonsense! Which African writer is better than Shakespeare?'

Mr Vuga kept quiet because he agreed entirely with Kafu in this, though he had not read any African writer yet. He said gravely 'They don't write well, sir.' Kafu sensed his agreement and asked, 'Now you see the harm being done, Mr Vuga?'

'I can very well understand, sir, but . . .'

'But what?' Kafu asked leaning forward suddenly, menacingly, 'The school was founded by the Church. Many upright white men died pioneering it. They were ministers of religion and they laid a sound religious foundation from which many people have benefited to the glory of the country and the Lord. I went to that school. Can you believe that since the government took over the school, no minister of religion has been appointed head? And to spite the Church Benjy Baisi doesn't go to communion?'

'This is an irrelevant point, sir. Government must manage what it pays for. Whoever pays the salary must appoint, sir.'

'Mr Vuga, what degree do you have?'

'MA, sir.'

'Is it a first?'

'Yes, sir.'

'Mine is a second. You probably took yours in Scotland. Mine is London. You must be careful how you argue with me. You may be old but I'm your boss. If you have any regrets, blame the people. Is that clear?'

'It is, sir, but still I don't think we have sufficient grounds for dismissing Mr Baisi. It will be highly irregular, sir.'

'Mr Vuga, your longevity in the world should not be the excuse for your stubbornness. I'll put all my cards on the table and my decision shall be carried out. Mr Benjy Baisi doesn't admit the children of old boys and those of churchmen. It's a deliberate departure from tradition and a slap in the face of the Church. I'll make him atone for it.'

'I remember when I was in the Department of Welfare Services and Pedagogy, this subject was brought up. Entry to the school was on a competitive basis, the Common Entrance Examination which is nationwide, and Mr Baisi went strictly by it, sir.'

'I see. Are you trying to hold a brief for him?'

'Not at all, sir. My job is to advise, sir.'

'Now advise on this. Mr Baisi took a bribe of five thousand cedis from the school bread contractor, Mr Anson Berko, to put up a house in the Adisadel area. As a result, the weight of a loaf of bread has been reduced for the boys. This reminds me. You must also write to Rev. Opia Dan Sese that Anson Berko must cease forthwith to be the school's bread supplier. He must be warned to learn to behave.'

'Here again, sir,' Mr Vuga explained, 'an anonymous letter was received at the Department of Welfare Services and Pedagogy accusing Mr Baisi. It was referred to us and I had an investigation made. The total cost of the house was thirteen thousand cedis. Mr Baisi raised a loan of five thousand from Mr Anson Berko. Mr Baisi's savings account confirmed he had eight thousand. There was documentary evidence to show that Mr Anson Berko was to give him five thousand, but he had in fact given him only one thousand six hundred at the time of the investigation. We advised Mr Baisi therefore to raise a loan of five thousand cedis from the State Insurance Corporation, repay Anson Berko his loan and repay the Corporation from rent accruing from the house. Mr Baisi as far as this ministry is concerned cannot be faulted, sir. The entire proceedings are on File MIW. 10/VOL.IV. I'll bring it up for your perusal, sir.'

'Very well put, Mr Vuga,' Kafu said rising from behind his desk. He started pacing up and down the office, 'How old are you?'

'Fifty-five, sir.'

'So you have a few days before you retire!' Kafu said with a steady smile, watching Mr Vuga.

'No, sir. I've five more years to do and my health is all right, sir,' Mr Vuga said. His glasses began to slide down.

'Your health is beside the point, Mr Vuga. My government is reducing the retiring age to fifty-five and I am going to press hard for it, you see?'

Mr Vuga was speechless.

'Now, Mr Vuga,' Kafu called in a tone of finality, 'write to Mr Benjy Baisi as I have instructed you.'

'Yes, sir.'

'You may go. I'll be back here in a week. Have Mr Baisi's

dismissal announced on the radio at one o'clock this afternoon; and let it go out on TV this evening, you understand?'

'Yes, sir,' Mr Vuga said feebly. It took him over a minute to rise from his chair. Kafu watched him without batting an eye. He turned in his chair and began to read the spines of bound volumes of legislative instruments and decrees while adjusting the knot of his tie at the same time. Mr Vuga had reached the door which led from the minister's office to his own. Kafu called him back and said, 'I understand you're a stickler for rules, regulations, discipline and obedience – a very rare characteristic. Is it true?'

'I try to do my best, sir.'

'Mr Vuga, I can see our first meeting has been fruitful. I admire people like you. Tell me, by the way, if a civil servant feels very strongly about a ministerial directive what does he do?'

'He must resign, sir,' Mr Vuga said, the perspiration now guttering like tears down his face. He adjusted the sliding glasses.

'Well, I expect to hear the news at one o'clock. Make sure this office is provided with a transistor radio, will you?'

'Very well, sir.'

'Good. I'll be back. My home telephone number is 82225. You can get in touch with me in case of emergency.'

'Yes, sir.'

Kafu walked out briskly. He descended the stairs ignoring everybody. Anyone who met him on the way stopped dead in his tracks to let him pass.

Mr Nutor Vuga started working on the release for the press, radio and TV. Speed was important, so he called W. W. Mensah to write to Baisi with a copy to Rev. Opia Dan Sese. Twice he started to draft the release but he felt so unwell that he could not. He called W. W. Mensah again and asked him to do both with dispatch to meet the one o'clock deadline. As soon as he had finished giving the instructions, he passed out.

7

It was in the afternoon, just after two. Mr Benjy Baisi had not yet gone home for lunch. He was reading history so as to teach one of the classes Kafu had left without notice. He found the topic absorbing. It was missionary activity in eastern Ghana between 1828 and 1928. What impressed him was the attempts of a man like Andreas Riis to buy huge chunks of land for large-scale Christian farm settlements. It reminded him of state farms and his own school farm. 'There is nothing new,' he thought. 'The form may be different but the substance is as old as can be remembered. My school farm must succeed. The boys have had a pleasant surprise. They did not know they could raise such beautiful livestock. They find the pigs most interesting. Pigs are. We should be able to feed on our own livestock for at least a term next year. I can make that our target. If it proves successful, we move on. How wonderful!'

There was a knock on the door, and before he was called in the knocker Anson Berko burst in panting. His head had been shaven clean and was shining like a mirror in the sun. His cloth was hanging loose on him, and one side of his body was showing naked but for the shorts he wore. His potbelly was well loaded and he carried it like a bass drum.

'Benjy, that boy is a worthless animal!' he said, hardly able to utter the words clearly for want of breath.

'Who is? And mind your language. You're on a school compound,' Benjy Baisi advised his friend with a smile. He often found something comic about Anson Berko which amused him.

'If I get at him, I'll beat him up. That's what he needs. I know he does...!'

'What are you talking about?'

'The trouble with you, Benjy, is that you waste too much time in this office. I have always told you that in this country if you devote your time and energy to the service of the state you will either be pushed aside, ignored, ridiculed, harassed or ruined. It's the thieves and crooks who get on. You simply look round the entire country and dare deny what I say! The law of libel must be scrapped. I say it must be scrapped!'

'And you'll be the first to be exposed! I'm sure of that, Anson. Now let me tell you something. As a country, we aren't doing badly. We can do better still by talking less about weaknesses and improving upon our strengths. We honour a few people each year for their honesty, or something good they've done, don't we? Do you know what is called self-denigration?'

'I don't know. Rubbish!'

'Yes, self-denigration is rubbish. I'm busy, Berko. What's your trouble? The school farm is beating all expectation....'

'Benjy, did you listen to the one o'clock news?'

'I didn't. Has something happened to somebody? Governments usually knock people out by that news. Who is it this time?'

'You!'

'Me? Impossible. I'm an obscure headmaster. No government has time for me. It's the politicians who fight among themselves. Dog bites dog. They're a funny bunch, aren't they? It may well be Paul Baisie who stood for the NUP in these parts. He's the managing director of the State Cassava Production Corporation. Poor fellow. What do they say is his crime?'

'If I get Kafu I'll beat the hell out of him! I swear I will! I don't care if I'm jailed!'

'Don't be foolish, Anson. He's a minister of state now and you must respect him.'

'That stupid bedwetter?'

'Never mind what he is. You must respect him because of his office. If a minister or a head of state is a donkey, blame the people. Don't pick on the walking embodiment. Kafu is not here, so you breathe fire. Let him enter this office and you'll begin to talk about contracts. Am I wrong, Anson the great? We've made politics a choice between money and guns and you want to beat up Kafu, too. Relax, Anson.'

'Do you hear that noise outside, Mr Preacher?'

'Never mind the sound. It's the motor-bike ᴏf Mr Martin Golder, the Peace Corps chemistry tutor. It's got a powerful engine and he seems to get limitless joy from the vroom alone. Anson, Kafu is gone and we've got to forget about him. I find you've improved the weight of the bread but can't you make it a little heavier still? Anson! Where are you going? I'm talking to you...!'

Anson Berko walked out from the office to the verandah and looked out. It was not Mr Martin Golder. It was a police dispatch-rider. He unfolded a bag strapped to the back of his motor-cycle and collected three letters from it. He came up to the office. Before he knocked on the door, Anson had gone in again and was sprawled in an armchair, exhausted. The policeman knocked, entered, saluted smartly and delivered the letters. He didn't say much because his English wasn't very good and he thought a school compound was not the place to make an exhibition of it.

'The headmaster of this school?'

'Yes, I am,' Mr Benjy Baisi replied.

'From Accra, sir. Rev. Opia Dan Sese is here?'

'Yes, he is.'

'This one for him, sir. You know Mr Anson Berko?'

'Here I am!'

'Oh, very good, sir. This one for you, sir.' He saluted smartly again and left.

'Benjy, I told you!' Anson said breathing heavily and sinking more in his chair.

'Keep cool, Anson. Let's see what's in mine.' Baisi then read his letter aloud:

'Dear Sir, I have been directed to inform you that you should cease, with immediate effect, to be the headmaster of National Secondary School, Cape Coast. You should hand over, forthwith, the administration of the school to Rev. Opia Dan Sese. You must vacate the school bungalow you now occupy within thirty-six hours and thereafter must not be seen on or near the compound of the National Secondary School, Cape Coast.

'2. I am by a copy of this letter informing Rev. Opia Dan Sese to take over from you as stated in paragraph 1 above. Rev. Opia Dan Sese should move into the headmaster's bungalow without delay.

'3. You are to note that the effect of the directive in my Paragraph 1 above is that you are to retire from the teaching service. In this connection, I should be grateful if you would forward, as a matter of urgency, Retirement Form 130 duly completed for necessary action.

'4. In view of the short notice, I am to request you to apply for alimentary allowance should you find yourself in sudden financial distress. Please acknowledge receipt of this letter.

'Yours faithfully,
W. W. Mensah for Permanent Secretary.'

'Benjy, I told you! According to the radio you are dismissed. This is incredible! But what the hell has Kafu got to do with me? Benjy, take mine and read it to me,' he handed over his letter to Benjy Baisi. The letter said:

'Dear Mr Berko,

'I have been directed to instruct you to stop supplying bread to the Ghana National Secondary School, Cape Coast. You are to comply with this directive forthwith. You must not be seen on or near the compound of that school until further notice, and you must ensure that your conduct, generally, is conducive to the public good and safety. Please acknowledge receipt of this letter.

Yours faithfully,
W. W. Mensah for Permanent Secretary.'

'Benjy, I'm not bothered about myself,' Anson Berko said, having now recovered his breath. 'It's you I'm worried about. You can't move into your house. You've signed a tenancy agreement with the Intercontinental Oil Company and there is no going back on it within three days. The louvre-windows have to be fixed and there is a lot of final painting to be done. And you've got to get out of here. Why not move over to my house? I've two spare rooms. We must hire a lawyer to fight your case in the courts. A man cannot be removed and retired without being told why. It's not right!'

'Thank you, Anson. I'll start moving my things to your house immediately. I'll need a week or so to sort things out. But why spread the fire?'

'Which fire?' Anson asked.

'Whichever lawyer takes up my case may be exposed to the

fire, and we must not forget the judges, too. They are independent and dependent at the same time. If I can be burnt this way I don't see how they can escape the same fate in the short or long run. Anson, I feel a load has been lifted off me. I don't know how to describe it, but I feel somehow relieved. Kafu has altered the course of my life and I accept it. Perhaps I'll have to leave the country. Anson, if I had known about the State Insurance Corporation, I would never have taken any loan from you.'

'But you've paid back every pesewa I gave you.'

'Of course I have; but the thorn in my conscience is that you shouldn't ever have given me or my wife any money when you were reducing the weight of the bread. This was your crime and I think I was your partner.'

'It was my doing. I don't deny that, but I have no regrets at all. I'm a business-man, and I spend long sleepless nights speculating. For any little investment, I must make the maximum profit before some lout like Kafu wrecks the entire enterprise – by a stroke of the pen. But it's all a ruse, Benjy. This school will have Kafu's own man as the next bread contractor. That boy needs money. He won't find another contractor for the school out of the largeness of his heart. I am going, but another vulture will soon land on this compound. I'm not going to starve either. I have six buildings, all let out; I supply the Cape Coast prison with meat, vegetables and other foodstuff and I don't lose money. I'll now enter the *gari* trade. Kafu knows he can't really get me, so he warns me about public safety. I don't know, but we shall see. Benjy, don't think of leaving the country. You'll get a new job all right, heh?'

'Anson, let me have somewhere to lay my head first. The rest will follow. I don't . . .'

There was a series of three quick knocks on the door which sounded more like bangs. Rev. Opia Dan Sese entered and found the two men. They looked calm, showing no signs of agitation at all. He ignored Anson Berko and spoke to Mr Benjy Baisi. 'I've heard the news, Benjy, is it true?'

He was given his copy of the letter and was asked to read it on the spot. He nearly jumped with joy when he finished reading it because of his personal elevation, but he realised quickly that it would be a terrible mistake to show any outward sign of pleasure, so he managed to look lugubrious at once. This was not hard to do, because he had always done it in the pulpit during Easter sermons, especially when a beautiful choir girl in the front row whom he loved winked at him. He said, 'What a shame, Benjy! What are you going to do?'

'Simply clear out by tomorrow afternoon, Opia. With your permission, of course.'

'It's all very wrong, Benjy. What are you going to do about it?'

'What do you, Opia, mean to do about it?' Anson Berko asked staring the Rev. Minister squarely in the face.

'This is not a meeting for contractors. We're dealing with high government policy.'

'Opia, you call a letter from Kafu high government policy? You're all right, aren't you, Opia? When you pray to God what do you tell him?'

'To save your soul, Anson Berko!'

'Gentlemen, let's talk business,' Benjy Baisi intervened.

'No,' said Anson Berko with great force. 'I shall leave this room. Benjy, I'm going to get my labourers to start packing your things. Don't worry, Benjy. You'll find me at the bungalow.' With that he banged the door and left.

'He's a coarse man, Benjy,' Rev. Opia Dan Sese said solemnly. 'He thinks of nothing but how to make money!'

'Opia, there's very little time,' Benjy Baisi said. 'I have to pre- pare handing-over notes quickly for you and pack up at the same time. It's a good thing you know a lot about this school already. I'll make the notes brief so that you can use them as guide- lines.'

'Thank you very much, Benjy. The boys want to stage a de- monstration to protest your removal. They are being organised by Osei Kwame. The government might think you are fomenting a strike. Would you like to talk to them?'

'Surely, I will. Tonight. The headmastership is like a little stream that serves a village. The waters come and go but the village remains. Osei Kwame likes mischief, but the top class are an understanding lot. If I were you, Opia, I wouldn't worry.'

'Thank you, Benjy. Thank you,' Rev. Dan Sese said, very much relieved.

Benjy Baisi moved out of National Secondary School before the expiration of the thirty-six hours. He was staying in Anson Berko's house thinking deeply what to do next. He needed no money to complete his house and the rent to be paid by the Intercontinental Oil Company was particularly good. He was not fifty yet and very fit. If he could get another job to tide him over his normal domestic needs, it would be most welcome. His gratuity alone could pay for a complete, modest new building. And this was what cheered him most. It did not look as if he would really be badly off.

Meanwhile, there was an acute crisis at National Secondary School. It was caused by the termination of the contract of Anson Berko. Bread was hard to come by because flour was scarce in the country and not every baker could get the same quantities of flour which Anson was supplied direct by the factory. It was extremely expensive to buy the total amount of bread consumed by the boys at breakfast in small lots from different bakers. The quality and taste of the different types were uneven and the supplies were irregular. All this infuriated the boys. They were becoming restless.

Rev. Opia Dan Sese decided to act. He discussed the matter thoroughly with his young wife, Vida, who was now heavy with child. It was decided between them that his wife should supply bread to the school. They would negotiate with Anson Berko and take over his bakery as well as the flour-supply contract with the factory. Rev. Opia Dan Sese decided therefore to unleash all his charm and astuteness on Anson Berko. For religious and other reasons Anson Berko had grown to love the school and was unhappy about the hardship there. The couple offered to buy his bakery, but Anson knew this would involve a huge capital outlay which they would find difficult to raise in a short time. The bakery would require the personal attention of at least one of them. Dan Sese would not have the time. His wife's pregnancy was too advanced for the strain. Besides, the job required expertise and supervisory experience, which neither had. Having taken all these matters into consideration, Anson Berko told the couple: 'I should like to give you the easiest of terms, though I know your husband doesn't like me.'

'Is that true, Opia?' Vida asked, not believing Anson. Dan Sese had told her long ago that Anson Berko was an irredeemable crook.

'Of course not. It's incompatible with the tenets of my calling. As a minister of religion, my job is full of this kind of hazard. I talk straight to people and they say I hate them. Nothing could be further from the truth!'

'You see, Mr Anson Berko, Opia likes you,' the wife said with conviction.

'Never mind that,' Anson said matter-of-factly. 'I intend to help the school and both of you. As I've said the terms I'm giving you are the easiest. You sit at home, do nothing and make money. I will supply the school with bread through your wife. Your wife's name will appear on the vouchers and all payments will be made to her. Her commission is 16%. Mind you, not 10%! The 16% is generous because it is worth two hundred and forty cedis a month. For the academic year, you make two thousand one hundred and sixty cedis. So you get two hundred and forty cedis every month just for signing papers, that's all!'

'What if it is reported to the government that it is you who in fact are supplying the bread? We'll all be in trouble, won't we?' Vida asked.

'Leave that to me!' Rev. Opia Dan Sese said with assuring confidence. He continued, 'Anson, I wanted to solve this bread problem quickly and you've offered a wonderful solution. May the Lord bless you. I, or shall I say, we accept your terms. You start supplying from tomorrow. You will have to get a new label for the bread. Make it "SDO ENTERPRISES".'

'Very good,' Anson Berko agreed. 'There is one small point, though. From the calculations, you'll pay me on average one thousand five hundred cedis a month. It's my policy that this amount should be paid in advance.'

'Oh yes, yes, yes. This is no problem. My wife will bring you a school cheque tomorrow. And lest I forget, have SDO ENTERPRISES painted on the delivery van, will you?'

'It shall be done, Rev. Dan Sese,' Anson Berko said, adjusting his cloth over his left shoulder.

As they drove back to the school, Vida said, 'Are you sure this arrangement is safe?'

'It should be,' Dan Sese told her. 'Now, listen. You will go to

Accra to Grace, Kafu's wife. Tell her about this arrangement and offer her her first monthly share of one hundred and twenty cedis. The school driver will take you in my car. I'll talk to Kafu before you go. He rang me up last night. I'll be seeing him myself very soon about Benjy. Grace needs money, and a hundred and twenty a month is better than nothing.'

'Oh, thank God,' Vida said. 'We are so very lucky!'

So Anson Berko continued to supply the bread. Kafu had resumed duty at the ministry. Mr Vuga had recovered. He had spent three days at the Ridge Hospital, Accra, under observation. Kafu called for the letters he had ordered to be written. He wanted to be sure that his instructions had been carried out. He was incensed by paragraphs three and four of the letter to Baisi. Those paragraphs pensioned him and offered him a gratuity and the option of an alimentary allowance. 'This is absolutely intolerable!' he said. He rose from his seat and violently opened the door leading to Mr Vuga's office. Mr Vuga took fright at once.

'Who retired Baisi?' Kafu bellowed.

'It was done in error, sir. I will write to rectify the anomaly, sir.'

'Look here, Mr Vuga, I'm not asking what you intend to do. I say who wrote the letter?'

'I fainted just when you left, so Mr Mensah took action, sir.'

'Is he your deputy?'

'Yes, sir.'

'Bring him here, will you?'

'Yes, sir!'

Mr W. W. Mensah was thirty-four years old. Promotions in the administrative service were rapid and he was now far ahead of his colleagues who were in the Department of Welfare Services and Pedagogy. This in itself was a great source of apathy, bitterness and laxity in the civil service. It was a situation that wrecked the individual as much as it hurt state business; for apathy bred both physical and intellectual atrophy. Many brilliant young men took to drinking and frittered away the most productive years of their lives, underemployed and useless to themselves and to their fatherland. The more they complained the more they were ignored, because they were thought to be of no use. In this respect, the service had become a vast accummula-

74

tion of human wastage where a few top men worked themselves to death and many potentially good personnel were condemned to idleness and a futile existence. They never fulfilled themselves till they retired. Their lives were without patriotic devotion or achievement – emptiness all around.

Not so with W. W. Mensah. He was a hefty and energetic man. He had read history and was two years ahead of Kafu at the University of Ghana, Legon. They sometimes attended the same lectures. He knew Kafu well and had no cause to have a profound personal respect for him. He was prepared to defer to him as his minister but he knew ministers could be extremely rude to civil servants. They could bully and treat them like dirt. But a lot depended, too, on the individual civil servant. Mensah seemed to love his job.

Mensah came to Kafu's office and said good-morning. Kafu ignored this and would not ask him to sit down. He said gruffly, 'Are you the Deputy Permanent Secretary here?'

'Yes, I am.'

'Did you write this letter?'

'I did.'

'Who asked you to retire Mr Baisi with gratuity and pension?'

'I used my discretion, sir. What I was told to tell Mr Baisi was that he should cease to be the head of a school because he had been relieved of his post as headmaster. That is neither suspension, interdiction nor dismissal. It couldn't be any of these because nothing had been brought up against him by which I could go. As an employee of the state he was in contractual agreement which was being violated, not to mention that he was also being denied natural justice, all of which are actionable in a court of law. As a compromise, therefore, and to save the face of the ministry, I decided to let him take his gratuity and pension which he had used his own salary to contribute to over the years.'

'But you signed for the permanent secretary?'

'I did, sir, because it's routine to do so. I accept responsibility for the two paragraphs!'

'All right. Go back to your work, Mr Mensah,' Kafu ordered him without looking him in the face. Mr Vuga was upset by Mr Mensah's boldness and felt angry, because if Kafu erupted he would suffer it alone. But Kafu was silent for some time and then told Mr Vuga: 'Go and write to Mr Baisi, withdrawing paragraphs three and four. Write yourself!'

'Yes, sir.' Mr Vuga went out to obey.

The letter was routed through and with a copy to Rev. Opia Dan Sese. He was unhappy about the withholding of Benjy Baisi's pension. He felt he must do something about it. He now had four things to see Kafu about: to thank him for making him a headmaster, to explain the bread-deal to him as a source of guaranteed income for Grace, to plead that Benjy must be given a gratuity and pension and, in addition, made managing director of the State Cassava Production Corporation and finally to invite Kafu to a thanksgiving service at Cape Coast to thank God for his having been made a minister of state.

Grace was as usual an excellent cook and she fed Rev. Opia Dan Sese well. He was very pleased with Kafu's circumstances. The beautiful, comfortable house, the air-conditioning which in spite of his baldness made him sleep well, the new Mercedes Benz 280SEL automatic, the servants – including an attractive girl of fifteen called Gloria Opoku, with whom he chatted for twenty minutes when she went to make his bed; the girl was titillated by his few but expert lecherous jokes – and, oh, the feeling that he was very much at home.

Three of the four points were satisfactorily disposed of. The thanksgiving service would be held the following Sunday. But Benjy Baisi's case proved a little thorny. 'Osofo, you don't seem to understand,' Kafu stuck to his position. 'I know I should forgive, but I cannot forgive any man who stands between me and my advancement in the world. This is how I see Benjy Baisi. There are too many of his type holding top positions in the country. They must be got rid of before they erect an effective barrier in the way of the upcoming generation.'

'Yes, I accept your thesis, Abraham. You have, in fact, removed Benjy. But why withold the money he has earned?'

'Osofo, I want him to feel the pinch of penury!'

'You mean he should earn no income at all?'

'Yes, Osofo. It will give him time to think over his misdeeds.'

'Abraham, I feel most unhappy about this. You're also not prepared to make him the managing director?'

'No!'

'Abraham, please, just a little compassion.'

'His pension, no; the managing director, maybe. Even here it's because of Paul Baisie. He is a political acrobat, surviving every regime. His corporation doesn't make a profit and he thinks he is clever. I will dislodge him!'

'Yes, I agree; and then you'll have Benjy Baisi appointed. He is very good at farm-management and the corporation will make a profit. Do please let him have the job, Abraham.'

'On one condition only, Osofo. He must come and ask me formally.'

'I'll arrange that for Sunday evening, after the thanksgiving service.'

'If you care to, Osofo.'

The thanksgiving service was simple but well organised. All the Liberation Party stalwarts of Cape Coast attended; so did the Rev. Sampson Abaka Kafu, Abraham Kofi Kafu's father, Mrs Edusua Kafu, his mother, and Veronica Kafu, unmarried, his only sister, for only the two of them were born to their parents. She was older than Kafu by two years and was now the matron of Effiakwanta Hospital, Sekondi. Rev. Abaka Kafu looked trim and well preserved. He was sixty-eight, of medium height, and very neat. His wife Edusua was tall and big and domineering. She was very proud of her son. The sister was dedicated to her work; indeed so dedicated that she could not relax fully with any man. She was attractive in her own right and had inherited her father's neatness. So clean were her lodgings, food and habits that the few men who drifted her way could not cope with them and withdrew. One of them, Amissah Brew, quipped after his withdrawal, 'Her room looked and smelt like a disinfected side-ward!'

Rev. Opia Dan Sese preached the sermon. His text was Psalm 127, 1: 'Except the Lord build the house, they labour in vain that build it: except the Lord keep the city, the watchman waketh but in vain.' He gave a brilliant exposition of the text, linking it with, among others, the selfless public service of the elder Kafu and that which his son had just embarked upon.

As he preached, his girl-friend in the front row of the choir, Miss Lydia Johnson-Baiden, a pretty petite and a fashionable seamstress, divided her gaze between him and Kafu. She successfully winked at both men without their knowing that they were being tantalised from the same spot. Kafu accepted the challenge.

He had not taken Grace to the thanksgiving service. The excuse for leaving her at home was the baby. There was no room at his father's so he used the guest-apartment of the Headmaster of National Secondary School's bungalow, which was semi-detached and self-contained. He spoke passionately to Opia Dan Sese about Lydia in the afternoon. In the evening Dan Sese went to talk to Benjy Baisi about Kafu's terms and to persuade him to accept them. His banishment from the school compound would be waived for the evening.

'Kafu means to humiliate and ruin me,' Benjy Baisi quietly told Dan Sese. 'He warned me but I did not understand then. Who knows whether this is a ploy to finish me further? I thank you, Opia. My mind is made up. I do not think the country needs me and I must go. I've got a teaching spell in the United States for eighteen months. I'm leaving with all my family in a month or two. Tell Kafu I thank him for the offer.'

'This is most disappointing, Benjy. I'll tell him. I wish you would change your mind. Think of your children and the disruption in their lives.'

'I have considered it all, Opia. I must go!'

'Very well. I must see you before you leave.'

'Thank you, Opia,' Baisi said, the tears welling up in his eyes.

As Rev. Dan Sese drove back, he went and picked up Lydia. He drove her to Kafu's lodgings. He had stocked the place with a wide selection of expensive drinks. He did not give Kafu Baisi's message. Instead, the three chatted till about twelve midnight. Dan Sese insisted it was too late to drive Lydia home so he left her with Kafu.

When Kafu was leaving at seven in the morning, he asked Dan Sese, 'What did Benjy Baisi say?'

'He's not keen.'

'I see. He can please himself,' Kafu said nonchalantly. He added as the car purred gently, about to move off, 'Osofo, if Lydia complains about pregnancy, tell her to forget about it. I took every precaution.'

'Leave that to me, Abraham. Expect nothing,' Rev. Opia Dan Sese told Kafu, who was driven away whistling contentedly.

8

When Rev. Opia Dan Sese visited Kafu in Accra, another thing that struck him was the peaceable nature of the Kafu household, especially the individual loyalty of the domestic staff to both Grace and Kafu..There was the cook, Afua Cudzoe, thirty-five, a second cousin of Grace, who had been deceived twice, first by a mechanic of the state transport corporation and then by a plumber of the water and sewerage corporation. Each man gave her a child; Grace rescued her just when she was finding it difficult to resist a third one, this time a Public Works Department carpenter. Then there was Frank Owusu, houseboy, a neat, meticulous fellow of average intelligence, eighteen years old, a middle-school leaver and undecided what occupation he should pursue permanently. There was Gloria Opoku, whose breasts, the beautiful breasts of a fifteen-year-old, had originally attracted Opia. It will be recalled that in their twenty-minute encounter, Opia managed also to touch her left breast, which tickled both of them a lot. Then she giggled, but did not recoil and said shyly, 'Oh, Osofo, I don't like that!' Then Opia counselled softly with his right forefinger on his lips, 'Shsss, don't let your boy-friend do that to you, my dear!' And she smiled. There was the chauffeur, Kofi Danso, twenty-six, inquisitive, showy, a tell-tale, loud-mouthed but prompt on occasion, a reckless driver when alone in the car or when giving someone he didn't like or respect a drive, or when he was either hungry or angry or both. Money under-pinned Kofi Danso's loyalty, particularly when given unexpectedly as tips. And finally Salifu Bukari, a handsome, well-built, tall man, some thirty years old, absolutely trustworthy and dedicated to his job and to the Kafu family; he loved Kafu Junior like a brother, a son or a friend, it was difficult to tell which when they were together. He was the watchman. It was a household of harmony, recruited from diverse sources when Kafu was appointed to the high rank of minister of state. Kafu received a big enough allowance to pay their wages, and the superior transformation in their lives was evident.

The transformation was, no doubt, equally demonstrated by

Kafu; for apart from his congenial domestic setting he had an excellent Lebanese tailor called Malik Ishmael, of Ishmael and Sons. The first day Kafu was introduced to him, he called him a friend and took the liberty of shaking Kafu's hand vigorously. 'My friend,' he said in a high-pitched, monotonous voice, 'I'm a Ghanaian now. I have a Ghanaian wife. I've been in this country for forty years. You see, you can be my son.' In saying the last sentence, he held Kafu by the left arm and put his left hand on Kafu's right shoulder. 'I'm glad you're a minister,' he assured Kafu. 'I'll make you look like a minister.' And so it was that Kafu's wardrobe became fabulously stocked. He received the first consignment of six well-tailored and fashionable suits, costing one thousand two hundred cedis, within a month. He would now put on a different suit each day. His skin was becoming polished and shiny and his gait a little more steady and jaunty. Even his teeth became whiter and reflectively bright.

He now plunged heart and soul into his work. One of his first major concerns was a five-point petition from the Accra Central constituency executive of the Liberation Party. The signatures under the petition included those of Mr Mills Blankson, Odofo Lamptey, Dr Mills Blankson, Salamatu and Nee Otu Lartey. It was a soberly and optimistically worded petition, demanding that Makola and Sraha should be demolished and rebuilt. In the meantime, the two markets should be provided with better lighting and more toilets.

Since the earthquake of 1937, Accra Central had steadily decayed, particularly at Atukpai, Gbese, Akoto Lante, Akugmadzi and James Town. Although these places were still teeming with people, that is, with the relatively poor, the new educated elite having fled to the new suburbia, the houses were generally no longer fit for human habitation. They pleaded therefore for slum clearance in stages.

There should be one good day secondary school for the five quarters. One or two acres was all the land that was needed. There used to be a secondary school in James Town, but since it was a bureaucratic policy that sixty acres of land should be used for housing a secondary school, whether day or boarding, the school was rehoused some four miles away; which was merely ridding Accra Central of a school. This must be remedied.

The Korle Lagoon had become a cesspool that stank horribly and bred mosquitoes generously. A major blot and source of pollution. Once upon a time, when a petition had been submitted requesting that the engineers should do something about it, someone had caused a picture of the Riviera or something similar to be published in the docile press – as Dr Mills Blankson often characterised the press – with a caption saying that this was what the Lagoon area would look like when the jet-set tourists came from Europe and America to sample the sunlight, comfort, health, hospitality, lushness and beauty of the Korle Lagoon–Odaw complex. Hopes were raised and dreams were dreamt and Mr Mills Blankson, on the advice of his doctor son, decided to establish a gambling casino in the complex. Nothing happened. Now all that the petition asked was that the engineers should permanently get rid of the mosquito-breeding, stinking expanse of water.

Finally the petition noted that kenkey was a high-sediment food. The people of Atukpai and Gbese areas were particularly fond of balls of the stuff; unfortunately they did not have lavatories in equal numbers. The beach under Usher Fort was not far away and was shielded from view by a high cliff. The people succeeded in converting it into a massive lavatory which polluted the sea in the area and made the fishermen's work difficult and unpleasant. Besides, when old and young wanted badly to shit, they had to cross the broad and busy High Street; and since they were being hard pressed by nature they were usually a traffic hazard. Sometimes, the descent of the cliff by itself induced the shit, and each day one or two individuals were embarrassed in this way. Their shit messed up the path and slowed down the progress of others who wanted to descend quickly to let loose. They swore and cursed but waded through. The smell did not leave their nostrils for a week. The petition asked for five new public lavatories. Just that.

What the petitioners wanted Kafu to do was to use his good offices, as their representative, to have these things provided for them. It was agreed that a meeting should be held in the house of Mr Mills Blankson. Kafu was expected at this meeting to explain what he could do.

Mr Mills Blankson's house had been built in the late thirties when he was a customs officer at Accra port. He worked hard, especially at detecting broken cases of tinned meat and fish which could be eaten on the spot. He gave a standing order to his wife to pack kenkey and ground pepper for him each morning. Fish or meat, no. He spotted broken cases every day, so he had two square meals a day at the port. He took no meals in the evening. He did not have to buy clothes, since he wore a government uniform, supplied free, to work. He had only two good suits which he had bought cheaply at the port when he insisted that they had been made wet here and there by sea water. In those days surf boats were used to unload ships; the surf was often turbulent and boats easily overturned. Customs officers dealt with losses or damage.

Dr Mills Blankson lived then in his father's house and paid no rent. At first he saved as a matter of course, but one day he realised that he had eight hundred cedis in his savings account. He loved this and so he increased his deposits. He made sure he did not go in for expensive or particularly literate women. He admitted one day when he helped himself liberally to someone else's whisky that he preferred women traders. One of them was bold enough to come and stay with him, and after some difficulty had a few children by him. He married her without ceremony when he was fifty.

Before he was forty, however, he had put up this house, a tall, two-story building, typical of the late thirties. He lived upstairs and let out the ground floor. Soon the reputation spread that he was a rich man. People came to borrow money from him. He would not lend money unless the borrower was a civil servant. For a small commission many paymasters in different departments did as he ordered them and deducted repayments from pay-packets on pay-day for him. He charged fifty per cent compound interest.

One customs officer, Mr Nelson Ofei, from Otublohum, who borrowed two hundred cedis from him for his mother's funeral, had to turn over his entire monthly earnings to Dr Mills Blankson and then re-borrow. So at the end of each month Dr Mills Blankson collected the interest and the same amount hung round Nelson Ofei's neck.

Nelson Ofei was married with five children. He did not feed

well. He was always brooding. He began to drink. He became alcoholic. He couldn't afford beer, so he drank Akpeteshi. Eventually he became a psychiatric patient and two weeks after his admission to the Psychiatric Hospital, Adabraka, his liver gave out and he died. He had been in debt to Dr Mills Blankson for eight years. When he died, Dr Mills Blankson, as he told a friend later, was compassionate, for he waived the payment of the interest and so on but demanded only the original two hundred cedis from the relations of the deceased, displaying the well-kept documents on the transactions. This was paid from the funeral donations. It was paid before Nelson Ofei was buried. He insisted on that. By the time the funeral was over, there was a deficit. Nelson Ofei's elder brother, Oswald Ofei, had to go to the only one he knew, Dr Mills Blankson, for a hundred and fifty cedis to defray the funeral expenses of his dead brother.

Mr Mills Blankson had become used to tenants. They still occupied the ground floor of his house when the meeting with Kafu took place. It was in his lounge, which was neat and functional but not comfortable. The chairs were made of hard, thick and durable wood but did not have enough room in them and the cushions were bulky and hard. Nee Otu Lartey, perhaps because of his height or whatever it was, looked as if he had been trussed up and was not sitting when he settled in one of them. Salamatu was sitting close to Dr Mills Blankson. Odofo made sure she sat alone by herself, away from Salamatu, the doctor and Nee Otu Lartey.

Salamatu avoided looking at Odofo, but whenever their eyes met she glared at her. Nee Otu Lartey avoided looking at the doctor, but whenever their eyes met the doctor scowled. Odofo deliberately cast seductive eyes at Nee Otu to embarrass the doctor, and once in a while looked at Salamatu from head to foot contemptuously. Meanwhile everybody managed to keep the conversation going. It was dominated by the old man Mr Mills Blankson himself. He said, 'Adjin Yeboah was the only fellow who seriously studied and understood our problems. He also felt them, I think. He was the best to help us, to get things done; but I didn't like the way he spoke. Why should someone use his brains and energy and acquire property just for the government to come round and seize it and share it out to some lazy lout who does nothing but breed with his wife? Why? When I was a young man, I decided not to have many children, so that I could look after them well. Children cost money. I had to control and deny myself and have got only three. Some said I was impotent, others said I was sterile. Now, go to Accra New Town; a labourer there who enjoys himself every night, when I don't, has eight children. And what happens? These socialist acrobats come along to tell me that because those labourer's children go naked, don't go to school, play truant and shit on garbage dumps, government should take my money and property to look after the good-for-nothings! Tell me, what silly nonsense is this? Yeboah did not think properly!'

'No, he didn't!' Nee Otu agreed with all his heart.

'It's a foolish upside-down business!' Mr Mills Blankson warmed up.

'Father,' Dr Mills Blankson said, 'what Adjin Yeboah meant was that people of your type must be held in check. Once they begin to make money, they don't know where, when or how to stop. They create social problems.'

'Dear me, Attuquaye!' Mr Mills Blankson turned on his son. The shiny skin on his bald head lost its lustre and creased up; his face looked suddenly old indeed. 'When have I ever created any problems for anyone? Tell me! Did I not pay hard cash to have you train as a doctor? Did I not starve to do so? What am I going to do with the money and property I have? Are they not for you and your brother and sister? Tell me, Attuquaye!'

'Paa,' Salamatu cut in, 'don't mind Attuquaye. He's like Adjin Yeboah except that he's in our Party, perhaps because of you or me. But we know the type. They go to expensive schools and universities, somebody pays their fees for them, and then they come out and talk about socialism, hard work, rot! All they know is book, food, women, drink, money and dress. Then talk, talk. They can't stand in the sun for five minutes and wield a machete. Useless people!'

'Exactly!' Nee Otu shouted and laughed loudly and rose and shook Salamatu's hand, mostly out of spite for the doctor.

The noise of the engine of a motor-cycle was heard from the street. Its siren blew to warn a driver who was about to park his car in front of Mr Mills Blankson's house to keep moving and give way to Kafu. Mr Mills Blankson rose and went and looked down from the window. The heat of the argument had not subsided in him yet, and when he saw that it was Kafu who had arrived he turned and told the gathering somewhat impatiently, 'This Kafu man, I don't understand him. We've invited him here without publicity and he comes with police out-riders, uniformed drivers and fanfare. What foolishness is this? I don't like waste. His new car alone can give us two lavatories. Where's the one we bought for him?'

'Well, well, Paa,' Salamatu tried to calm the old man, 'this is not the time to talk about the car. We bought it for him. Let him keep it. Paa, I've brought you some palm oil and okro stew with snail, *wele* and pigtrotter inside, and *banku*.' She spoke in a cheerful, innocent voice while her eyes twinkled with mischief. Nee Otu's mouth watered, the doctor held Salamatu's hand and pressed it, Odofo looked impassive and rested her chin in her cupped hand.

'Where is it?' Mr Mills Blankson asked delightedly.

'It's on the table in the corridor.'

'Good girl! Good girl!' Mr Mills Blankson said, completely gratified; he looked vastly young now, especially with his perfect set of teeth.

Kafu entered briskly. He was in one of the new suits and looked elegant. His hair was slightly disorganised but not unkempt, his voice had deepened a little more. He looked like someone who would not tolerate much argument.

'Hello, everybody,' he said with a tinge of cheerfulness, 'how are you?'

'Everybody is well, Kafu,' Mr Mills Blankson said on behalf of himself and the rest.

'Good. I'm glad to hear that. Odofo, you look withdrawn, what's the trouble?'

'Nothing, Kafu,' she replied off-handedly.

'I hope not. Well, now, ladies and gentlemen, let's go through your petition item by item.'

'Why, Kafu,' Nee Otu interrupted, 'this is not a cabinet meeting. You can't do this sort of thing here. All we want to know is, are you prepared to use your good offices to have these amenities provided? If you are, what are the details? How and when are they going to be provided? Who are to be awarded the contracts? You see what I mean?'

'Do you have the money for all these projects?' Kafu asked.

'Who?' Nee Otu asked, so surprised at Kafu's inability to catch his point that his mouth stayed open for some time.

'Those of you assembled here and any others.'

'You mean I should use my own money to build a lavatory for some bloody ass to go and ease himself inside? Look, Kafu, let's talk business, you understand?' Mr Mills Blankson said angrily, adjusting his trousers, which were frayed at the bottom turn-ups but otherwise well starched and ironed.

'Now, ladies and gentlemen,' Kafu said like some chairman at a board meeting, 'if you are not going to use your own money, then we must go through item by item. The first is the rebuilding of Makola and Sraha. I must inform you that it has been decided to build a new market-complex at a different site altogether, a few miles away. When this has been done, appropriate measures will be taken to improve the present state of these markets.'

'You mean nothing is going to be done?' asked Dr Mills Blankson.

'The answer is yes and no,' Kafu fenced. 'It is not planned yet to rehouse them where they are, but provision will be made to ensure that they are clean and well lit.'

'How about more lavatories for Makola?' Odofo asked him.

'The matter is receiving urgent attention.'

'By whom?' she pressed.

'By the appropriate authority,' Kafu answered and continued, 'Now with regard to the slum clearance, as you are all aware, there is at present a housing scheme in progress at Dansoman; until that is finished, there is no intention to proliferate government commitments.'

'Kafu, you don't intend to do anything about our slum, is that what you want to tell us?' Nee Otu asked. He was disappointed.

'No, no! This is not the impression the government or I would want to create. It will certainly be done when the necessary funds are available. The same applies to Nima, you see!'

'Kafu, I'm sure you know whom you're talking to,' Nee Otu asked.

'Indeed, sir, I'm perfectly aware who you are. It is not the

86

policy of the government to provide a secondary school in a locality unless the locality has a minimum of fifteen middle schools to service the secondary school. My understanding is that the five areas under reference don't have between them more than five middle schools.'

'Whose fault is that?' the doctor asked.

'That will be looked into, I can assure you.'

'Now, Kafu, when there was a secondary school there, it was over-enrolled. You can't come and deceive us, you know,' Nee Otu challenged.

'Mind your language, Nee Otu. A day secondary school must have a limited and geographically contiguous catchment area. We don't want pupils to walk from Labadi to the Lighthouse area as they did in the past. It was an unnecessary marathon.'

'By the way,' Mr Mills Blankson interrupted, 'what kind of English have you been talking?'

'Don't mind him. He has seen there are women here. He wants to show off!' Nee Otu said, almost angry now. He scratched his head.

Kafu ignored both and went on, 'Government is prepared to do something about the Korle Lagoon. A third bridge will span it at a point in the Industrial Area. It will make access to Lartebior-koshi and Link Road easy and break the bottleneck at Abossey Okai.'

'Who asked for that?' Salamatu queried.

'Just a minute,' Kafu said. 'It will be dredged.'

'But that has been done before. Will it not silt up again and stop flowing and then breed mosquitoes?' the doctor asked.

'The technical details are being worked out,' Kafu informed them and then added, 'I'll see to it that one new lavatory is sited at the beach to stop the nuisance.'

'In the sand?' asked Nee Otu, who was wondering whether he should force a quarrel with Kafu.

'A suitable site will be chosen. Now, ladies and gentlemen, what I want you to understand is that Accra has benefited for too long and too much in development at the expense of the rural areas. You'll have to wait until we bring up the rural areas a bit!'

'Look here, boy, if I had my way, I'd remove you from office

87

right now!' Mr Mills Blankson said, thoroughly disappointed.

'Kafu, don't you want to stand for elections again?' Odofo asked, wondering whether Kafu appreciated the consequences of what he was doing.

'Elections? When do you hope to have them?' Kafu asked with a faint smile.

'You mean you're not stepping down after five years?' the doctor asked absolutely scandalised.

'Of course I'll step down! All of us will have recovered our election investments then and your father will have made enough profit on the present lot to enable him to back the next horse!' The smile on Kafu's lips was now so derisive that the doctor sat bolt upright, staring straight ahead like a man who had received a spiritual revelation.

'Kafu,' his father said after heaving a sigh, 'we will not quarrel with the government for doing something for the rural folk. I have lived in Mayera and I know what it means, but you'll agree that some buildings here are as bad as those there. We don't want everything overnight. Can't we clear this slum bit by bit? This is all we ask for.'

'I'll see what I can do,' Kafu said, rather as if he had softened up a bit. He could not endure the disappointed gaze of Odofo and the apparent, even if temporary, disenchantment of Nee Otu Lartey.

There was silence all over. No one seemed to have anything more to say. Time was needed to absorb the shock and the meeting would have to wind up. Mr Mills Blankson was in fact the first to recover. He winked at Salamatu who rose and went into the next room and came back with a parcel. She looked at Mr Mills Blankson, who nodded. She stood erect with her hands clasped behind her as if she was standing at ease. She still looked sinuous and fetching. She said, 'Well, Kafu, this meeting has not been as fruitful as we expected. People think we are interested in money only. It's not so. We are also interested in the public good. You've given us excuses but we hope you will not confuse government policy with political indifference. You may wish to justify your stewardship to us and to the country. There's time yet for you to reconsider the stand you've just taken with us. However, since you were elevated to your high office, we have not as a

88

group, congratulated you and wished you all the best. We are doers, not talkers, and to show our appreciation I have been asked to present this parcel to you on behalf of all of us here. Here you are,' and she lifted the parcel and gave it to him.

Kafu impulsively rose to make a long, emotional speech. Nee Otu suspected this and said, 'Why not see what's in it?'

'You're right, Nee Otu,' and he carefully opened the parcel. It contained four cartons of Rothman's cigarettes, two double-pint-size bottles of Black Label Johnnie Walker whisky, two large and expensive bottles of eau de cologne, wigs of four different expensive types for Grace and six bottles of Stork gin. 'Good gracious,' he cried, 'these are smuggled!'

'They are. I suppose you will find them useless?' Mr Mills Blankson asked, watching the obvious confusion of the young man.

'I know,' Kafu replied, 'that habits die hard. Ladies and gentlemen, your gifts are very welcome. Thank you very much. I'm sure Grace will love the wigs. She's been pestering me to get her some for state functions. But why do you deal in smuggled goods? It's not right. You know I'm a Minister and you're my friends. You can see the danger, can't you?'

'To whom?' Mr Mills Blankson asked. He turned his head from Kafu's gaze and laughed.

'To me and to yourselves,' Kafu replied.

'My friend, you must learn to worry about yourself. Watch your fortunes, Kafu. They take some watching,' Mr Mills Blankson told him.

'In fairness to myself, I'm embarrassed also,' Kafu continued.

'Embarrassed?' Nee Otu asked. 'If you want us to use our common sense in a different way, Kafu, let Nigeria join Dahomey and Ghana join Togo. Not the other way round. Then let the federation of Dahomey–Nigeria and the federation of Togo–Ghana work out common tariffs. In the meantime, may the Lord bless the smugglers!'

'Amen!' the rest responded.

'May the Lord bless us who condone and connive at smuggling.' Salamatu invoked.

'Amen!' the rest responded, except Odofo.

'And may the good Lord bless all those who through private or official means actually consume smuggled commodities in one way or the other in this country,' the old man intoned.

'Amen! Amen!' was the prolonged chorus.

'Oh Lord make haste to save us!' the doctor sang, Anglican fashion; they all chanted the response and clapped and laughed. It was so beautiful. Drinks were served and Kafu made an appointment with Odofo while the others conversed noisily under the happy influence of the drinks.

9

On this Sunday evening Odofo had been to a women's fellowship meeting of her church. She returned home at about eight o'clock, washed and had a cold light dinner all by herself. After that she sat on a rocking chair she had bought at an exhibition mounted by the Accra Polytechnic. There were several useful, rough and ready items there, but it was the rocking chair that caught her fancy. She had never regretted buying it. It was very comfortable. She hardly had time to use it, but would sometimes force herself to sit in it when she wanted to collect her thoughts and enjoy the little bit of idle comfort she thought she was entitled to.

She had the vague feeling that Kafu would call. She wanted him to very much, for there was so much to discuss. There was a knock on the door and she said without rising, 'Come in, Kofi.' For some reason she was becoming fond of him. She liked and was deeply charmed by his upright upbringing which he rather hated and was determined to cast away. This tended to make him seem unreal, and she found it extremely puzzling. She felt Kafu should have been her brother. Except that she was light-skinned, there were resemblances between the two of them, especially the cheeks and the hefty body. What she liked most was that Kafu had so far never tried to use false pretences to take money from her as other men had done.

She knew her education was not up to much, though through sheer grit she had learned to speak good English, write good letters and keep her business books. She belonged to the new generation of Makola women who knew what they were about, though their mode of trade resembled the old pattern. She regretted however that she had not had the same kind of elitist education as Kafu; it commanded respect and in these days guaranteed a life that was insulated from the uncertain rough-and-tumble, the hustle and bustle and wheeling–dealing life of the rich textile-market woman. In this respect, not only Kafu's upbringing but also his formal education made him a dedicated, innocent man living more on knowledge than by knowledge. She was sorry she had not had this type of opportunity.

There was some hesitation. The person who had knocked was not entering. She said again, 'Kofi, come in will you?' The person came in. It was not Kafu. When Odofo saw him she was so upset that she nearly fell from her chair. When she rose she forgot to gather her cloth round her properly and her wonderful body showed in parts. 'Get out!' she shouted.

'Please let me explain! In the name of Jesus, let me!'

'Explain what? I say, get out! Quick!' she cried.

Kafu's 204 was heard outside. He was driving it himself. He had had a lot of beer but was not particularly drunk. He entered the house and made straight for the room with the briskness he had cultivated recently. When Odofo saw him, she appealed, 'Kafu, make this man get out of here!' And Kafu, without asking question, said casually, 'Mister, vamoose!' And the man, hopelessly frightened, scurried away like a rat. He recognised the Minister of Internal Welfare.

'Who is he?' Kafu asked.

'Conception Contractor!' Odofo replied, half crying, her breast heaving.

'Why do you consort with such a type?'

'Your life has been laid on for you, so you may well ask, Kofi.'

'How is that?' Kafu was puzzled.

'You remember I told you about the different kinds of men who had come my way?'

'You and your different men! Where did you keep your judgement?'

'You make me want to cry, Kofi. Why? I could perhaps have been as good as you. You've got both parents living. They care for you. I'm sure they pray for you before they go to bed every evening. I was left alone to fight it out – an only child with jealous relations who would have taken my mother's property from me if she had not made a will; so they left me alone to play it out, thinking I would never make it, praying I would never make it. Kofi, come and sit by me!'

Kafu obliged and went and sat by her on a couch. He thought she was in some distress.

'Kofi, please put your head on my lap – or is that asking too much?'

'I don't relish women asking or telling me, but never mind, if it will make you happy. I'm a little tired, though – ah, that's good. You've got a comfortable lap, my Big-Thighs!'

'Kofi,' she called tenderly as she caressed his head, 'the human body is nothing. I think men sometimes seem to know this better than women.'

'Why do you say so? Is it in connection with the different men who have come your way?'

'Maybe yes, maybe no. Can I ask you a question?'

'Of course.'

'Have you ever been loved?'

'I suppose so.'

'By whom?'

'At least by my wife.'

'Are you sure?'

'We aren't divorced yet!'

'Why does she love you? Do you know?'

'I think she feels she needs me and perhaps I feel the same about her most of the time. But why do you ask?'

'I want someone who can excuse my money, and my body and love me. Someone who finds the totality of me, his conception of me, the idea of me inexpungeable from his mind.'

'That is academic.'

'I don't understand, Kofi.'

'I mean you want someone who can intellectualise you and

gloss over your physical presence. It will be a flop. You can't expect that from the man who has just run out like an animal?'

'No, I know, and that's where you don't want to understand me and show pity. What would you like to drink?'

'Beer, please.'

'You and your beer. Some day the doctor may ask you to quit it, heh?'

'I shall be dead by then. Odofo, what did that man do to you?'

'A moment, please. Let me finish serving you.'

'Won't you take something?'

'I have to watch my figure.'

'Damn you women and your figures!'

'You men take account of it, though.'

'Perhaps!'

'Ah, perhaps. You're all the same. Here you are, darling. Is your head well rested? Are you comfortable?' she asked possessively.

'Don't worry, dear. Anyhow, you could have been more choosy. I wasn't impressed by the look of that character,' Kafu said, determined to condemn her for her want of discrimination as he had seen it so far.

'I know what you mean. It was so difficult. I came across him at the spiritualist's. She's very well known at Kaneshie. Have you heard of her?'

'No.'

'She's called Madam Bampo. She is a fully qualified midwife and a public health nurse. She did not like men and set up a highly successful practice as a private midwife. A herbalist managed to break into her cocoon and destroy the inside. They had a child and he ran away. Disappointed, she turned to the Bible and prayers, and, according to what I was told, received the gift and became a prophetess. I've told you I have no child, haven't I, Kofi?'

'You have.'

'I went to her for help. There I met the rag you saw here.'

'What did he do to you?'

'It's a long story, so I'll give you the bare outline. He's about my age, unemployed now, but he used to be a Methodist catechist. His real name is Ofori Nortey but we call him Conception Contractor.'

93

'Why?'

'He spends his entire time hunting for well-to-do women who are finding it difficult to have children. You'll find him in the homes of prophetesses. There are many in Accra these days, and that's where such women are to be found. He's good at feigning serious prayers, at singing, at playing the tambourine and at receiving the gift of tongues. When he is in glossolalia some of his predictions come true, whether by chance or by intuition or experience or insight or wisdom, I can't tell. But he has managed to give a child to two or three women after he had persuaded them to desert their husbands or whoever their men were. On each occasion, he pretended he would marry them and performed customary rites but never a wedding.'

'And what happened?'

'He rolled in the women's wealth and then abandoned them when he was gratified, satiated.'

'Didn't you know of this?'

'I did but I . . .'

'Thought in your case it might be different?'

'Yes, but I didn't allow him much. I threw him out before he could make it. It hurts him, and once in a blue moon he shows up. Each time he looks more pious. He asks that we kneel and pray together. He begins with a powerful prayer calling the name of Jesus forty times in a minute. He has no beard and his face bears the innocence of a six-year-old. But I was and am determined, come hell or high water!'

'He might have won in the long run,' Kafu teased her.

'Not when you're around, dear.'

'By the way, tell me a little more about Prophetess Bampo. Who really finances her?'

'Why, everybody knows in Accra. Don't you have these prophetesses in Cape Coast?'

'I never really bothered about them.'

'Well, I was supposed to give one-tenth of my earnings to her.'

'Did you do that?'

'It was very hard.'

'So you got no baby?'

'Not that. I needed the right man. I couldn't get one, either at her prayer sessions or outside. I had heared about Conception

Contractor and was in doubt and confused. But after some time I realised that Madam Bampo was not always inspired and many of her prayers were put on. It takes time to know the difference but I found out initially on suspicion.'

'And later?'

'Half the time she prayed, she was actually thinking of trade, Kofi. It started one evening when the prayers were intense and many people were jabbering and grovelling, she came and tapped me on the shoulder and said, "The Lord says rise and follow me!" I did, full of expectation. I thought she had some good news from the Lord for me.'

'What did she say?'

'She said simply: forget about those people praying there, Odofo, they've not been paying their dues. I suppose they expect me to feed on the air. Odofo, why not give me some of your textiles to sell? I have been selling provisions in my stores. So I asked her: do you have a store? And she said yes, I've two. One is called The Lord Will Provide and the other The Lord Is My Shepherd. They are doing excellent business and I want to diversify. So I helped her. I still supply her. You know, Kofi, she's bought an estate house at Teshie-Nungua, and is putting up a huge building at Dzorwulu.'

'Did you have any regrets?'

'I don't know. My hopes were not fulfilled and I returned to my old church.' There was some silence and then she said, 'Kafu, I hope you will not disappoint us?'

'Now, now, now! This is a little serious. How come?'

'Why did you ruin that headmaster?'

'Ruin? I simply sacked him!' Kafu replied with some passion and rose from her lap.

'It's the same thing. I hear he was efficient. You weren't working hard, and when he complained you hated him.'

'That's not correct. He refused, I say he refused to recommend me for promotion.'

'But you were not working hard enough. You hated him, darling!' And she rose and kissed him.

'I hated him with all my heart! You see, nothing causes as much frustration and bitterness in this country as education. When you're in education, the country thinks you are a fool so you aren't paid well. When you're due for promotion, those responsible dilly-dally. Even when you move to the next salary point, there is no distinction between the very lazy and the very hard worker. Everybody gets the same cash. My father worked hard, what's his reward? And yet the people, the thoughtless pigs, want me to educate their masturbating progeny for nothing because I'm stupid enough to choose to go into education, and my ancestors were stupid enough to work in education as national slaves! Let me tell you...'

'Enough, dear, I only wondered why you picked on ... what's his name? Mr Baisi.'

'He is atoning! I saw him as a symbol of the idiocy of the whole country and I laid him flat, you see? Laid him flat! My father will die a pauper because he helped to raise people's bastards. Their fathers never came forward but their mothers were related to him. I refuse to be played down like my father so I hit him and hit him hard! I did! And I've no regrets!'

'And you've solved the problem, dear?'

'And I'm purged, darling.'

'Kofi,' she said when they disengaged.

'Yes?'

'You know you have children and I don't?'

'What about it?'

'I feel I must be useful. I must help my colleagues at Makola. I must leave some monument behind. I hope you understand?'

'Of course I do.'

'Will you help me?'

'I'll do my best.'

'How?'

'I'll talk to the city authorities and my colleagues. It's really because of you, dear.'

'And yourself, too, darling.'

'It's my father I'm worried about.'

'Why?'

'We have no home. He lives in a rented house. If he or mother dies I've had it. It will be a disgrace.'

'Tell me, dear, what did he do with all his earnings? He wasn't the only poorly paid teacher and minister of religion.'

'You're right, but as I've said, he looked after too many female relatives' children without reckoning the consequences. When we were old enough and saw the danger, we spoke to him. I mean us, his children. He told us God would provide. God hasn't done so yet.'

'Too bad.'

'Can you help me?'

'You've arranged more import licences for Salamatu than for me. It's not my business how much she gets or imports, but if you want me to help you, then you must help me to help you, dear. If you like, I'll split the profits fifty-fifty with you, for your sake and your father's. Is it a big house you want for him?'

'I don't think so. Something modest, I suppose. Say three bed-rooms, lounge and dining-room, kitchen and conveniences. No expensive interior appointments.'

'You'll probably need some eight thousand cedis.'

'Yes, I'll talk to Nee Otu. I'll arrange a big licence for you.'

'Thank you, Kofi, but Nee Otu isn't happy, you know. He's getting hard up for money and he thought you let him down badly when you refused to help us with the amenities. They would have entailed a lot of contracts that would have made a real difference to his finances.'

'Refused? I didn't really refuse. I stated government policy.'

'Kofi, are you convinced we need them?'

'Morally yes, politically no.'

'Kofi, I'm not giving up. I must either have a child or leave my name with something.'

'You can bequeath your property to the Society of Friends of Mentally Retarded Children.'

'And what would you like to bequeath, my dear, hatred of the education set-up and your beautiful wife and children?'

'Don't be cruel, darling,' and he embraced her firmly and dragged her to the couch, where they lay together.

When Kafu returned home it was one o'clock at night. On the way, not far from Odofo's house, he saw someone who looked like Ofori Nortey. He was grinning. He wondered why, and thought of stopping but instead drove on.

Grace would not go to bed and was slumped on a sofa in the lounge, fast asleep. All the lights were burning and the TV had not been switched off for three hours. Bukari was not asleep and was as alert as ever, though he did not and could not know the state of affairs where Grace was concerned. When Kafu parked the car in the garage, he hurried to open the car door for him. The night was chilly and he wore an old army pullover and a woollen pair of trousers given him by Kafu and a woollen head-piece which Grace had knitted for him. He was fond of this head-piece because it was given him by Grace, which made him feel very much a man of consequence, and also because it was extremely comfortable, particularly in the small hours. He wore also thick, old army socks into which he had tucked the bottoms of his trousers. He had on a pair of brown, aged gymshoes. He held in his hand an ancient, stout bow with the arrows in a pouch slung over his shoulder. Seen from the distance, his aspect alone could frighten a hardened burglar. Kafu took a good, long, look at him and his bow and arrows and asked smiling, 'Bukari, what do you do with these?'

Bukari laughed readily as was his nature and said, 'Master, this one self tiefman fearam bad!'

'But nobody uses bows and arrows these days, Bikari.'

'You see now, master. Only police say make we no use gun or pissly.'

'What's pissly?'

'The short one you shootam ide make paii! Na him good. You shoot one for tiefman bottom, he go fit run for him house before he die there self, so policeman no come and halahala you.'

'But what you're holding is dangerous. It can kill a man on the spot.'

'You see now, master, ibe true you de talk. Even if ino kill you at once self, the poison iday for the arrow go kill you some time.'

'Look, Bukari, no watchman uses this sort of thing these days. We hang it in a room to make the inside look nice. Can't you use a big stick or a truncheon?'

'Master, dis our house iday for place people tink everybody day dere ibe moneyman. So the tief iwant come here no fear big sticki. Ibe dis one when he see den his heart comot! You see now master? Anyway, master, just now you be gofment. Like you want me use pissly, you go fit bringam? Then I go leave this one for my room. No be so, master?'

'All right, Bukari, I'll see what I can do.'

He went to the main door and banged on it. Grace started and rose. She was sleepy and confused and came and opened it. When Kafu entered, the first thing he did was to go and switch off the TV and then some of the lights. There was as much cold anger in his eyes as there were regret, anger, confusion and slumber in Grace's. He noticed how Grace felt but pretended he didn't care. He thought Grace should on no account use TV's and electric lights to protest against his late homecoming.

'You could at least have switched off the TV and gone to bed, Grace.'

'Kofi, you could either have come home early or rung me up to say where you were. You have no right to leave me and the children imprisoned here!'

'Right?' Kafu asked with a sarcastic gleam in his eyes. He sat in a chair and crossed his legs. 'Did you think of what you were saying before you said it?'

'Of course I did,' she replied, more out of spite than conviction.

'Then get this straight, woman,' Kafu said coolly, anxious to school her into accepting his incipient irregular habits. 'As a politician my life and time are at the pleasure of others. You come second. I have to account to them, any time. I need not and will not do so to you!'

'You're right, Kofi,' her big, distressed eyes rolling half-drowsily in his direction, 'the politician's first domestic obligation is to some woman in town who keeps him till after midnight! You know you don't even want to touch me these days.'

'Come on, have you any proof of what you say? This is not the time of night to pick quarrels.'

'I've no proof, Kofi, except that that perfume makes me sick! At first you brought some home saying it was a gift, but now it has become such a magic concoction that it stays fresh on you even after midnight!' She was not used to violent quarrels with him yet. She felt she had made her point and was anxious not to lose her self-control and disturb the night, though she was very angry with him. Odofo in her enthusiasm had sprayed too much on him as a parting shot. It was the same eau de cologne given him by the group.

'Thank you for the insight, my wife!' Kafu said, half subdued and half defiant. He stretched his legs fully and crossed them at the ankles. 'Did anybody call?' he asked.

'Nee Otu was here.'

'Did he leave a message?'

'He said there ought to be some urgent consultation between the two of you. It's about our house, Kofi. It appears he's run out of money. He says it will cost thirty-six thousand and he's got halfway through with eighteen. Even then you owe him some four thousand or so.'

'I know, Grace,' Kafu said thoughtfully as he wiped his face with his handkerchief, though the air-conditioning was on. 'And there is my father's house, too. I want to discuss it with him.'

'Your father's house, Kofi?' Grace asked and sat down, completely surprised. She sat so loosely before him that he could see straight and far in between her well-tapered thighs. 'You've never discussed this with me.'

'I'm sorry, Grace. I'll tell you all about it tomorrow. Let's go to bed!' He grabbed her left arm and flung it over his left shoulder from across his back and then held it with his left hand. He then threw his right arm round her waist and almost carried her into the bedroom like a hurt star footballer going to be stretched down flat for treatment.

In the morning Kofi Danso was sent to go and collect Nee Otu Lartey. Kafu wanted to have preliminary discussions in the house with him before they went to his ministerial office together. On the return journey, Nee Otu sat in front by Danso. He wanted to be sociable so he remarked, tongue in cheek, 'Your car pulls beautifully, Kofi Danso.'

'You've said it, sir. This is the fastest of the government cars. I've handled it from when it was brand new and I've trained it. No car can overtake it on the straight drive!'

'How about petrol consumption?'

'Very good, sir. Very good for its size. It takes the least in its class. The other drivers dispute it but I know. Any car I handle doesn't guzzle, no matter what!'

'I see,' Nee Otu said and asked no more questions. He was getting bored and began to think about his problems.

Kafu had breakfast with him and mentioned the house for his father. Nee Otu was not opposed to the idea. Obviously a minister of his standing must have a home. He reasoned that in these parts politics was either a lethal or at least an unpredictable business and anyone who went into it must watch the stakes in spite of the commissions of enquiry. But matters of this nature hinged on money, which, in this instance, must come in fast and plenty. 'I must tell you, Kofi,' he said to Kafu, 'you really disappointed me the other day. Why did you do that?'

'Odofo has told me. I spoke the truth. That was all. I thought you asked for those projects for their own sakes and hadn't tied them up with your business interests.'

'They surely were tied up with business, Kofi, as well as the social considerations. Since you came to power, your rural policy has slowed down the building industry in the urban centres. You've got to do something about it, otherwise it will be pretty bad for some of us who have large overheads – er – business-wise and domestic-wise.'

'I see what you mean,' Kafu said, holding the cup of tea halfway between the saucer and his lips for some time.

'And you know, Kofi, your building is only halfway through. I've added my own four thousand to the fourteen thousand. We've just finished, luckily, with the roofing and ceiling, but what remains is what makes a house and we've got to find the money. You made a sad mistake, you know.'

'Why?'

'Rebuilding Makola alone could give you your own finished house and your Dad's house in six months. Have you a life insurance policy?'

'No, Ataa Otu.'

'I thought I advised you to insure your life and that of your kids. You'd better do it while you're playing hanky-panky with your buiding projects.'

'But we can start modestly, don't you think, Nee Otu?'

'How? Come out with it and let's see.' Nee Otu's face lit up a little hopefully.

'Technically it is the responsibility of the city authorities to provide the lavatory at the beach. I'll tell Mr Vuga to draft a memo that the local community is prepared to start putting it up so the government should set in and help. How much do you think the structure will cost, altogether?'

'Eight thousand should be all right, Kofi.'

'I think we'll make it twelve thousand to give us four thousand. You take two, I take two. Let's go to the office.'

At the office Kafu called Mr Vuga. He practically rushed in and sat down, pencil in hand at the ready and his huge glasses sliding down his nose until he began looking at Kafu from above them.

'Mr Vuga, I want my ministry to provide twelve thousand cedis for a community project to erect a lavatory at Accra beach. When will the money be available?'

'Are we going to use the amount to buy materials for the project and then provide technical guidance for a good structure, sir?'

'No, Mr Vuga. The twelve thousand should be paid to this contractor, Mr Nee Otu Lartey.'

'Then we must tender, sir.'

'Mr Vuga, I hear when you were in the Ministry of Trade, you unwittingly gave a licence worth a fantastic amount to one Kwahu trader alone. It must have been interesting!'

'It was investigated, sir, and I was cleared, sir.'

'I know. I wonder if it should now be properly investigated under due process?' Kafu said slowly and almost in a whisper, his eyes steadily fixed on Mr Vuga's glasses, which were becoming misty, 'Er, arrange to have Mr Lartey get the contract, is that clear?'

'Yes, sir.'

'You may go!'

'Yes, sir,' and he left, pulling up his trousers which had become suddenly loose and were dropping.

'Nee Otu, the rest of the job is yours. You'd better set about it. Incidentally, you must put up a strong building, though. We don't want weak walls collapsing at the least earth tremor. You know what Accra is.'

'Don't worry, Kofi, you just come to the site in a month. Seeing is believing!'

10

'Why don't you want to confess so simple a matter, Kofi? I know you're in love with her.'

'No, Salamatu. It can't be. I'm properly married.'

'And you spent a whole night in her house?'

'It's not true. You're being vulgar.'

'Let me put it this way, Kofi. Is Odofo not fond of you?'

'I can't tell, but I know we like each other very much. Now look, suppose she is fond of me, what's wrong with that? What's your interest?'

'I thought you would have to choose between us. I have been told how you spend the whole time there. I wouldn't be surprised if she has put some love medicine in your food and drink. Tell me, Kofi Kafu dear, what is it at all you see in Fat-Thighs?'

Kafu suppressed a laugh, as Salamatu seemed dead serious and could become hysterical. He wanted to defuse the emotional atmosphere so he asked calmly, his arms folded on his chest, 'Do you know a man called Ofori Nortey?'

'You mean Conception Contractor?' Salamatu asked, with a start at Kafu's question. Her face dropped and then quickly resumed its charm.

'Yes, I know him. Why do you ask?'

'Does he visit you often?'

'No, on and off. But why do you ask?'

'Is he your spy on me?'

'I'm not answering, Kofi.'

'Do you think a woman of your standing and beauty should tolerate in her house such a verminous sex hunter and make him her spy, too?'

'I don't tolerate him. He comes to beg for money. I don't just give it him. I make him run little errands, that's all.'

'Maybe, but I wonder if I can have much respect for any woman who embraces that man!' Kafu said with a smile. His eyes were steadily fixed on hers. He thought there was something in his vague suspicion and it made him angry.

'I don't!' Salamatu cried. For the first time Kafu saw from the encroaching but indistinct lines on her face that she was not that young and fresh.

'Of course you don't. Dr Mills Blankson is not used to supping from the same bowl with worthless beggars, or is he?' Kafu now had his hands on his hips, still staring in her face.

Salamatu was standing near a five-foot-tall tapered stool on which stood a huge, exquisite vase loaded with showy roses from her own garden. She was in tight slacks and an equally tight blouse that was even tighter around her bust. Her brows were pencilled and her lips were painted red to contrast beautifully with her lighter red skin – the type Kafu found difficult to resist. Her hairstyle on this occasion was 'Try Again'. The beads holding the hair in a bunch at the back of her head were beautifully wrought. Kafu admitted to himself that in this type of hairstyle and dress she looked simply wonderful, especially from a distance.

While she was pumping him about Odofo, she had both arms on her hips and was full of confidence, but now her legs could no longer carry her and she simply folded up like a boneless creature into a nearby chair and propped her chin in her hand while her languid eyes were helplessly fixed on him. Then a sudden powerful feeling surged up in her and she asked him, 'Ofori Nortey is worthless, how about Mr Baisi?'

'Get your thinking right, mistress, I never played around with Baisi!'

'Of course he was a good man, so you wouldn't, would you?'

'And Ofori Nortey is a rogue, so you would, wouldn't you? It's a neat little piece of argument you've got there, Lady Salamatu. I'm terribly impressed!' Kafu answered, still staring at her with a contemptuous smile.

Just then two visitors arrived. They were a man and a woman. One would have thought they were married, but they were not. The man was Amega Amenu, an ex-soldier, ex-policeman and now 'a private business-man', as he described himself in his passport. He was forty-two, with a chocolate-brown skin. He was very neat and dapper; his hair looked as if it had been brushed a minute ago and he had a beautiful set of extremely white teeth that reinforced his neat appearance. He was tall and stout. He wore an expensive and attractive Patapata shirt and a fashionably cut pair of trousers, French style, and held in his right hand a well-loaded, commodious shoulder-bag. He did not seem to be happy about Kafu's presence in Salamatu's house.

His companion was called Mercy Mensah. She worked as an executive clerk in the Ministry of Interior but found the salary, as she told a female friend, below the poverty line because she had three children staying with her mother and she had to provide for them and her mother as well. The children's father would not look after them. One of his reasons for not doing so, as he alleged to her family, was that he believed he was the father of only one of the three. The family was disappointed but did not take the matter to court. Once, when he was drunk in a beer-bar, he said loudly that he felt Mercy Mensah was so resourceful that she would never lack money to look after the children. Actually, he was himself doing well as a salesman when the economy was booming, but during the middle sixties, when the economy turned sour, he lost his job and was now working with an Italian building contractor whose contracts were not being paid for regularly by the government, especially during Kafu's regime.

It was a fact, though, that Mercy Mensah was an extremely beautiful woman; the type that Kafu would want to ravish in an instant had society not worked out elaborate systems for going about these things. He bit his lips and swore to himself as he took a good look at her. She was twenty-six, well-proportioned, tall and fair-coloured. She had a broad back and a slender waist. Her legs were well-rounded and her arms were shapely, though Kafu thought they could easily be used for rough work if it came to it. However, what Kafu found most interesting about her was her face: it was beautiful but not charming, compassionate but at the same time disconcertingly tough. In other words, Kafu estimated, Mercy was a woman who knew her bearings no matter what you thought of her. She seemed an independent character with attractively full lips that were shut tight, a fine nose and bushy eyebrows. She wore a long, Patapata maxi-robe that was tight at the waist and back with generous floral designs in it. The flappy sleeves hung gracefully on her arms and her heels were four inches high. She had on an enchantingly fresh hair-do called 'Guarantee'. She also carried a synthetic leather bag.

Amega and Mercy said good evening to Salamatu and Kafu

almost at the same time. Salamatu responded but Kafu did not. As a minister of state he deliberately used this kind of reaction to reinforce his status. Salamatu thought it was phoney and was being used primarily to impress Mercy, for she was watching Kafu very closely indeed and was reading his thoughts. She said, 'I've been expecting you all this afternoon so I didn't go to Makola. How was it, did you have a good consignment?'

Kafu felt insulted because Salamatu was deliberately ignoring him. He put his hands in his trouser pockets and said, 'I've some urgent work at the ministry, Salamatu, you can ring me up there. Will you?'

'Oh, I'm sorry,' Salamatu said, her face lit up with mischievous glee. 'This is Miss Mercy Mensah and Mr Amega Amenu. Mercy, this is Mr Kafu. He is our minister. He doesn't tolerate indiscreet women, you hear? And Amega, he doesn't like hanky-panky business, you understand?'

'Don't be silly, Salamatu, there is no point talking like that to the lady! I must be going.'

'Must you?' Salamatu asked. She added, 'All right, I'll come over there by seven o'clock.'

As Kafu was leaving, and while his back was turned, Mercy drew near to Salamatu and whispered, 'Sala, you're doing well. Is he on our side?'

'Don't worry, Mercy, I'll work him over!' Salamatu assured her with a confident smile.

Soon they all heard two people talking outside. It was Kafu and Ofori Nortey. As Kafu got into his car he had seen Ofori Nortey in the driving mirror, lanky, neatly dressed in white shirt and brown trousers. His thin, smooth and handsome face and voluptuous mouth were very noticeable. He was stalking into the house. Kafu instinctively reacted against his entry – it simply filled him with hate. So he bounced out of the car and intercepted him. Ofori Nortey took fright when he saw Kafu suddenly. He had not recognised his Peugeot car. He would have liked to bolt away. Kafu confronted him squarely, chest out, trying to tower over him, though he could not make himself taller than him, and peering into his face. Ofori Nortey stood at stand-at-ease, both hands firmly placed on his hips shivering. Kafu glowered, 'Look here, man, what's your name?'

'Ofori Nortey, sir.'

'Any previous names?'

'No, sir. No, sir!'

'What's your job?'

'Er, I beg your pardon, sir.'

'Don't be silly. I say what's your job?'

'I'm looking for one, sir.'

'In a woman's house?'

'Pardon me, sir?'

'Look here, the next time you say pardon something, I'll have you locked up in a police cell, you understand?'

'Yes, sir.'

'Have you ever slept in one before?'

'No, sir.'

'Good Lord, you need to. Now tell me, and no beating about the bush, are you looking for a job in a woman's house? Yes? No? Answer straight!'

'No, sir. I swear, sir.' Ofori Nortey said, and beads of perspiration appeared on his upper lip and nose.

'Liar, I didn't ask you to swear,' Kafu said. He became more and more angry as he looked at what he considered the insignificant and worthless body of Ofori Nortey. He asked, 'You realise you're a foolish man?'

'Yes, sir,' Ofori Nortey answered, till standing at ease. He was beginning to hate Kafu but was for the moment riddled with fear.

'Is a woman's house a Labour Exchange? You bedbug!'

'No, sir!' Ofori Nortey answered, feeling desperate. A minister could wield immense power, he knew.

'Look, now,' Kafu said, his voice full of threat, 'if by day or night or any time whatsoever, I see you not at a work site but stalking round women's homes, I'll get the Bukom boys to whip you. That will be stage one. Have you ever been in an army camp?'

'No, sir.'

'Good. I'll have you sent there. They will shave your hair. You will lie on the ground, you will roll on the ground, you will crawl on the ground and you will be booted in the arse! You will see blood. Is that clear?'

'Hm-m-m. Yes, sir,' Ofori Nortey said and farted. Kafu heard it. He was both happy and disgusted. He thought the man was a chicken-hearted, good-for-nothing, odious sex adventurer. He would teach him.

'The army camp will be stage two. You will then be taken to Nsawam and put in a maximum security cell, where they put those awaiting the hangman's noose. You will then be charged formally with subversion before you're ...'

Ofori Nortey fled.

Kafu went back to the lounge in haste, wanting to pick a loud quarrel with Salamatu. He was dead angry. He cried at her, 'You women are useless! How on earth can you accept such a lousy, wretched, hopeless, cringing raga ...'

'Oh, Allah, enough, enough, Mr Great Man Minister! There are visitors here. Why make a scene?' She got hold of him and kissed him and said, 'Keep cool, darling, take me to your office. We will settle everything there!' She then told Mercy and Amega, 'Don't you go away, will you? Find something to eat and drink. Wait until I return.' They smiled dutifully at her instructions and Kafu drove her away.

Ofori Nortey soiled his pants as he fled. He ran straight to his single room. There he undressed, washed his clothes and himself quickly and put on clean clothes. He set out again for Salamatu's house. This time he did not go through any of the two gates of the house but climbed over the wall, after a great deal of reconnoitring to ensure that Kafu was nowhere near. When he entered where Mercy and Amega were he was panting. Amega asked him, 'What have you done to that man?'

'Nothing. Nothing whatsoever.'

'But how did he know you?' Mercy asked.

'Oh, you see, you see, I mean ...'

'Speak up and stop this "you see" business,' Mercy snapped. 'When you corner innocent women, the words flow like a June rain, you sucker!'

'Actually, heh, he saw me at Madam Odofo Lamptey's house. Odofo was shouting as if I was a thief and he asked me to clear out. Then I suppose he saw me again when he was driving away from her house. It's all very wrong. He thinks I'm a criminal or something!'

'What did you go to Odofo's house for anyway? If I were her, I'd box your ears and smash all the teeth in your deceitful mouth!'

'Why, Mercy, I only went to try my luck,' Ofori Nortey said, looking in the direction of Amega with a smile.

Mercy rose and rushed at him. She grasped him by the neck, shook him violently and pushed him into a chair. His mouth hit the arm of the chair and his lower lip bled. She said in a voice that sounded masculine: 'You know Odofo and Salamatu are no friends and you crawl between the two of them. You have been selling whisky, gin, perfume, everything, cheap to her and then she resells them, making a profit from all of us, while you want her body too, you snivelling, smelly cockroach!' And she went over and punched his face like an expert boxer. She cried, 'I'm an Asere! Real Accra! No nonsense, you swine!'

'Do you do this to me because you want to make love to the minister?' Ofori Nortey asked as he wiped away the blood on his lip. Mercy was going to beat him up again but Amega intervened. Ofori Nortey began to shed tears and said as he sobbed, 'If I get him, I won't spare him!'

When Kafu and Salamatu got to the ministry at six-fifty, Mr Nutor Vuga was there still, working away at the thirtieth cabinet memorandum; none of them had brought about a single breakthrough since Kafu took over the ministry. Kafu felt in his bones that Mr Vuga was selfish, anachronistic and obstructionist and thoroughly despised him, but he did not know how to get rid of him or make him run the ministry efficiently. Mr Nutor Vuga knew how Kafu's administration could be undermined by a show of obedience and diligence when in fact there was nothing but carefully concealed passive resistance, carried on by sending long policy circulars to the regions and districts asking for acknowledgement of receipt in the penultimate paragraphs but no followups unless the minister remembered; suppression of new ideas from senior staff to the minister; playing off one senior staff member against another so that there was no esprit de corps among the staff, and lying to senior staff if any of them mustered courage to complain about their promotions. He told them the minister did not like them. Above all, he loaded the minister with a lot of clerical work so that all decisions that should have been disposed of by the permanent secretary or his deputy were passed on to him. The minister even had to write down whether or not a senior officer should go on leave. The result was that the minister was nothing more than a permanent secretary himself and many crucial programmes were either stillborn or not pursued in the field for lack of time. Everybody was holed up in ministry offices, talking, writing – about nothing.

Kafu felt all this and complained to him one day that he was getting no help from his staff and was becoming disillusioned. Mr Nutor Vuga was happy. He said under the shower one morning, 'Whoever wants me to retire prematurely will quit first!' And he laughed gleefully.

When Kafu and Salamatu settled down in the minister's office, he went over and asked, 'Did you call me, sir?' He very well knew he hadn't been called. Kafu replied, 'No. By the way, when are you promoting those ten officers?'

'They have all refused transfers, sir. I don't recommend promotion until they have gone on transfer and acted in their new posts for some time, sir.'

'Why? Is that fair? Why should a man risk transfer if he knows he's not going to be promoted, his children's education will be interrupted, he will have little social amenities and he will lose money, too? Mr Vuga, is this the way you people handle morale in the civil service?'

'Sir, the officers are lazy, irresponsible and money-minded. They come to work late. They don't stay after work to clear files. They do nothing but grumble about promotion!'

'Are they all the same?'

'No, sir. Unfortunately those who are reasonably good are far down the seniority list. If we promote by merit, the public services committee will ask so many ugly questions in respect of the lazy ones that we might as well let things be.'

'So are we or are we not promoting them, Mr Vuga?'

'I don't recommend promotions just yet, sir. We will see whether they show any improvement during the financial year, sir.'

'Have you told them their shortcomings?'

'I've told them to stay after working hours and come to work on holidays, sir.'

'And what's the response?'

'I'm the only one left in the building now, sir.'

Salamatu was getting bored with the shop-talk. She disliked Mr Vuga at first sight and wanted him to leave. Kafu realised there was no point pursuing such a matter at great length before her. He told Mr Vuga, 'All right, Mr Permanent Secretary, you may go home. All the best to you and yours!'

'Good night, sir,' Mr Vuga responded. When he closed the door, he muttered to himself, 'Bloody fool! We will see who retires first. They are all the same. They think running government is barking orders, drinking and wenching. We'll see! I'll dodge my wife into the study tonight and take whisky to celebrate this evening. The fool doesn't even realise that I'm taking some of his whisky home! Why should a small boy of thirty-two make more money than myself when I do the donkey work? "Monkey de wok baboon de chop!" I'll tell W. W. Mensah that the minister says he doesn't want any promotions because the officers don't deserve it. The news will spread!' He let go a high-pitched laugh. Kafu heard it, opened the door and asked, 'Anything wrong, Mr Vuga?'

'Everything is in order, sir.'

'Good. Sleep well, Mr Vuga.'

'Yes, sir!'

When Kafu returned to the office, he sat by Salamatu on a settee. They were having scotch. Salamatu gave him a loving smile and asked, 'Do you like Mercy Mensah?'

'An indecent question. Ask another.'

'She has money, Kafu.'

'So?'

'Oh, yes, she has!'

'How did she make it?'

'She is a tough, business-woman.'

'In clothes?'

'No, no. Drinks, perfumes, cigarettes, wigs, wrist-watches, Java prints, the like.'

'God Almighty, she's a smuggler. Along with that nice-looking man?'

'They're tycoons!'

'Impossible!'

'Never mind. They have more cash in hand than you and your "family" combined.'

'Possibly!'

'What would you do if their names were brought up? The guards are pretty smart these days. We need advance signals to know how to manoeuvre.'

'Why would you expect me to relay signals? We need the revenue to develop the country.'

'True. Including your house?'

'Haa! That's a sad story!' Kafu sipped his whisky.

'How much more do you need?'

'Sixteen thousand.'

'What does Nee Otu say?'

'He's broke.'

'And you?'

'Broke.'

'And Odofo, your sweetheart?'

'Keep her out of it!'

'I won't,' and she turned and pressed her bust against his shoulder, took hold of his chin in her hands and kissed him. For a few seconds Kafu was paralysed.

'Well, darling, Mercy will give you the sixteen thousand, eight of which actually belongs to Amega.'

'Any conditions?'

'No conditions except that they would want the same amount back through herself, Amega, you and me. In other words, you repay only four thousand out of the sixteen within a year from now. Your building should have been finished by then, shouldn't it?'

'It should have been. The terms are reasonable. When do I get the money?'

'Tomorrow, dear, but I'm taking you back to the house. Did you see those bags they were carrying?'

'I did.'

'They contained gifts for you, dear. Let's go and collect them.'

'I'm grateful.'

'Kafu, why can't you spend a little more time with me?'

'Sala, we'll see!'

11

As Kafu was driving Salamatu back home, she asked, 'What sort of man is the Permanent Secretary — what's his name?'

'Vuga.'

'Yes, that Mr Vuga, who is he? What sort of man is he?'

'Why, you don't like him?'

'Does he like you?'

'He is not supposed to like or hate me.'

'Is he not a human being?'

'He is, but the rule for civil servants is that they must as far as possible neither like nor hate. They must be disinterested. As a matter of fact, a good many of them have become uninterested, too. I've been thinking of what I can do about it.'

'Kafu, I wonder whether what you're saying is strictly practised by Mr Vuga. He doesn't like you.'

'How do you know? Why state it so positively?'

'I was watching his face, his eyes, the way he looked at you. He deeply resents you.'

'I can't take what you're saying seriously. You women can sometimes generate expensive trouble. In any case, assuming what you say is true, it still has nothing to do with the work. I'm the boss, you see. He does as I tell him.'

'And you can't tell him to promote those people?'

'You keep your Makola nose out of this. Running a ministry is more complicated than supervising the activities of a couple of smugglers.'

'Kofi, you sometimes make me feel you don't love me. Is it because of Odofo?'

'Sala,' Kafu said to her a little compassionately, while adjusting his tie with one hand, 'a man can't love more than one woman at the same time!'

'Kofi, who do you love now?' her breath was quickening.

'My wife!'

'Liar!' She drew close to him. His driving became impaired but he could not ask her to push off. He felt he must change the subject because she had begun to squeeze his thigh. He asked,

'Sala, is it true that provisions are scarce these days? What's happening?'

'Yes, Kofi,' she answered rather anxiously, letting go his thigh and easing away. 'I have been wanting to tell you all along, but each time we meet something makes me forget. Now let me see – there is no milk. I think baby milk in particular. There is no sugar. There is . . .'

'Sala, is it a long list?' he asked realising at that moment that his bladder was full.

'Kofi, it isn't long but as you know, it's a dangerous short list. Are you politicians not informed about how the people are feeding?'

'We are, but many of my colleagues feel that sardines, for example, are not essential. They're expensive and almost a luxury in most of the so-called developed countries.'

'I believe you, but I think they can get fresh fish all the year. But here, what do we have now? No meat, no fish. Only kontomire and palm oil.'

'Which are very good, though.'

'I agree, but palm oil too is in short supply. Most of it is being used by the soap factories. Kontomire is expensive and tomatoes are scarce. The yam and plantain that should go round are being exported. As a woman I feel it's the baby milk that's most serious.'

'But you have no child.'

'Kofi, you can be as cruel to me as you like but we'll see! I'm not talking for myself. If a mother has no breast milk what happens?'

'You must think of yourself.'

'Think of myself? Is it not true, Kofi, that when one is in politics one must think more of others?'

'The most important rule for a politician is that he must consolidate himself.'

'What does that mean, Kofi?'

'Here we are. Back at the palace of the great queen Salamatu!'

They laughed and got out of the car. Amega and Mercy were there. They had had dinner and were taking brandy and ginger ale. Ofori Nortey was there. Amega had asked him to wait until Salamatu returned. He was sipping Gordon's gin, neat. The gin helped to make his thoughts about Mercy and Kafu more bitter, dark and sinister while he also chafed at his helplessness. When the voices were heard, he uttered a frightened whisper, 'Good heavens, the minister is back!'

'Go and hide in the kitchen. Quick!' Amega advised him.

'No. Don't go there. A kitchen is too big for a hiding place. Get into the lavatory and hide behind the door,' Mercy ordered him.

'Jesus Christ, I will!' and he dashed into the place after quickly emptying the glass and depositing it on the sideboard as if it had not been used.

When they entered the room, Salamatu asked, 'Have you had anything to eat and drink?'

'We have, but I would have preferred roast pork. Reserve some for me next time.'

'But, Mercy, you know there aren't enough pigs in the country and the roast pork sellers are being forced out of business. I suspect you want Kafu to know about the problem!'

'Me? Just to let me know about the problem?' Kafu took it up without waiting for Mercy to explain to Salamatu. 'Is it the responsibility of the government to raise pigs and provide roast pork and expect the Moslems to ask God to preserve it in power?' He cast a furtive glance at Salamatu to see what she would say.

'Kafu dear, please keep my people out of this,' Salamatu pleaded. 'I know you would seize on any opportunity to tease me. We Moslems don't like pork but we haven't said those who like it should be deprived of it.'

'Why should the government raise pigs? This is my question,' Kafu pressed, stroking his chin.

'I think,' Amega began to reply instead, 'that governments of this country say a lot. They give the impression they have the means to provide everything. The people know in their heart of hearts that no government has got all the means but they continue asking, demanding, blaming, blackmailing!'

'I appreciate your contribution, Amega,' Kafu said feebly.

'And you know,' Amega warmed up, 'the government continues lying as if it can provide for all of us. And the press too joins in spreading the lies and when the people are disappointed in the long run, they begin to wish for the end of the government;

and when it is toppled, they are delighted and look forward to the next one that will continue the same lying. It's a bad habit!'

'Like smuggling!' Kafu snapped. There was an uproar and Ofori Nortey laughed softly in the lavatory. He was a good laugher, especially when someone was being discomfited.

'Sir, we smuggle out of desperation,' Amega said, looking uncomfortably at Kafu. 'It's not at all safe. Some have been shot, some have been arrested, many have drowned in the Volta estuary. It's hazardous!'

'And very profitable!' Kafu cut in, winking at Mercy. This upset Salamatu, so she asked, 'Amega, have you parcelled out the Minister's gifts?'

'Yes, I have.'

'Good. We will not open them here. The Minister will do that by himself in his bedroom!' Everybody laughed at the last sentence, but Ofori Nortey clenched his teeth, waved a fist in the air and whispered, 'Look at that! The uncircumcised lecher talking to the beautiful ladies! They give him gifts! Je-e-sus Christ! The day I get him the angels will sing hallelujah!'

Mercy said, 'Mr Kafu ...'

'Don't call me mister. Either Kafu or Kofi will do.'

'And that makes Mercy number three. Not so, Kofi?'

'Don't be jealous, Sala,' Kafu replied nonchalantly.

'Sala is jealous, but it's so hard not to be,' Mercy spoke as if she was speaking more to herself. 'The best thing is to know what you want from your darling and coax it out. Kofi, would you like an Omega watch?'

'Why not?'

'Take this one. Ask no questions. No thanks. It's between us!'

Salamatu hated Mercy's move but had no grounds for open protest. Amega was impassive.

'Je-e-sus Christ! The rascal has got an Omega watch, too. When I get him, I'll punch him under the belly, like this!' And Ofori Nortey demonstrated it and smiled happily, for his mental picture of the act and the rehearsal of it were so clear and precise.

He then heard Salamatu say, 'Amega, Mercy, I've told Kafu about our offer. It's sixteen thousand cedis altogether. The three of us are providing twelve thousand as a gift. It's understood that the remaining four thousand will be paid back to Amega within a year. Actually it's money that's meant for safe keeping because Amega, like any of us, doesn't want to keep all his money with the banks. As soon as there's a coup and there are commissions of this and that all your accounts lose privacy. There's no point keeping four thousand idle when it can help Kofi. So, Kofi, use it but make sure you pay it back. Amega can be tricky when it comes to money!'

'I suppose so. Most people are!' Kafu replied casually with a short, pointless laugh.

'Jesus in Jerusalem! They are heaping money on the womanising upstart! Ahaa! After I've punched him in the belly, I'll tweak his fat nose – like this,' which he demonstrated and then laughed slightly audibly, 'Hi, hi, hi, hiii! And he will groan! Lord, have mercy upon me and let my plans prosper! Please, damn the rascal's soul! Please, do! Amen,' and he bowed his head as he said the amen.

'Salamatu, my bladder. Your toilet?' Kafu asked.

'Straight. Last door on your left.'

Ofori Nortey's heart jumped. He looked at the two little windows. They were hopeless. They were burglar-proofed. He thought hard and fast what to do. Fight? Run? What? Kafu switched on the light. Too bad! He entered. Saw him. In a flash! Like in a dream! He cried, 'Wha-a-a-t! ! Ofori Nortey! Again?' He tried to grab Ofori Nortey, but Ofori Nortey broke loose and dashed out. Kafu chased him through the narrow corridor. In a second they were in the lounge where the others were. Ofori Nortey was yelling. '*Adzeii! Aagbemi eii!*' Kafu caught up and tripped him. As he was in the process of falling, it was clear that it was going to be a somersault. Mercy was so thrilled with it that just as he was landing, she shouted, '*Zeleen!*' to synchronise with his landing on the carpet. Kafu wanted to pin him down, but Ofori Nortey was as slippery as a cockroach being chased in a bedroom. He dodged, rose, wove through the furniture and was gone.

Kafu had not run for a long time. He was in one of his Ishmael and Sons suits. The arms of the coat had moved up the sleeves of his expensive shirt and the diamond cufflinks shone. He was panting. He had got a shock. He wanted to talk but couldn't.

Mercy went and practically carried him on to the couch. She got two cushions, piled them into a pillow and rested his head gently on them. She was going to loosen his tie but Salamatu cried, 'Enough! Leave him to me!' Mercy recoiled. She did not utter a word.

Salamatu went and sat by him and said, 'Mercy, go to the bathroom, soak a towel, squeeze it and bring it to me.'

Mercy did as she was told and sat down. Amega filled her glass. Salamatu gently wiped the perspiration off Kafu's face. He recovered his breath and senses slowly, then said, 'Mercy, beer, please!'

Salamatu was furious but said nothing. She looked at Mercy with cold, menacing eyes. Mercy saw it and gave her a quick defiant look in return. When she brought the beer and glass she gave them to Salamatu to serve him and then fetched a coffee-stool for the refreshment to be put on it. Kafu took a long, cool, soothing mouthful and then asked, as if to nobody in particular, 'What happened?'

'Nothing,' Salamatu said casually and cheerfully and took his hand and rubbed it. 'You were taking some exercise.'

'In your lavatory?'

'Oh no, in the corridor.'

'I will kill him, that boy!'

'What has he done to you?'

'I don't want to see him, that's all. I feel I must twist his neck. Can't you feel how I feel?'

'I'm trying to!'

'No, you can't. You don't understand. You simply don't. Let me warn you! As Minister of Welfare I don't want to see unemployed layabouts hiding in lavatories. This is what he has done to me, if you want to know. I'm going!'

'Where?' Salamatu was uneasy.

'To Grace, my wife!'

'Can you give us a drive home?' Mercy asked, smiling, with a mischievous glance at Salamatu.

'Who?' Kafu asked unenthusiastically.

'Amega and me.'

'I surely will.' Kafu obliged because of Mercy. He had forgotten all about Amega. He asked, 'Do you live at the same place?'

'No,' Mercy answered.

'Splendid, let's go.'

'You will come back here, Kofi?' Salamatu asked.

'Of course not!'

'Of course you will.' She quickly dashed to her bedroom, came back and sprayed the perfume Grace hated on him. 'This will stay on you for three hours. The money is here. I give you fifteen minutes. Mercy, you understand? You will be sorry if he delays! Kafu, your dinner will be ready. It's your favourite. Roast chicken, sauce and mashed yam and a little Bols wine to help the digestion!'

'I don't know,' Kafu said, still aggrieved. 'Mercy, Amega, let's go!'

They drove off. Kafu said, 'You say the people are unhappy, food is scarce, prices have soared. There is widespread unemployment when there are large tracts of uncultivated land. I can't understand it. Self-unemployment? Laziness? What? Why blame the government?'

'If you wouldn't have me placed under detention, sir, or in protective custody, I would say that the governments of this country talk too much. Haven't the civil servants anything to do but write speeches, sir?'

'Of course they have a lot more to do than that, Mr Amega,' Kafu answered, now bored with the theme.

'Yes, sir, but the governments try too hard to woo the people. If a wooer talks too much, he makes promises he can't fulfil. He becomes a deceiver. The people know the empty promises – the lying that has become endemic. If you talk openly against it, it is subversion. If you are fed up with it and show no interest, you are called unpatriotic. Who cannot love his country, sir?'

'I'm trying to understand you, to sympathise with you, Amega,' Kafu replied, subdued and pensive. 'I forget, but I think it was the Greek orator, Pericles, who once said something like this: "We alone regard a man who takes no interest in public affairs not as a harmless but as a useless character." Public speeches started long ago, Amega. You simply can't stop them just because the people have not enough to eat.'

'Kofi, I hear you're very learned?' Mercy asked. She did not relish Amega's vehemence and wanted to cool it off.

'I don't know whether I'm learned but I did spend a long time at school, at public expense, since you ask me.'

'And, sir, they say all your colleagues in government are learned?'

'They're well educated, yes.'

'Then why do we have so many problems?'

Kafu smiled and said, 'You can know all about Greek speeches and great men like Plato, Socrates, Shakespeare, but it doesn't mean you can get rid of the mosquito. Maybe we have to stop talking.'

'And laugh,' Mercy quipped and they all laughed.

'Mr Amega? Is this your place?' Kafu asked as he pulled up.

'Yes, sir. Thank you very much. I'm sure we'll meet soon. Good night, sir. Good night, Mercy.' He got down and said to himself, 'He's a simple, jolly nice fellow.'

As the car moved for Mercy's place, Kafu was silent, obviously thinking. Mercy after some time became uneasy and asked, 'Kofi, did Amega annoy you with what he said about the government? He likes this government, you know.'

'Never mind. What he said stirred up memories. He is not the first person to have said it. A student girl told me almost the same thing at the point of death.'

'Was it Miss Ghartey?'

'Yes.'

'Maybe you were entranced by her. Couldn't concentrate on the driving?'

'No, never! When she spoke I thought it was just a violent student reaction. Students so often see political, social or other issues as either black or white. Their solutions may therefore allow for no cautions or concessions. Perhaps one must listen to them. It might prove useful. So I did, but I regarded our conversation as academic. I think I know now. I suppose it's serious, Mercy.'

'Oh yes, it is, Kofi. If the government either has no money to buy drugs or it no longer intends to provide subsidised drugs, it must say so. But when there are no drugs either in government hospitals or in private drugstores – in fact no drugs anywhere in the country – and then some minister says drugs have been bought and dumped into the Akosombo Lake by saboteurs and that a shipload of drugs is arriving in the country and has reached Half-Assini, surely the people know the story is too political to be true. They know the minister has bad political manners but they must endure him until he liquidates himself. The tragedy is that many people get hurt for nothing before he goes! You see what I mean, love?'

'Mercy,' Kafu said, still thoughtfully, 'suppose your picture is overdrawn – perhaps just to make the point? Essentially, it's a problem of communication. The government must keep the people in the know. It must be with them.'

'Yes, like the confidence between a man and a wife, not like a father taking his under-ten-year-old kids for granted. And you know something? Even that doesn't work nowadays!'

'What should we do?' Kafu asked as if he needed real help from the woman.

'If only we could get half of your colleagues interested instead of, for example, driving a useless person like me home!'

Kafu laughed heartily and said, 'Mercy, I like your sense of humour. How far do we have to go?'

'The next gate, right ahead there,' she pointed.

When they got there, Kafu said, 'I don't think I can come in. I must go home. My wife is expecting me.'

'Your wife?' Mercy raised her eyebrows, wondering. 'Has she still not got used to your hectic ministerial life?'

'She's trying,' Kafu said defensively, to play her off. She noticed it and retorted amiably. 'Good girl!' Then she said persuasively, 'You've got to see where I live, if you understand what I mean. Remember Sala's perfume? Kofi, I want to talk to you!'

They went to her room. It was simple and neat. There was not much there, but whatever there was was the best and most expensive. Kafu loved the freshness of the room. He was given a cool, soothing beer in a silver mug. Kafu looked at the mug admiringly and asked, 'Where did you buy this?'

'It was given me by a minister when I was in the civil service. Mr Twum Addo – he was so fond of me. Platonic love, you know!'

'Don't worry about what kind of love it was,' Kafu said and flashed one of his disagreeable smiles, 'it must be a priceless gift. How well do you take care of it? Serving me with it?'

'And telling you the truth about it!' They both laughed softly, warily. Then Mercy asked, 'Incidentally, when do I see you next? Next Saturday?'

'Why?' Kafu asked, half interested, half apprehensively.

'Simple! We must have a full night. You and me. Odofo is happy. Sala feels on top. How about the crumbs? Of course if either catches me, I'll be torn to pieces! Have you ever been to the casino at the Hotel Continental? Not everybody can afford it there. At least, not Ofori Nortey. Privacy, not bad! A good dinner, then the casino.'

'What sort of place is it? Forget about your friends and Conception Contractor. It might be interesting.'

'It is, er, let me see ... Yes, there are two rectangular salons that intersect. Walls and floors decorated with big black and red squares, low ceilings and on one side a semi-circular bar. Many tables, I mean gaming tables, for roulette, chemin de fer, black jack. No chairs. Bets are placed standing. You'll find nice little young girls as croupiers, they'll rake in the money you win – for you! If you like you could make one of them deftly deal the cards for black jack and rake in the winnings for you!' And she touched him gently on the chest, adding, 'You could try the roulette, too.'

'What time Saturday?'

'We'll start late. Ten? You could tell your wife you're going to a political harvest rally at Mpraeso and you'll return the next day. She can pack your suitcase. I'll take care of it in my room here.'

'I bet it'll be quite an adventure?'

'Yes, sir! You'll have everything – everything! Including cash and an old maid like me to warm you up as the ... climax? Anticlimax? Epilogue? Whichever way you like it, dear!'

'Let me think now,' Kafu said, working out some of the raw details, 'How about the money – for the bets?'

'Sala is giving you quite a lot. Just take five hundred out of it. You might go back home with an additional thousand!'

'Or empty-handed.'

She smiled beautifully and said, 'Not when I'm with you! So Saturday, ten at night. Till then?'

'Yes, I'll be right here,' Kafu promised.

Then she said, 'Oh, wonderful!' went up to him as he reached the middle of the room, stood squarely in front of him, quickly slipped her arms under his armpits, hooked his shoulders and drew him to her, and gave him a good kiss. It was a fast, expert operation and Kafu was a mixture of paralysis and satisfaction. He was quiet and stood motionless. She repeated it, this time, thoroughly well. She was pleased with her performance and spoke softly into his ear, 'You have a father to intercede for you on the day of the last trump. Don't forget to plead for me when you've been saved!'

'I won't,' Kafu said feebly, shaking his head.

As they got on to the verandah, she observed the sky and said, 'Kofi, it might rain, you know, you'd better hurry up.'

'How do you know?' Kafu asked, doubting.

'Look towards Osu, the clouds behind the castle. That's it. It'll surely pour, probably after a thunderstorm. The sort that rips the roof off the grandstands at the Independence Square.'

'Ah, yes, that reminds me! It's my responsibility to ensure that the roofs are durably done. I've kept postponing the instructions!'

'I know. It's a busy job and so many appointments,' she said and gave him a little but deft good night kiss.

Just as Kafu was about to stop at the gate of Salamatu's house, a thunderstorm broke. The wind blew ferociously, tree branches groaned and snapped, roofs were being torn and telephone and radio poles and wires were being brought down by falling trees. Salamatu rushed out of the house and shouted, 'Drive the car in! There could be a flood!' Kafu obeyed. As he was getting out, some dust was blown into his right eye and he called, 'Sala, help me. I can't see!' Salamatu held him by the hand and took him straight in to the bathroom, where she dealt with his eye. Kafu was relieved and was happy. Her touch was most soothing.

After the excellent dinner, they sat on the carpet hand in hand, drinking and talking at a leisurely pace. At one point Salamatu said, 'I know you'll find it difficult to believe me fully when I say I love you. Maybe for two understandable reasons. I don't care about the first because I love you as Kafu and not as a minister.'

'Let's hope so,' Kafu answered. His voice was a doubting one but Salamatu ignored it and continued, 'The second, I know, is Dr Mills Blankson.'

'Of course,' Kafu said curtly and stroked her hair.

She replied, 'Attuquaye has not been a man of conviction – to me. He's in our Party because of his father's money, but his heart is with NUP. He fears his father's anger and any possibility of his being disinherited.'

'Is that all?'

'Of course not. I know, and he knows I know, that his father wouldn't like him to have a child by me because of my name and religion. But he lies and says that it's because he's married.'

'He may be lying, but what he says is the proper thing, though!'

'Yes, but he can't have it both ways. I have a soul. As a human being, I have full rights. I'm not a mere pleasure vessel!'

'But I think you like me because of your senseless rivalry with Odofo.'

'Maybe you're right, maybe you aren't. She and I are no spiritual enemies. We seem to be able to spot the same chances and get in each other's way and on each other's nerves. I believe that's about all. But she can't steal a march on me. She is surprisingly very calm and contented these days. You've worked a magic on her. You continue being wicked to me, insulting me, teasing me, spurning me, oh . . . !' She broke down and her body shook with the silent sobbing.

As Kafu consoled her, there was a brilliant flash of lightning. The thunder cracked, a squall blew and all the lights in the house went out. They lay prone. Then they embraced. On the carpet.

124

12

Rev. Opia Dan Sese had put on weight. Two years of headmastering had not been bad at all. He still profoundly disrespected Anson Berko, who in turn judiciously tolerated him because of money only. But it must be put on record for the sake of posterity – since Rev. Opia Dan Sese would not tell his friend Abraham Kofi Kafu, whose dislike for Anson Berko had not diminished with the passage of time – that Anson Berko, in spite of everything, had freely and diligently helped Rev. Opia Dan Sese to put up his four-flat, single-building complex which he let out to four bachelor members of his staff even before full completion of the building. He used school money to furnish the flats luxuriously, including curtains, fridges, gas cookers, cutlery, crockery, table-lamps and specially designed bookshelves in the fourth bedroom which he fitted out as a study. The young men had never had it so good and were more than satisfied.

His wife, Vida, had also put on weight, especially after she acquired an enviable collection of jewellery brought to her as security in her prosperous money-lending business. She had begun this humbly with the wives of members of staff and now extended it to all and sundry, including the wives of policemen. The police barracks was pretty close to the school and many of the wives were church members. She once told the police sergeant who had borrowed two hundred cedis from her through his wife that she was too busy to find time to register as a moneylender. 'You see,' she said, 'my husband and I are so busy providing for the children and for the future. You should be doing the same, you understand? You're too slow in paying back. I accept your explanation. If you can pay a hundred cedis the day after tomorrow, I'll drop the other hundred. But I don't want any of your corporals to come and ask me silly questions about a money-lending licence. As the wife of a minister of religion, I don't intend ever to turn professional. It's against our church rules.' The sergeant was pleased with the rebate and dutifully warned the corporals.

In the same manner she showed great concern for the inner

needs of her husband's tenants in the flats and supplied them regularly with bread and other provisions, payment for which was deducted at source in lump sums by the school bursar at the end of each month. In view of all these services and the quality of the flats, the rent was three times higher than what should have been charged, but since the rule was that no member of staff should spend more than ten per cent of his salary on rent, his tenants suffered nothing and the school stood the difference. No doubt Vida's own posh house would be completed within a month. So Dan and Vida were a very contented couple. He decided to have a grand speech and prize-giving day, with Kafu as the guest speaker. And so with this and other considerations in mind, he came down to visit the Kafus over the weekend.

On his way, he bought some forty balls of Fante kenkey and lots of sugar-cane and coconuts at Yamoransa. At Mankesim he bought some hundred oranges, ten pineapples, cassava, tomatoes, and a lot of other produce that happened to be on display and pressed by the women sellers. The two fat bars of chocolate were carefully wrapped and hidden in his briefcase. He was determined to be generous to the Kafus; but, to impress Gloria Opoku, he was resolute. It was the thought of Gloria that influenced the quantities of the gifts bought along the route to Accra. A showdown there must be. He had for too long dreamt, imagined, loved, missed her.

As it was a Saturday, Kafu was late in coming home; indeed he never came home until nine on Sunday morning. He told Danso to take the car home. That was all. Grace did not know his whereabouts and no one else in the household knew. Salifu Bukari was depressed because he felt to the core Grace's almost permanent state of worry over her husband's transformed life.

After breakfast, Grace told Opia, 'This is the life I have been enduring. For six months now I've been ringing you and telling you, Osofo, but you don't seem to understand.'

'Oh yes, I understand you perfectly well.'

'But you only try to console me, that's all.'

'Actually, that's my sole reason for coming to you this weekend. Oh yes, it is. It's terrible the way you sometimes cry on the phone!'

'And then you hurry up the conversation and hang up on me.'

'Well, you see, your husband is a minister of state. Even if your telephone is not bugged, one can't tell. There can be so many ears. I got worried when I heard in Cape Coast that Abraham was leading a reckless life.'

'Not only that, Osofo, I've been receiving anonymous telephone calls in which I'm insulted and all sorts of filthy things are said about Kofi. In one call a man threatened to bomb this house. Bukari was worried and said we must ask for police protection. But Kofi hates the police, just as he hates the army — as you know. He simply can't see why a policeman should be stuck at his gate. He wouldn't hear of it, so poor Bukari is on the alert day and night. I feel so sorry for him. He's lost weight. He hardly sleeps.'

'So have you. You've also lost weight.'

'I know, but I don't care about myself, Osofo. You remember I told you about an anomymous letter to me. I'll let you read it for yourself. It says Kofi has got girl friends. He spends all the time with them. He can't take decisions as a minister and hardly sees any programmes through. He's always distracted. What disturbs me most, Osofo, is this: the letter says Kofi is gambling at the casinos at Hotel Continental and the Ambassador. He's been borrowing money from people. The letter mentions one Mr Mills Blankson, one Amega. I forget the others.'

'Oh, but this is impossible!' Rev. Dan Sese said, not that he felt Grace was framing her husband but that the details of the present story were hard to believe.

'You mean you don't believe me, Osofo?' she asked with a tear in her eye. As she wiped it with the used, crumpled table-napkin, she rose and went to the bedroom and fetched the letter, which she had carefully hidden. She gave it to him, saying, 'Please read it for yourself.'

It was a longish letter and Rev. Opia Dan Sese pored over it very carefully. He wanted to know all the facts so as to know how best to tackle his friend. He found some of the details lurid, others disturbing. Taken all together, it was a pretty nasty business. 'Hm-m-m-m,' he sighed when he finished reading. 'Did you show it to Abraham?'

'He refused to read it.'

'Why?'

'He said it was all lies. It was all part of the price I should expect him to pay for being a successful minister.'

'I believe he has a point there, Grace. Of all the ministers, he appears most on TV these days, giving speeches – good speeches, I think, Grace. He knows how to exhort the people to work hard – you remember what he said the other day? "If you want to have your cake and eat it, then produce more than you can eat!' You can't better that, Grace. Then he tells the people to tighten their belts. This is a developing country – there should be less eating, more mortification of the flesh and sound moral life. Your husband is a great orator.'

'But Osofo, I'm his wife and I believe that however poisonous this letter may be, not all it says is lies. Can you believe that Kofi finds it difficult in spite of all his big income to provide money for running the house? We are living now from hand to mouth. Today he says take this ten cedis, then tomorrow he says can you lend me five cedis? By the end of the month, whatever he gives me, he has taken back. If it hadn't been for the money I get from Vida, which she kindly increased when I told her a little of my story, I would have starved with my children!' And she began sobbing and her little daughter started crying.

After cheering her up expertly, for he was extremely deft with women – more so with those in distress – Opia asked, 'I suppose Abraham didn't say who in particular must have written this letter?'

'No. All that he would say was that it must have been written by Mensah Quartey, national secretary of the National Union Party. He says that that man by nature is prone to extravagant, mischievous pranks. He says that that was one of the qualities that made the opposition appoint him as national propaganda secretary. Besides, politically he's not above subversion.'

'Very well, Grace,' and he handed back the letter to her, 'leave it to me. I'll sort it out with him. I hope you'll come to the speech day?'

'No, I can't, Osofo. He hates going out with me unless it's a state function and it's a must. I've gone through the humiliation of too many refusals to ask again. Osofo, what I need now is some more help from you. Can I ask?'

'Grace, if I can help you, I surely will. Yes, I think I can be of use to you.'

'I'll need a little house, a little roof over the heads of my children and me. I feel I must have it, Osofo. I wouldn't be surprised if he kicks me out of this house some day. Osofo, right now I'm more of a housekeeper than a wife. It's true, Osofo. It is!' She broke down but soon recovered herself.

'How much have you got in cash?'

'Four thousand two hundred. My father gave me a piece of land just behind Mr Benji Baisi's house. We can use that.'

'You've done well, Grace, to save so much. I'll tell Vida. We'll do it for you. Something modest. Not more than six thousand. We'll halve your bread allowance to pay for the difference of one thousand eight hundred. Oh yes, Grace, we'll do it for you.'

Grace was so happy that she took Opia's hand impetuously and kissed it, and then kissed her daughter, who smiled cheerfully. And she got up from the table so jerkily that a saucer fell and broke.

The evening before, Rev. Opia Dan Sese had contrived to effect the desired contact with Gloria Opoku. Right from the time he arrived and his car was unloaded of the gifts, he cleverly and surreptitiously watched the movements of his heart's desire. And the moment came. She had gone to do up his room. He was talking with Grace, then asked to be excused. He went to the toilet only briefly, then slipped quietly, tiptoeing, into his room. The young girl was spraying the room with air-freshener when he suddenly held her by the shoulders. She gave a cry of fright, but he had put his hand on her mouth and that was it – no noise was heard! Then he asked her, 'Did you miss me all this time?' The girl had actually never thought of him but did not want to be unkind to him, so she said, 'I don't know, Osofo.'

'O-o-o-h!' Opia said in a well-cadenced voice, 'So you think only of your boy-friend and leave me out?'

'I've told you I don't have a boy. Missis has warned me against it. She has asked me to sleep upstairs with the children so that no one interferes with me.'

'I see, my beautiful one. Did you enjoy the chocolate?'

'Yes thank you very much, sir.'

'Oh, don't thank me. It's nothing. Take this,' and he flashed thirty cedis in bright new ten-cedi bills.

'It's too much,' Gloria said, though from the sound of her voice Opia felt strongly that she would very much like to have it. He had little time. His move had to be fast now.

'It's for you,' he said. 'Don't worry. I've some more. I can give you some more. Hei, hei, hei? My dear!' He kissed her. It was adroit, anaesthetic. She did not resist, and he turned off the lights.

The next morning when Grace broke the saucer and Gloria came to clear the mess, she could not look him in the face and was a little nervous. Grace noticed it vaguely and wondered at it, but she had more pressing matters on her mind and never gave it another thought.

It was not long, then, after breakfast that Kafu arrived. Rev. Opia Dan Sese took a close and hard look at him. He found that Kafu had lost weight. He was tired and listless and not very much in the mood for a relaxed, serious or prolonged conversation. Grace was carrying their daughter and was looking at him distantly, pityingly and also querulously. When Kafu noticed this he cast a sharp, hostile glance at her and she lowered her eyes and left.

Notwithstanding this, he was heartily pleased to see his old friend looking so well and prosperous, his hair meticulously dyed so that he looked quite young, as usual. Kafu pleaded he was tired, exhausted. He would go to bed for two or three hours and then they would talk. It was obvious he needed sleep, for his eyes were bleary and he was yawning constantly. There was lipstick on his shirt collar.

When he had woken up and taken his bath and they went to the study downstairs to talk, Kafu was refreshed and exuberant. Opia noticed though that he drank more than before in a short space of time. When he was at Cape Coast he had been good at nursing his drink. 'Osofo,' he said, 'rain or shine, I'll be there. I'll give them a good pep talk. Any government that ignores the students is running a serious risk. This is one of the abc's of modern politics. I'll be right there!'

'By the way, will Lydia attend?'

'Who is that?' Opia asked, his mind preoccupied with Kafu's problems.

'I mean Lydia Baiden-Johnson, the chorister.'

'Oh yes, yes, yes! She will, Abraham. She looks terribly pretty these days! The dainty petite!'

'Will you lay her on?'

'Aren't you coming with Grace?'

'No, she complains too much these days. She gives me funny looks in public when she disapproves of my behaviour or utterances. No, she's an impediment. Home she stays!'

'Yes, I see. I suppose she wants to protect you. I've heard all sorts of things being said about you – gambling, running after women openly, that sort of thing. Is it true, Abraham?'

'It's all spoof, Osofo. Grace gets nasty phone calls – even a stupid and dirty letter. It's the opposition. They use things like these to discredit the government, to win over the masses and topple a government that is the choice of the people, that won a landslide victory. But they are joking. We know we'll be in power for at least fifteen years. The rural folks are with us. We've given them roads, water, health clinics and what have you!'

'But I hear they don't get pilchards and sugar.'

'We know,' Kafu said heatedly. 'It's the opposition – the saboteurs – they've been hoarding. They've been diverting the goods to other countries. We know those who are doing it. We'll smoke them out. Do you know who wrote that filthy letter to Grace, a minister's wife? It was Mensah Quartey, the national propaganda secretary of the NUP.'

'Oh yes, ye-e-s,' Opia responded, slowly and thoughtfully running his hand over his bald dome. 'I don't believe that. I'm sure he's too decent to do that.'

'Have you read the letter?'

'Yes.'

'Grace showed it to you?'

'Yes.'

'This girl Grace! Anyhow it's not the work of a spook. My government has its intelligence service. I know it's Mensah Quartey. I was advising my colleagues in cabinet to have him detained for endangering internal security.'

'Abraham, you shouldn't do that.'

'Why? We are the government. The choice of the people. We must do what we think fit.'

'But not that which will alienate huge sections of the people. Already the government is no longer popular and er . . .'

'Are you sure, Osofo?'

'Yes, this is my impression at the moment. If you detain a man of the standing of Mensah Quartey you'll provoke trouble. I suppose governments are nowadays influenced or even ruined more easily by world opinion than by that of its own people. Detention is a touchy world subject. If you touch him world opinion will lash out at you. The people will be afraid, and out of self-protection some of them will band together and kick you out. The army and police, for example. They do it sharp like an amputation,' Opia said with a non-committal smile.

'It's a pity one always has to look over one's shoulder to see what the army is up to. That's no comfort, really!' Kafu said sadly and lit a cigarette.

'Yes, Abraham, all this will end some day.'

'How?' Kafu asked, brightening up a little.

'God knows!' Opia said, looking as bland as ever, while Kafu looked up at the ceiling as if he was working it out with inspiration from there. He heard Opia ask in a voice that sounded miles away, 'Abraham, dear, will you stop gambling?'

'I beg your pardon, Osofo,' and he cupped his ears.

'I say will you stop gambling?'

'I don't gamble. No, I don't. Who said I do? I don't!'

'Do you need money?'

'I'm broke, Osofo. Very broke. I don't even have a cedi in the house. Any help?'

'I'll give you two hundred,' he counted it there and then and gave it to him, 'but please don't gamble it away.'

'Thank you, thank you very much,' Kafu said quickly, pocketing the money fast with trembling fingers while he cast quick furtive glances to see whether Grace was anywhere around, near enough to see the gift. Then he added slowly, quietly, 'Gambling is a funny business – so easy to get in, so hard to get out – well, well, well! I'm not a gambler, Osofo. I'm not. Whoever says so is a liar! I swear!'

'If you say so! You'll come on Friday evening and leave on Sunday morning. I mean the speech day. Will that be all right? Lydia will be thrilled to see you!'

'I have an appointment at the Hotel Continental on Friday night. Let's make it Saturday with Lydia. Then back on Sunday morning. All right?'

'Yes, yes. That's all right, Abraham.'

Kafu himself prepared the speech. He knew the National Secondary School, Cape Coast, well and he told Mr Vuga he needed no dreary, platitudinous civil-service script shorn of humour and insight. Besides, he had his own gambit. So as he stood sprightly and dapper, before the admiring audience that Saturday in one of the best Ishmael and Sons suits, Lydia wondered whether ministers were ordinary mortals or God's chosen few. Her admiration for him was absolute. A mere association with him was in itself a distinction, a paradise. Kafu saw how helplessly she hung on his words and he pulled out the throttle:

'Mr Chairman, Distinguished Guests, Ladies and Gentlemen – The Liberation Party government derives its mandate from the people. It is a full mandate and it is an absolute one. No one has the right to change it except through the will of the people and the ballot box. Materialism or no materialism, the will of the people always remains supreme. We are doing our best. The cities have been enjoying the amenities while the rural folk who generate the national wealth are ignored. So their children, when they get the slightest education, come over into the cities in the hope of enjoying whatever there is. We are determined to reverse the trend; and the feeder roads, the clinics, good drinking water – these, I say these testify to what we have been doing. So those of you who are in the cities and do not see with your own eyes what we've done for your brothers and sisters over there must stop maligning the government. You simply wish to see this government out! Why? If your child is no good you reform him, you don't throw him out. The best way to reform a party is to vote for another one next time. If we are misbehaving, tell us. Don't keep quiet. I know this has been said before and editors have been ruined. So you leave us to destroy ourselves, not so?' There was a rumbling response of suppressed laughter and Kafu exploded, 'We intend to stay in power for as long as we can. There shall be no hunger. We shall start within two months a twenty-million-cedi ranch in the Accra plains. Corned-beef production for the entire requirement of the country will start in a month. A sardine-processing complex so huge that it can supply all the sardines we can eat plus a substantial surplus for export to earn foreign exchange will be commissioned in two weeks. Large quanties of milk have been ordered. They will arrive in the country in a week. However, you have to work hard and eschew laziness. You must be honest. You must not try to get rich quick. You must avoid bribery and corruption like cholera. You must not lie. You must exercise self-discipline.' Then he turned to the pupils, 'Now, boys, I must also tell you : there is only one thing a man needs above all else. It is character, character! Without character, this nation will continue to struggle – unabated. Meanwhile, I find, my friends, that the school has no up-to-date encyclopaedias. I promise you a cheque for five hundred cedis for the acquisition of a new edition!'

There was wild applause. His mother, father, and Opia beamed with satisfaction while Kafu himself grinned, childlike, and then winked at Lydia as he pretended to wipe his face with a spotlessly white handkerchief. He was as pleased as Punch, so also were the pupils.

Thus Lydia was so good that instead of returning home on Sunday, he drove straight to his ministerial office on Monday at ten.

Nee Otu Lartey was waiting for him. He had not lost weight but his left foot was bandaged and he was limping. A scaffolding plank had fallen on it as he went to inspect the final painting of the lavatory. The shell had been finished more than a year ago but paint and other accessories were in short supply. He had also run out of funds for the final assault and Mr Nutor Vuga had to write him several letters (he thoroughly enjoyed writing them), most of which were very threatening, before Nee Otu was able to complete it. His relations with Kafu were not now as they used to be. The warmth had cooled somewhat. Kafu still owed him money, though his building was almost finished except for the finishing touches and furnishing. Kafu said, 'Nee Otu, I haven't seen you for two months.'

'You people say we should tighten our belts, so I've tightened mine. I can't move about comfortably.'

'Do you want money? Here's fifty cedis.' It was half the money Opia had given him again that morning.

'Fifty cedis is nothing, Kafu. We're friends still, I suppose? The lavatory block is finished. There must be some sort of ceremony to open it. It will be good for the image of the Party and government.'

'I agree with you, Nee Otu, but are you sure that building has a good foundation? I went to inspect the site when you started work and I thought the foundation was far too shallow but, heavens, I forgot entirely to tell you to deepen it. I remember I made a note of it in my diary. Anyway, when do we do it?'

'That's for you and Nutor Vuga to arrange. The man is full of spite. He wrote to me polite letters but they were full of abuse underneath. He thinks I don't understand English, to the extent that I wouldn't detect the veiled insults he heaped on me. I don't blame him. He's all right. Party or no Party, politics or no politics, he's here. So fix the time, arrange it with all concerned and the constituency executive will be there.'

'Good. You leave everything to me, Nee Otu.'

There was no doubt that the lavatory block looked nice. It was well designed and stood there white, neat and trim. Mr Mills Blankson was present at the commissioning ceremony; so also were the other stalwarts: his son, Odofo, Salamatu, Doku Lamptey, who had installed his own address system, Odoi Hammond and even Araba, the pig-trotter dealer. Then there were old men, young fishermen who would not stop talking and a whole ragtag of children, some looking intelligent and others bovine.

There were three speakers. The first was Mr Mills Blankson, who traced in great detail lasting over forty minutes, including several repetitions, the history of how the building came to be there. This was followed by Nee Otu Lartey, who managed to connect the Party and the government's achievement in providing the amenity with the insolent behaviour of some public servants. 'They think they are the masters of the people. They have benefits but do not learn to respect. We shall show them!'

Nutor Vuga, who sat close to Kafu, simply pooh-poohed Nee Otu's threat in his head and muttered to himself with a wry smile, 'If you play the fool again, you'll get worse stinkers!'

The long and short speeches over, the tape was cut, but no one could, of course, use the place immediately. All that happened was that Kafu, Mr Mills Blankson, Nee Otu Lartey, Odoi Hammond, Mr Nutor Vuga, Dr Mills Blankson and Doku Lamptey went over, as was explained later to the press, ceremonially to inspect the inside. When everybody was leaving, Dr Mills Blankson lingered behind, looking closely at everything. Nee Otu Lartey, who wondered what he was up to, asked, 'Aren't you coming out with us?'

'Mr Lartey,' he said haughtily, 'I'm a medical doctor. We live in an age of preventive medicine. I must satisfy myself that you've done a good job!'

Nee Otu Lartey did not reply. He was not in the mood for an argument. Just as he got out and Dr Blankson was about to leave, there was a brrr-o-o-m! and then boom! boom! a whole wall collapsed, burying the doctor underneath.

At first everyone was stunned. Then Nee Otu Lartey recovered and shouted 'Call the ambulance! Everybody, come on! Let's clear the rubble!'

The young men who had the stomach for it set to work. Mr Mills Blankson had swooned and Salamatu was sobbing. Kafu removed his coat and worked as if he was possessed.

Then the ringing of a bell was heard: clang! clang! clang! It was the fire service. It happened that one of the illiterate fishermen had been to the booth and lifted the receiver. When the operator asked him the number he said, '999.' Then a pause. The operator, an otherwise sweet-voiced lady, was apparently tired and hungry now. She shouted extremely harshly and impatiently, 'What is it you want, fire?' And the fisherman confused by her harsh voice answered simply, 'Yes, Atukpai tiafi hee!'

Kafu cried, 'The fool! Will someone who speaks English please call an ambulance? Oh Lord, maybe he's gone! I feel I'm dying myself,' he whispered and then suffered a short blackout.

The firemen were going to pick a nasty quarrel but realised the situation was too grave for that. They joined in the clearance and worked with precision and zeal. By the time the ambulance had arrived they had got to the body, but there was no life in it.

13

'You were here yesterday evening, weren't you, Kofi Danso?'
Odofo asked as Grace looked at her coldly but closely, studying
her in every detail on first seeing her.

'Yes, madam,' Kofi Danso answered politely, since Grace was
in the car.

'What did I tell you?' Odofo asked.

'You said he was in your house for a short while and left.'

'And he hasn't returned home yet, Mrs Kafu?' Odofo asked
Grace in a voice meant to indicate commiseration. But Grace
would not reciprocate. Her eyes and face showed nothing but
controlled hostility. She replied, 'Perhaps he'll be *home* by the
time we get back. He wasn't there, that's why we came here.
Thank you.' She stressed the word home as she spoke.

Odofo wondered what she meant by this stress and smiled de-
risively. Grace noticed the smile, felt it was insolent and resented
it. Then she thought, 'Why this smile? I'll lose my self-control if I
don't go away. This woman seems to know a lot and probably
doesn't think much of me. What else? I can't think.' She told
Danso, 'Please, drive away to the next woman's.' But Odofo did
not hear her instructions.

When she was driven off, Odofo went back inside. Kafu asked
her, 'Is she worried?'

'What woman wouldn't worry, Kofi? Your wife is well-
behaved. She looks a good woman.'

'And you are sweet!' Kafu said with undisguised fondness and
took her by the waist, his round cheeks showing nothing but complete satisfaction with being where he was, so insulated and
nursed like a three-year-old. Odofo was now fondling him. She
asked, 'Any drink?'

'If you want me to, dear.'

'But, darling, no spirits, no beer, orange squash only, right?
You've had too many strong drinks.'

'Then a cool one, Odofo. Nothing, just a really cool one.'

'Jolly good,' she said, and went to the fridge and prepared it.

When she brought it to him and he took the first sip, she asked, 'Good?'

'Excellent!' Kafu replied.

Odofo's face turned serious. She took Kafu's hand and caressed it. She said, 'Kofi, honestly, you must go home on the third day. It's not fair to keep Grace in this state for more than three days.'

'I would prefer a week,' Kafu said, his arms folded. 'What about all the people calling on me to repeat the same story over and over again? Sheer waste of time. Some would take advantage and come and sit down for hours in order to finish whole bottles of whisky before they went home drunk. They wouldn't even be interested in the tragedy. All they want is the comfort of a minister of state's house, his drinks, the opportunity to talk rubbish non-stop. No, I won't have it! I'll go home after the funeral.'

'Yes, but you've got to ring Grace and tell her that you're alive and well and everything is fine. She is suffering.'

'Suffering? Let her,' he said casually.

'Kafu dear, get up, take the phone and tell her.'

Kafu waited for an hour or so until Odofo had ordered him again, this time more firmly, and spoke to Grace. He did not give her the opportunity to ask questions. He would not say where he was. He was all right. He was helping with the Mills Blankson funeral and all was well. He would be back home after seventy-two hours.

Before the phone call, Grace had been to Salamatu's and Salamatu was more alarmed than herself. It occurred to her that Odofo must have engineered something, so no matter how much she was bereaved, she took action.

While Salamatu was giving instructions, Odofo was in deep conversation with Kafu. She said, 'My uncle has done well to finish the house. Your parents can move in next month. You haven't introduced me to them, Kofi.'

'I will.'

'Every time you say "I will".'

'You know I'm forgetful, Odofo. I shan't forget this time, I tell you. By the way, what did you say the name of your uncle was?'

'Kofi, how did you manage to stay on at school? You're so forgetful. I told you he was Gilbert Lamptey, storekeeper, Cape Coast, my father's youngest brother, a good, honest man. You owe Nee Otu money, so I asked him to supervise the construction, no contractor business. Listen, Kofi, for the last time. I won't tell you again if you ask.'

'But Odofo, darling, you didn't show me the plan of the house, why?'

'What you said you wanted was clear enough. The design is beautiful. It's a nice little house and solidly built. I'll show you a picture of it.'

As she left to bring it, Kafu went to the fridge and took out a bottle of beer. When she came back and saw it, she said, 'Kofi, you've been drinking too much.'

'Odofo, just this one, to celebrate.'

'Well, Kofi, this is a picture of the house.'

Kafu was amazed. He cried, 'My word, this is really beautiful!' He kissed her and asked again, 'Where is the plan?'

Odofo replied, 'Kofi, I want to ask you something.'

'Go ahead,' he said cheerfully.

'What should be the name of your first son?'

'His name is Kafu Junior, why?'

'I don't mean that. It's only a repetition of your name. What should have been his own?'

'Oh, I see. Ebow. But why?'

'And how about a first girl?'

'Let me see . . . I suppose Essi.'

'I can see you don't really know. Why not ask your parents?'

'Why should I? I've got a boy and girl already. That's all I need. I don't want any more. Why bother?'

'Kofi?' she called quietly.

'Yes?' he responded convivially after taking a long sip.

'I'm expecting your baby.'

'Impossible!'

'True!'

'Why me after so many?'

'What do you mean?' she asked calmly, though offended.

'I'm sorry,' Kafu said and fell back in his chair, looking rather helpless. 'Has the doctor confirmed it?'

'Yes, three months ago.'

'And why haven't you told me all this while?'

'Your child is yours, Kofi, time has nothing to do with it. Now you know. Aren't you happy?'

'If you are happy, what can I do?' Kafu asked and rested the back of his head on his folded palms on the back of the chair. He belched before he could control it.

Odofo resumed caressing his hand. He did not withdraw it. Then she said, 'Kofi, you know something? The name on the plan will be that of our child. I wouldn't like him or her to have the same name as that of any of your children with Grace. If it's a boy we'll call him Ebow Lamptey-Kafu and if a girl Essi Lamptey-Kafu. One of these will go on the plan. I've asked my uncle to plead with the city authorities to be patient with us since this is an important matter. Any objections?'

'So the house is not for my parents after all?' Kafu asked rather sadly, which puzzled Odofo.

'Kofi, your parents will not live for ever. The child is your own. The property is yours and secured for yours.'

'Ah, well! I wish you had told me earlier,' Kafu said dejectedly, his head resting on his chest now. He hiccupped and his head dropped back on his chest.

'It makes no difference, my all,' she said passionately, 'It's been no cost to you and I am happy.' She kissed him and said, 'Food is ready. Let's eat and then go and visit old man Mills Blankson.'

By the end of the third day, in the evening, when Kafu was about to go home – which he was reluctant to do, because he actually had a lot of his clothes in Odofo's house and could stay on – he had recovered fairly satisfactorily from the impact of the news of Odofo's pregnancy. As Odofo saw him off and he sat in the taxi, whose engine had been running for two minutes now because of the deep conversation and the unwillingness of the two to part, he turned his head intuitively and looked back. There, in the distance, some hundred feet away, was Ofori Nortey, neat as always, his trousers were well pressed, grinning. Kafu was very angry but showed no outward sign of it for Odofo to see. He was driven away.

It took well over a week to prepare for the burial of the body of Dr Mills Blankson. Rev. Opia Dan Sese came all the way down from Cape Coast to attend. Such was the sensation the death had caused all over the country and such was the shock with which people received the news of the collapse of the lavatory wall that for the first time in some two years the *Morning Herald* and the *Liberator* were locked in a journalism that stirred the country. The *Morning Herald* had charged that the general shortage of cement plus the shoddy work of Liberation Party contractors were the root cause of the disaster. The contractor involved had put up a few lavatories elsewhere and conservancy labourers must be on the lookout. Aroused, the conservancy labourers petitioned that the occupational risks of their job had been made worse by the authorities concerned, so they were entitled to an immediate wage increase or they would go on strike. The *Morning Herald* supported them strongly. It asked rhetorically in an editorial on the subject: 'Why should the government jeopardise the lives of lowly paid, sacrificial workers whose miscalculation in life, so the government seems to tell the nation, is that they have made the removal of human waste their entire life career? Either the government protects these people by giving them better wages or it must not be surprised if these conservancy labourers take the most obvious course of action open to them. We are sorry to say this; for we know that what is needed most in this country is stability, but the truth must be said and damn the consequences. We shall overcome!'

The *Liberator* opened up and accused the *Morning Herald* of inciting sections of the public to treat constituted authority with hatred, ridicule and contempt. 'There is a mouthpiece of the enemies of the peopple,' it said, 'whose sole aim is to undermine the republic and bring this great nation of ours into international disgrace and to its own destruction. Government is advised to review its press laws so as to curb the satanic machinations of our detractors. The struggle continues!'

It was partly this press battle which persuaded Rev. Opia Dan Sese to come over to Accra, since among other things it highlighted all the more the importance of the funeral. And of course, because of the inherent crisis if the conservancy boys struck, it was perhaps also well worth it if he could give his friend the benefit of his advice.

So after the funeral Grace, Kafu and himself sat in the lounge, thoroughly exhausted after the long, slow, solemn, sad, unforgettable, gruelling day. They would not talk, everybody was going over the experiences of the day in his mind and enjoying the refreshing drinks. This lasted for some twenty minutes until Opia, sufficiently rejuvenated, called suddenly, 'Abraham?'

'Ye-e-s,' Kafu responded absent-mindedly.

'Do you hear me?'

'Of course I do, Osofo. What's the matter?'

'Abraham, I thought you were not with us, but now I see you are. I'm talking about the promise you made at er-r . . .'

'Which promise?' Kafu asked completely unaware of any promise.

'I mean the encyclopaedias for the boys, er, for the school. Can I have the cheque before I leave?'

'Good Lord, Osofo, it was a political promise. I didn't mean it at all. I didn't expect the boys to expect anything. Why, the boys are daft!'

'Yes, yes, y-e-e-s,' Opia said, very disappointed. He ran his hand over his bald top, making sure he did not disturb the sides, the hair on which was carefully dyed. 'Abraham, the boys took you seriously. Very seriously. They look forward to them,' he said slowly, pleadingly and painfully.

'Tell them to forget about it,' Kafu said impatiently with a wave of the hand.

'Yes, Abraham. It will be difficult.'

'Well, they can please themselves.'

'But, Kofi, if you knew you wouldn't buy the books for them, why did you promise them?' Grace asked. 'Have you never been a boy?'

'Grace, I promised them! Now you ask me why, post facto? I say I've no encyclopaedias to give away just like that. A minister of state doesn't mint money. Are you sure of a good dinner for us, madam housewife?'

Grace did not reply, but left them. She went and sat on her bed, thinking.

Opia continued, 'Abraham, so you have no money for the encyclopaedias?'

'I have absolutely nothing, Osofo. Even if I had, I wouldn't buy them. I made that statement off the cuff. It was not in the text. Why bother? No problem.' He started laughing as if Opia was a fool to raise the subject at all.

'Well, Abraham, you see, the *Morning Herald* spread it on the front page, you remember? So also were your corned-beef and sardine factories given prominence. You meant those anyway, didn't you?'

'Why, Osofo, with due respect, are you getting old?' Kafu asked in genuine amazement. 'How can a corned-beef or a sardine factory be commissioned in one or two months? I was merely employing hyperbole in my speech and the fools took me literally. Osofo, you are not teaching the boys well! These literary gadgets must be thoroughly taught, hei?' Kafu said these accusing sentences slowly and menacingly, to stop Opia from pursuing the matter further.

But Rev. Opia Dan Sese refused to be cowed by his friend. 'Y-e-e-s,' he said, also slowly and deliberately, 'but why didn't you refute it when the press, too, reported you literally?'

'The press?' Kafu asked contemptuously. 'They are always either politically praising or condemning, misreporting or causing a hollow sensation. Have you ever found them level-headed, Osofo?' Kafu was now sure he had cornered his friend and he stretched his legs fully forward, folded his arms and laughed softly, mischievously.

Opia noticed it and decided not to answer. He said instead, 'It will be embarrassing if the boys don't ever see the encyclopaedias.'

'Why not use school money and present them in my name? That's the best thing to do. How can I use my money to buy books gratis for schools? If I do it this time, the next time another school will expect a gift of bags of cement, then another will ask for roofing materials and so it goes on. I need money myself, I've told you, Osofo. Help from you is always welcome. Very welcome!'

Rev. Opia Dan Sese sighed deeply and said nothing more on the subject. He saw no point in pursuing it, so he asked, 'These conservancy boys, what happens if they go on strike? There'll be an outrageous outbreak of disease.'

'They can't! They shouldn't! No, they can't,' Kafu took it up impulsively. 'The law forbids strikes. If they try to, they will be firmly dealt with!'

'How?' Dan Sese asked.

'I'll see that they are jailed. The whole bloody lot of them.'

'And who removes the night soil from the houses?'

'Osofo, you have a point there. I must approach this matter gingerly. You know something, Osofo?' Kafu said eagerly, like a boy who had just solved a difficult mathematical problem, 'We will infiltrate their ranks. We will alienate the leadership from the rank and file. Once there is no solidarity, they can't all go on strike at the same time. And if it comes to it, we will then harass those who go on strike, promise those who don't go on strike that they will be made headmen and supervisors and then add a few pesewas, just one or two, you know, and, hey presto! no problem, no problem at all, Osofo!'

'Well, Abraham,' Opia warned, 'if ever you talk to them, try to be tactful, conciliatory, empathetic. It's a slow, misty process, but it pays off in the long run. I'll have to leave early tomorrow morning, at about five.'

'Now, Osofo, let's drink some more, and don't forget to give my love to Lydia, you know? She was damn good the other day. Really nice and wholesome. Gosh!'

Rev. Opia Dan Sese did not reply, but he was amused and he nodded twice. He knew as much as his friend. It was simply the superfluity of being reminded.

Two weeks later, the conservancy boys gave a press conference. The points they made were reported in great detail and in bold type, front page, by the *Morning Herald* and hardly reported at all by the *Liberator*, which merely said in tiny type in the centre pages that they had spoken to the press and had threatened to strike. According to the *Morning Herald*, though, they stated that the cost of living had spiralled while their wages had not kept pace. They could not get food to buy, whether the food was national, foreign or from the antipodes. They said meat was meat, milk was milk and sugar was sugar. To their thinking, it was nonsense to call sugar or milk in particular foreign this or that. It was plain human food which we could either find for ourselves or buy from elsewhere. If we could not buy it we must shut up and stop giving it names. Their work was hazardous and they needed food, nourishment. Their job was a health hazard, for human waste was a veritable source of all sorts of disease. They needed wellington boots and proper clothing for it. Besides, they worked mostly either in the evening or in the early hours of the morning to minimise the malodorous pollution of the air caused by the waste in between houses, along back alleys, cul de sacs, pathways and streets. Finally, their job was vital but they got nothing but disrespect from the community. Children called them names. Adults sneered at them for fouling the air, and to add insult to injury they were poorly paid. Someone needed to be reminded. They would strike! If other people were suffering in the country and they would not talk loud and bold, they, the scavengers, the conservancy labourers would! The *Morning Herald* came out with a shrewd, carefully worded and underhand editorial virtually supporting and encouraging a strike no matter whether or not the labourers had a case.

Kafu felt the die was cast. He must show his hand, for if these labourers were allowed to succeed, others would follow. 'Mr Vuga!' he called, loudly and disrespectfully. Mr Vuga jumped from behind his table and rushed to Kafu's office, a huge fanciful ballpoint pen and a pocket notebook at the ready. Kafu wanted to joke about the pen but thought it would be infra dig. He ordered, 'I want you to bring here all the headmen and supervisors of those shit carriers. If they play the fool, I'll have them locked up, you understand?'

'Yes, sir,' Mr Vuga replied dutifully. Within an hour, they were all present in Kafu's office. Some fifteen of them.

'Who is your chief here?' Kafu asked brusquely and crudely, like an army officer on parade.

A thin wiry man of about fifty, his teeth worn short by excessive pipe-smoking (most conservancy labourers smoked to offset the smell), his hair cut short and matted, got up and said in a slightly shaking voice, 'I.'

Meanwhile W. W. Mensah and Nutor Vuga himself had begun diligently taking copious notes, so that every word that fell from the mouth of any mortal there would have a worthy place in the history of the government of the country. Otherwise, they were not interested.

'Now look here, what is it you've been telling the press?'

'Our grievances and what we intend to do.'

'Have you got a reply from me on your petition?'

'No, sir.'

'If not, why do you want to strike?'

'The reply has delayed for too long, sir.'

'How long? Ask these two gentlemen,' and he pointed a derogatory and accusing finger at both W. W. Mensah and Nutor Vuga, which infuriated Mensah and frightened Vuga. 'Ask them how long it takes to do government business. Ask them! I deal with the welfare of all workers. Not yours alone. You can't petition today and expect a solution the next day. If we increase your salary today, other workers too will ask. The money will not be forthcoming and there'll be trouble. You fellows here have got to be careful. Has the opposition been telling you to give trouble? Who is your strike leader?'

There was no reply.

'I say, who is your strike leader?' Kafu thundered.

No reply.

'Everybody, walk out! Go and find your strike leader and come back in fifteen minutes to tell me.' After they had trooped out disconsolately to consult, Kafu sent for their chief, who being alone with him was completely subdued and had become cringing. The setting of the office and the ministerial presence contributed greatly. Kafu spoke softly, in a conciliatory and very friendly fashion. 'Now see, my friend, you scratch my back, I scratch your back, you understand?'

'Yes, sir.'

'What do you want?'

'Justice, sir. Even if you add fifty pesewas to our daily rate, we wouldn't mind, sir.'

'My friend, don't talk about justice. Nobody eats justice. You want money, I'm sure?'

'Yes, sir.'

Kafu put his hand into his coat-pocket and drew out an impressive five hundred cedis in ten-cedi bills which Salamatu had advanced him. 'Take this, my friend, and pocket it quickly! Come on!' And before the man could protest he had thrust the money into his pocket.

Kafu then had everybody called back. He asked, 'Have you found your leader now?'

One of the men replied, 'We have only one chief, sir, and he leads us in whatever we do. We do not have a strike leader as such, sir.'

'Good,' Kafu said with confidence, 'Mr Conservancy Chief, are you people going on strike or not?'

'We will think it over, sir,' he said politely.

'Right. You go. I'll talk to all of you this afternoon,' Kafu dismissed them with aplomb.

As soon as they got back to report on their meeting with Kafu, a quarrel arose and the movement split in two: those who were opposed to striking until after further negotiations, and those who pressed for it immediately. The schism was deep.

When Kafu appeared to address them, there were not only mixed feelings in the hearts of those who had asked for a postponement but also anger among those itching for a strike. As he mounted the platform, one of them said, 'Look at him, he's all right!'

'True,' said another. 'I hear he has got ten houses since he came into office. Ten houses in two and a half years, all for one man. Two in Cape Coast, eight in Accra, they say!'

Another said, 'They say he likes Makola women!'

'Don't mind him! I hear he beats his wife!' somebody contributed. Then another took it up, 'And then he drinks plenty of beer!'

There was an uproar in the area and the police on duty shouted 'Order!' And someone said, 'As for the police, when someone is a minister, they open his car for him and salute. As soon as there is a coup, they slap him.'

'Very bad!' another reacted.

They laughed again and Kafu saw it. He thought it was an act of disrespect to a minister of state. He shouted at the hushed lot, 'You shit-carriers must behave. If you want to play politics with your job, you'll be sorry! Your leaders don't want a strike, but some of you have been bribed by the opposition to foment trouble. These are the people who will betray you and the country. But we will jail them. I say, we will jail them before they upset people's habits! You can't play politics with shit. Any fool who

147

dares to try will be vigorously suppressed! Think about it. Goodbye!' And he left them.

The men believed Kafu, and a scuffle nearly broke out between those who were instantly suspected to have taken bribes from the opposition and those who accused them. As the noisy fracas raged, someone said, 'Why should we allow a small boy to abuse us like this?'

'I hear he takes bribes himself,' another replied.

'They say he's got over five hundred thousand cedis in overseas banks. In fact, in Switzerland,' another put in.

'While we are suffering? This would pay us for more than two years. When will they get out of power?' a young man asked.

'Out of power? They'll harass you if they find you want them out,' an elderly one cautioned.

After a day or two the strike threat fizzled out. The chief to whom Kafu had given the money banked it with a view to adding more savings to it and buying a low-cost house in the future at Dansoman. Thus he lost all interest in wage increases. Kafu's treatment of the chief conservancy labourer was successfully leaked by Mr Vuga, and caused widespread resentment in the country. Then also the opposition and the *Morning Herald* were disappointed. Some were particularly disappointed at the way Kafu had shattered what they had expected to be the beginning of a countrywide political holocaust. So, two or three days later, the *Morning Herald* wrote an editorial lamenting the whole affair. Kafu took the paper to Salamatu's house to read.

14

'Kofi, why not let us discuss it and finish with it?' Salamatu said loudly.

'I've told you I'm reading – or is it that you want to pick a quarrel? This is the wrong time, Sala,' Kafu said, still reading the *Morning Herald* editorial. He was reading it carefully and didn't care much about whatever she wanted to say. But Salamatu wanted him to listen. She said, 'There's nothing wrong with the time. Why, are you afraid?'

'Of what?' Kafu asked rather mechanically. He was absorbed by the editorial. He said, 'Sala, listen to what these people say.' And he read to her this extract: 'We know for certain that the strike action failed not because the workers lacked the will or had second thoughts in view of the enormous hardship it would have caused, but because of the immoral stratagems of certain individuals who are not above bribing just causes out of existence and who, above all, do not scruple to dispose of their amorous rivals by laying lethal traps for them. Woe betide a people whose governance is full of moral irresponsibility such as we have indicated above. We shall overcome!'

'Sala, don't you think this is slanderous bombast?' Kafu asked angrily.

'I'm no lawyer,' Salamatu replied. She was more anxious to discuss what was on her mind.

'Don't be cheeky, Sala. Try to understand. What the editorial is saying is this: the labourers were bribed to drop the strike. Fair enough. Who wants a strike? I don't care. There's peace now. But to say that Attuquaye's death was engineered by me is a serious personal accusation. Is this what people say?'

'Yes, Kofi,' Salamatu said quietly. She hated the subject and didn't want it to be raised at this time.

'What exactly do they say?' Kafu looked more upset than angry now. He seemed to be afraid of this fodder for public discussion and opinion.

'Would you like some whisky?' Salamatu asked him calmly,

fondly – to ease him up. She did not like the way he had tensed up.

'Yes, I could do with a good drink. A good, strong scotch,' Kafu replied, and sighed. He read a portion again, aloud, slowly, '. . . to dispose of their amorous rivals by laying lethal traps for them.' The drink was brought. He took a large sip and said, 'How could the wall of a lavatory be built so that it would kill nobody but Attuquaye? This is nonsense. But I'm sure people believe it, don't they, Sala?'

'I'm afraid they do,' Salamatu reluctantly told him.

'Was it not Nee Otu who was his rival? Nee Otu himself told me he was!'

'Are you asking me?'

'Of course I am!'

'Do you think this is a fair question to ask a woman?'

'I don't care what you are! It's all because of you. If it had been done, it would have been done by Nee Otu, not by me. You should know that?'

'What exactly have you come here to do, Kofi?'

'I've come to tell you that your five hundred cedis has been profitably used.'

'Do you know where I got that money from?'

'Of course I do!'

'Where?'

'From your business!'

'No, Kofi. When Attuquaye was alive, believe it or not, he gave me two hundred cedis a month. Since I gave myself up to you, you have been enjoying that money. That newspaper accusation you shout about, has it mentioned your name? It could be either you or Nee Otu. You know as well as I do that it's neither of you. You've become unnecessarily edgy these days. Neither of you would kill him. The NUP merely wants to taunt you, to provoke you into doing the wrong thing. If you swallow the bait, you'll ruin yourself and hurt the country! Oh, what can I say? I expect to see ten governments before I die. I'm about halfway through. I've lost so much in so short a time: both money and a good man. I live in uncertainty now. Kafu, keep cool. Don't leave me. I've seen it before. You go through it and you're never the same again – something indefinably good goes with an abundance of rottenness. But can it be all goodness, can it be all rottenness? Is there any choice? Is there no suffering for the right choice? Is there no suffering for the wrong choice? Which is the right suffering? Oh God, where am I?'

'Are you talking about a coup?'

'I don't know. All I'm saying is that you should drop this matter!'

Kafu shook his head several times and said with determination, 'Not me, not Abraham Kofi Kafu, son of Rev. Sampson Abaka Kafu. The child that does not want its mother to sleep, does not sleep either. I won't let blood. The people don't like bloodshed, but I'll teach them. I can and I have to. The editor at least won't go scot-free. If I take legal action, the case will drag on and on. Some opposition lawyer will ask me embarrassing questions and celebrate my embarrassment with his colleagues later. I will act! Oh-o-o!' and he raised the glass of whisky, looked at it and smiled. 'I will knock them out flat and they will never forget it!' he said slowly.

'And it may cost you!'

'I don't care!'

'Well, Kofi, always remember one thing: I told you. Now I ask my question. Where did you stay for three days after the death of Attuquaye?'

'Nowhere! I mean where I should have stayed!' he said loudly.

'Nowhere? Your wife was here looking for you.'

'What did you tell her?' he asked in a soft voice.

'What could I tell her? You weren't here and I said so, but she didn't seem to believe me. Tell me, Kofi, which of us is your wife?'

'Look here, Sala, don't ask funny questions. I come from a Christian home. We don't mess around with polygamy – overheads and turnovers of women, that crazy arrangement! I have only one wife, you understand? And she is Mrs Grace Kafu. Customarily and legally married to me!'

'But Odofo is now your wife. Doesn't Grace know?'

'How? Liar!'

'You spent those three days with her!'

'Suppose I did, what has it got to do with you? I'm a free man.

I choose to be here. I can leave you this minute and I intend to do so. Ask the furniture where I'm going next!' So saying, Kafu took his coat and trotted out. He was breathing heavily, like a mating bull. Salamatu had not expected him to do that, and was taken by surprise. Before she could utter a word he had got into his car and was driving away.

When he had driven a short distance, he saw Ofori Nortey with the usual trade mark – a grin. Kafu grimaced and became so furious that he shifted the gears quickly into reverse, nearly running into the gutter, and drove back to Salamatu. She was sitting crying in a chair. He bellowed at her, 'Why did you engage Ofori Nortey to spy on me at Odofo's place? Why do you always ask him to spy on me? See, when it comes to decency, you're not fit to kiss the feet of Odofo. I am fed up with you! And this is the last of me – here!'

He was going to get out briskly, but Salamatu said, 'I may be worthless but you have no right to leave me!'

'Wha-a-a-t! No right to leave you? Now tell me, who do you think you are? A great market woman? Smugglers' agent and a spy manipulator, or trash?'

'Your woman, of course,' Salamatu said, having determinedly suppressed a cry of protest.

'Maybe yesterday. But not today and not tomorrow. Our foolish acts are always past! Learn this one, too. You may not come by it easily again in your foul life!'

'I may belong to yesterday, Kofi, but not your child, you know?'

'I agree. You aren't my child!' Kafu said, his face turned away from her to demonstrate his resolve that all was over between them.

'I mean your child by the worthless woman!' Salamatu said, and broke into fits of weeping; but this did not last long, for she was resolved to face him. She knew her problem was that she had grown to love him, perhaps too dearly; and now that she carried his child, she felt she had simply become part of him. Meanwhile, Kafu got confused by the sudden revelation. He shouted, 'Ah-a-a! You too?'

'What do you mean by that, Kofi? What's wrong about Grace expecting a child?'

'Never mind. I'm sorry. Never mind.' He sat down, removed his coat and asked, 'Is my drink finished?'

Salamatu threw away the little that was left in the glass and served him afresh. Kafu did not say a word. Salamatu thought she should not disturb him, so they sat silently, each wondering now and then what the other was thinking. When she felt he had cooled down, she asked, 'Kofi, even if you don't accept me, you'll accept the child, won't you? It doesn't have to be cared for by you and Grace. It will be a human being like you or Grace or any of your children, won't it?'

'Sala, drop the subject, will you? Kafu said, and went to her and kissed her. She began to cry, this time uncontrollably.

During the week or so that followed, Kafu devoted some real time to his work. Mr Vuga had reminded him that a lot of work had piled up and that the flow of policy decisions was grinding to a halt. Already he had some hundred files in his study at home. Many of these contained vital decisions on whether people should be promoted, whether appointments were ministerially approved, whether certain alternative courses of action should be pursued. These were creating human misery in some cases. Of course the human suffering did not much bother Mr Vuga. He had seen so much of it with different administrations, which, to him, were always the same, that he had stopped bothering. He was in fact more interested in finding subtle ways of proving to Kafu that he, Vuga, knew better than Kafu did.

And in connection with this, it happened that while Kafu was working one morning at the ministry he remembered what Salamatu had said about Vuga and about the promotions. He called Mr Vuga and asked, 'How about the promotions, Mr Vuga?'

'As I said the other day, sir, we will have to wait till the end of the financial year.'

'And you say you must transfer them before you promote them?'

'Yes, sir. This is very important, sir. It will enable us to see whether the officers can perform competently in the new grade into which they will be promoted.'

'Who made this rule?'

'I don't remember, sir.'

'I don't like it because it can be abused, but it sounds sensible, though.'

'Very sensible, sir. Very much so, sir!'

'Mr Vuga, I understand in the world of management one of the fads these days is the Peter principle which is said to hold that each man is promoted to the level of his own incompetence. Is this what you are practising, and have you told the officers concerned?'

'Sir, matters of promotion are strictly confidential and are not supposed to be discussed with subordinate officers.'

'So what do we do, Mr Vuga?'

'We wait, sir.'

'I see. You can go.'

'All right, sir.' As he left and closed the door, he laughed aloud heartily. 'Damned fool!' he said. 'He can't take decisions and talks about St Paul's principles just to show off! To show me, Vuga, he's been reading up on management! Tch-a-a! Running a ministry is not teaching form five boys why some Ewes have Akan names or where Anlos settle when they retire. Stupid. We shall see!'

But Kafu heard the high-pitched laughter. It grated on his nerves and he called Mr Vuga. 'Who was laughing?' he asked angrily.

'Mr W. W. Mensah, sir!'

'I don't believe you. That man has a broad chest. I think I know his voice. The voice was ugly. I don't like it. It must stop. Tell whoever it is.'

'Yes, sir.'

'Now, Mr Vuga, another thing. The Morning Herald has been writing seditious and defamatory stuff clearly aimed at toppling the government. I always try to distinguish in my mind between open discussion and incitement to subversion. After a careful study of recent editorials, I'm convinced that the paper is canvassing the overthrow of this government. I know that a newspaper can eventually cause the downfall of a government. We must act, now! The Morning Herald must fold up. Let the editor be arrested and roughed up for seven days. And ... let me see ...
Mr Mensah Quartey must be detained for a week or two and

grilled thoroughly for writing anonymous letters to ministers' wives.'

'Sir,' Mr Vuga began, timidly scratching his head with his fanciful ballpoint pen, 'the Morning Herald is extremely popular. The people are not happy these days. If the Morning Herald is banned, it will deepen their frustration. If the editor and Mr Mensah Quartey are arrested all sorts of rumours will spread and stir up the country dangerously. Let's use the law courts, sir. That in itself will strike fear into the two gentlemen.'

'Let's use the law courts, sir. That in itself will strike fear into the two gentlemen,' Kafu repeated quietly and slowly, his generous cheeks moving up and down and quaking with controlled deep anger. 'A pious sermon as usual from the democratic exponent, Vuga!' He pulled his desk drawer and took out a letter mailed from the United Kingdom. He studied it for a minute or two.

Meanwhile Mr Vuga was muttering inaudibly to himself. 'This is a serious affair. I'll minute my advice on it on file NOCOT/ 568/Vol. X, for posterity to see how strongly I opposed high-handed directives.' When Kafu had finished re-reading the letter he gave it to Mr Vuga and said, 'Read this. It is not signed, but never mind.' Mr Vuga read the letter three times. On each round of reading, he sweated more copiously, so that he had to remove his glasses and wipe off the vapour which had formed on them with a wet handkerchief held in a clammy, shaking hand. Kafu watched him, patiently but showing no pity. Then he asked gently and again slowly, 'Is it true? Answer yes or no only!'

'Yes, sir. It's true.'

'I see. Ten thousand pounds sterling in a UK bank – a wee bit of money salted away by a poor civil servant. How come?'

'My brother, sir. My brother is a structural engineer. After the course, he stayed on in the UK for several years, working. It was arranged that I should pay his remittances to our mother in local currency and he would bank the sterling equivalent there for me.'

'The usual explanation. Very satisfactory, too,' Kafu said with the smile Mr Vuga secretly feared. 'Ten thousand is not much money, Mr Vuga. Your brother was generous to your mother. He didn't starve himself, or did he? The law courts are there. The people are tired of being milked.' Kafu then took his normal-size ballpoint pen and started scratching his head with it, imitating Mr Vuga. He asked, confidentially, bending forward as if to whisper into his ear, 'Shall I send it to the Special Investigation Branch?'

'No, sir. Please, no!' Mr Vuga pleaded.

'Very good!' Kafu said. He leaned back in his chair and lolled back and forth. His voice was deep and clear. 'You would not advise me to ruin your career. Oh no, you would not. And what do we have here? Infringement of currency regulations – under-invoicing, over-invoicing, generous import licences, kickbacks, mysterious outside banking based on fraternal arrangement. And then the business pals, masonic pals, lodge pals, church pals, professional pals – the dazzling elite decorating the country. All very nice! The *Morning Herald* folds up. The editor roughed up just a little and Mensah Quartey politely, or if you wish humiliatingly, reminded to behave. Any more technical advice ending up in a long memo on a file, Mr Vuga?'

'I was merely suggesting an alternative course of action, sir, but I fully appreciate yours, sir,' Mr Vuga replied as he got up and pulled up his trousers, which were slipping down.

'Righto, man!' Kafu said with a smile as he wheeled full circle in his chair and then lolled. 'Now we understand each other! Keep a watch on the people's reaction, though!'

'I will, sir,' Mr Vuga replied. As soon as he closed the door, he said, 'And may their reaction blast you to hell!'

Kafu then shouted, 'Come back, Mr Vuga!' Mr Vuga gave a start, his notebook dropped from his hand and he pulled his trousers up again with trembling hands: he thought he had been heard. He managed to pick up the book quickly and virtually crashed through the door into Kafu's presence. Kafu was lolling still in his chair. He pretended he had not noticed Mr Vuga's ruffled state, and said: 'Well now, Mr Vuga, add Anson Berko's name to the list. I mean the Cape Coast contractor. He's very well known to the police there. He's been boasting that before I entered politics, he told me to my face that it would be all flim-flam. I understand he gloats in drinking bars that he's been proved right. Let him be locked up in a police cell for a couple of days so that he can tell the big bedbugs and the cockroaches there his story.'

'Yes, sir,' Mr Vuga replied with alacrity.

While all this was taking place, Amega booked a special appointment with Kafu's secretary in order to talk fully with Kafu about his money. The time agreed upon had expired and he had been going about the recovery of his money to no avail. Even more frustrating, as Amega told Ofori Nortey – whom he now found a sympathetic confidant in this matter of Kafu's indebtedness to him – was the fact that Mercy had told him bluntly that he should not press for the money, because Kafu might inform the police and that would be the end of the entire smuggling syndicate. This would ruin many people, including the venerable and now ailing Mr Mills Blankson. Salamatu, too, had become uncooperative. Kafu's car would be parked right in front of her gate and yet when he went to ask he was told Kafu was not in the house. On the advice of Ofori Nortey, he appealed to Odofo to put in a word, but Odofo said this was Salamatu's affair. 'Take this from me,' she said, her voice soft, mellifluous and contented, her hands resting on her lap, 'the whole thing was conceived and carried out by Salamatu as a competitive move against me. God knows – she brought in that compulsive hard gambler, Mercy, and she has messed up Kofi. He has no money. Why not drop it, Amega?'

'I simply can't.'

'Why not?'

'I don't like the state of affairs in the country. If the army steps in, our business pattern may change for the worse. Forty plus is enough. I must settle down now as a landlord. I need the money. At least Ofori Nortey believes I must get back what's my own. He insists it's a matter of principle. He says an understanding is an understanding.'

'Look here, Ofori!' Odofo exploded, closing in on him to hit him. Ofori Nortey saw it, he began to back out of the room and said with great force, his hairless face pleading for mercy by its sheer look of innocence, 'Je-e-sus Christ! Amega is lying! How could I meddle in the affairs of big people?'

Ofori Nortey's denial made Amega laugh heartily. When he had laughed enough, he asked Odofo: 'So, is there no help you can give?'

'Amega, please drop it. We make big money, we lose big

money. That's the nature of our business. Why not lose this one gracefully? You may regret it, who knows?'

'I've a feeling I simply must pursue it, though. I think I might not get it, but I must try, Odofo.'

'Please, for my sake, drop it.'

'I don't take your advice lightly, but let me try first.'

It was because of these setbacks that Amega decided to go and see Kafu in his ministerial office, where he might succeed in persuading him to pay back. When he was ushered into Kafu's presence and he saw the dignity and splendour of the office, he thought, as he later told Ofori Nortey : 'I can't see why this man should climb down all these stairs to the bedroom of a woman like Mercy. I wouldn't even climb up to her room. I respect myself, Amega!' To which Ofori Nortey replied eagerly, 'Yeh, yeh, yeh! He frightened me, Amega. He chased me out of the lavatory!'

When the conversation started, however, Amega felt that in spite of the charm, gentleness and humour, Kafu must be a shaken and worried man beneath. He felt vaguely that Kafu seemed to have lost control of something and was searching for a solid prop which he couldn't find. He really had no pride or confidence. Whatever pride he showed was synthetic, or perhaps a mere gimmick of his office. After skirting round the subject with his usual quips, Kafu said, 'Amega, tell me honestly, between the two of us, do you really, very badly, need this money?'

'Since you've asked me, I must be honest with you, sir. In a way, I don't need the money. I don't. I have three solid houses and I collect a total rent of – now let me see – seven hundred and thirty cedis a month on them. I intend retiring from this business. I entered it for money and there's no point inviting an arrest when I can live comfortably off my property; but, sir, I have four children, two boys, two girls. My ambition is to leave a house to each of them some day. This ambition is within reach. I've started the fourth one and I need the money to complete it.'

'Yes,' Kafu said, chewing the end of a pencil, which made him remember Benjy Baisi with mixed feelings, 'you have three already. I haven't even completed one. Is the four thousand too much to forgo, Amega?'

'It depends how you look at it, sir. At the moment I find it a large sum because I need it. The price of cement has doubled on the hoarding market. Hasn't a contractor told you, sir, that the price of building materials has doubled and tripled in some cases?'

'I've heard, but no one had told me how grave it is.'

'I suppose, sir, that's because you're a minister. If they tell you the truth, perhaps you'll have them arrested.'

'Amega, I won't do that if they are sincere. What we are opposed to is spreading alarm deliberately just because prices are high and there are shortages. There are those who do this to discredit the government with a view to having it overthrown somehow. This is where we shall hit hard, make no mistake!'

'Sir, just now people are afraid of you!' Amega said boldly, but Kafu told a colleague subsequently that he felt he looked sympathetic all the same.

'I expect so,' Kafu said without mincing words, and began to bang and thump the table. 'We are in government and we must stay in government, today and tomorrow! We will destroy all our enemies before they get at us!'

'I see, sir,' Amega said, rather upset at Kafu's sudden determination. He rubbed his hands timidly and asked, 'So when do I expect the money sir?'

'Don't worry, Amega, and don't come here again. I will ask you to come and collect it,' Kafu promised.

'Thank you, sir,' Amega said with relief.

As he was leaving the office he saw Nee Otu Lartey, who was the next caller after him. He looked business-like, unsmiling. As soon as he entered the office, he started straight off without ceremony: 'Kofi, you're making dangerous mistakes!'

Kafu was caught off guard and asked ingenuously, 'What have I done, Nee Otu? Has any of the women been to complain to you?'

'Even if they had, I wouldn't talk. You pushed me out and you are riding high, right on top, Kofi!'

'I'm sorry,' Kafu said nervously and wiped his face.

'No, no. No, no! I'm all right. I'm not complaining. Not at all. What I'm seriously objecting to is your treatment of Mensah Quartey and Anson Berko. What have you got against them?'

'Got against them?' Kafu said heatedly, banging the table and flailing the air with his clenched fist. 'Mensah Quartey wrote a dirty, criminal letter to Grace saying all kinds of horrible, unbelievable things about me. And as for that fat sack, Anson Berko, I've simply settled old scores. I'm the Ghana elephant – a good, long memory, Nee Otu! He's been mouthing it in Cape Coast that I'm a political weakling. He'll get his thinking straight in a police cell. He won't have any beer for a couple of days. It'll do his distended belly some good.'

'Is this all you have to say for locking up the two gentlemen? Both have some standing in their own right, if you don't know.'

'Standing? Rubbish,' and he banged the table. 'One is a political rascal, the other a social nuisance; together, they need only one thing: a warning they will not easily forget. It'll also surely keep them out of mischief for just a while.'

'But you forget a number of things.'

'Tell me, honourable Nee Otu, the great political adviser.'

'Even if Mensah Quartey is wrong, you break the law yourself by having him arrested without a charge. You are making a political martyr of him – a thing that hurts governments fatally. You're alienating whole sections of Accra. And this can spread. Any government that underrates Accra will always regret it, and this is what you're doing.'

'And what about Anson Berko?' Kafu asked, his arms folded on his chest. He looked every bit unrepentant.

'The case of Berko is rather odd, Kafu. You dislike him, that's all!'

'Of course I do. And, Nee Otu, you are convinced he likes me, aren't you? This is the first time I've seen you getting really ludicrous, my friend. My decision is irrevocable.' He banged the table and thumped it and then waved an admonitory forefinger at Nee Otu. 'I don't want any interventions. They will be futile!' He said the four words of the last sentence slowly, each by itself, to signify a cold-blooded determination.

Nee Otu Lartey knew Kafu well enough, so he moved on to the next subject, 'Kofi, I've an important proposal to make.'

'Come out with it, let's see.'

'Good. I want us to start a business. You and I.'

'Why?'

'We must secure ourselves, Kofi. The times are bad. You might not be able to return to teaching.'

'What's all this about the times are bad, the times are bad?' Kafu said with irritation. He got up from his chair and came from behind his desk to stand with his back against the door leading to Mr Vuga's office. 'If this were said by an opposition adherent in this office or anywhere else, I would have him locked up at once. Tell me, Nee Otu, there is a law called misprision. It carries a terrible sentence. Now, who has been planning the downfall of the government?'

'Kafu, I'm not afraid. I was born in this country and brought up here. I know the signs. They are there now.'

'But who are those that really want to do it?' Kafu asked rather calmly, smoothing his ragged hair with both hands.

'You should know.'

'You mean the army?'

'Of course!' Nee Otu said matter-of-factly and with strong emphasis as he sat up in his chair, his feet, naturally, not reaching the floor, and his trunk looking longer than that of a short man. 'We must start this business. I'm taking no chances.'

'Not so fast, Nee Otu,' Kafu interrupted him. 'Try to think it out. Democracy is a discipline, the army is a discipline. Discipline overthrowing discipline is not natural.'

'So what?'

'Once it starts there is no end to it. Those who start, no matter how well they perform in government, cannot tell what will happen next. They can only hope to do their best.'

'So?'

'Nee Otu, you don't want to listen?'

'Kafu, I'm a practical man. In business we say the best way to solve problems is to foresee them before they become problems. Kafu, if this government is toppled, you'll lose your house. They might set up impeachment committees which might recommend state seizure. Transfer it into the name of Odofo. It will secure it for . . .'

'Nee Otu, what has this government done?' Kafu interrupted him. He was agitated but defiant. He adjusted the knot of his tie.

'You should have asked me this long ago, Kofi. An overflow of

161

commitment. Don't you think so? I suppose the bridge to link the Industrial Area with Lartebiorkoshi and Link Road is still a coming thing, isn't it?'

'What do you mean?'

'I thought you had sharp ears.'

'You don't intend to be rude, do you?'

'I don't care a damn. We must start a haulage business. Big articulated trucks to cart goods and cocoa. What interest have you shown in your constituency?'

'But I tried to. . . .'

'What? Tragedy? That reminds me, Kofi. I've had the wall rebuilt. Let me tell Mr Vuga myself. These civil servants are unhappy these days. I must confess, Kofi, that though I had people like Vuga in mind when I urged salary cuts, it has really hurt many of them.'

Kafu called Mr Vuga. Meanwhile he told Nee Otu, 'Don't worry your head about them. They are obsequious but arrogant. Even if you spot those who are good, it's impossible to make full use of them and pay them for it. It's a really fossilised caste system that requires...'

Mr Vuga entered and Nee Otu said, 'I've had the wall rebuilt, Mr Vuga . How is life these days?'

Mr Vuga pretended he had not heard the question and asked Kafu, 'Is that all, sir?'

'Yes, Mr Vuga, you may go.'

When he left, Nee Otu told Kafu, 'I told you. These people are disgruntled.'

'They can go to hell,' Kafu said with a shrug. He was biting a fingernail, thinking, and said, 'Nee Otu, commitment means, I suppose, that all your personal priorities must go by default. It's hard. I believe. . . .'

'Kafu,' Nee Otu called, his short-fuse temper running out, 'I didn't come here to play with words. My contracting business is ruined. Your house is not furnished. Are you or are you not going in for the haulage business? Forget about being a minister.'

'Why not let me sleep over it? It will require a lot of capital.'

'And that's why I've come to you. Influence!' and Nee Otu flashed a fraternal smile.

'But I'm in debt, Nee Otu,' Kafu explained, still biting a fingernail. 'My total overdraft is thirty thousand. The bank will hesitate.'

'Yes, but if you are not prepared to come along with me, then you must put in a letter of introduction on my behalf. It should instruct, though!'

Kafu sighed and said, 'All right, I'll do that for you. The idea sounds attractive but let me think it over, as I've said.'

'Very good, Kofi,' Nee Otu said, 'I'll come for the letter tomorrow morning.'

That evening, Kafu took ten files home. He now had some a hundred and twenty there and work was being gravely hampered. He had therefore begun to work for a brief spell in the evenings if possible and for some two hours at dawn to clear the backlog. The next morning about seven-thirty while working on them in the study, he heard a frightening commotion in the house.

15

'She is unconscious,' Grace panted.

'Where's Danso? Have you checked her pulse?' Kafu asked.

'Yes, it's somewhat faint. Let's send for Dr Ayitiah.'

'No,' Kafu said firmly. 'We might as well use the time he'll take to get here to take her there. Who knows, she might require the facilities at Korle Bu. Now, Danso! Danso! Where are you?' Kafu shouted.

Danso climbed the steps by leaps and bounds. When he saw her state, he rushed down without being told, pulled out the car from the garage and in a few minutes they were at Korle Bu. The place was as congested as ever with the usual faceless mass who seemed to be irrevocably glued to the hard benches lined up in front of the consulting rooms, but there was a doctor at the casualty ward. Dr Ayitiah had left for Kumasi that morning.

The doctor who examined her was young, relaxed and completely and pleasantly unassuming. It was a welcome reception, Danso told his wife later, for in the past, he recalled glibly, and even now, there were many doctors who were so haughty, aloof, overbearing and awesome that the patient died several times before he recovered – if ever. This young doctor did not frown at Danso, the driver, for helping to bring her in. He greeted Danso and Grace instinctively in Fante and told them politely that they shouldn't worry, she would be all right. They should wait outside.

A few minutes later, a green uniformed nurse, smallish, meticulously neat, came for Grace. Gloria Opoku was being taken post-haste to the operation theatre of the maternity hospital. The complications arising out of an induced abortion would be taken care of there.

Grace felt Gloria's pregnancy was an act of disloyalty to her. Gloria had lost both parents while a child. Grace's parents adopted her, brought her up and gave her a smattering of education. Grace, who had always been fond of her and indeed regarded her more as a sister, had always asked her parents to let Gloria come and stay with her. Her parents had consistently refused her request because, as they explained, they couldn't be sure whether Grace could give her as much protection as they had provided so far without mishap. It was when Kafu became a minister that they relented. Grace therefore always kept an eye on her. The man she always suspected was Danso – for two reasons.

Kafu had told her during one of his relaxed moments at home, in the lounge, that drivers, especially chauffeurs, were no respecters of the status of women. They would have a try at any woman at all, and the more expensive the car, the higher they moved up, and if it worked, the deeper they sucked. Danso was talkative and she often saw him teasing or joking with Gloria. Sometimes he seemed simply playful, but she couldn't be sure whether Danso's playfulness was a well-laid-on ruse or whether it was part of the gregariousness to be expected of a peaceful household. All the same, Grace was always profoundly suspicious and she instituted all sorts of subtle checks, protection devices and surveillance techniques. Latterly, she was getting tired of it all, for it required eternal vigilance, and she had told Kafu that they should send her to the Abokobi Vocational Girls' School to specialise in roadside catering; but Kafu had put off a decision and she would not decide and act on her own initiative either. Now she thought, 'Danso has ruined my innocent girl. What will Dad and Mum say when they hear of this? How could Danso be so wicked? Why should he give her medicine? Suppose she had died? Danso is unreliable, dangerous. I'll tell Kafu to sack him at once!'

'Madam,' Danso said as they had just crossed the stinking Korle Lagoon, 'the doctor was a pleasant fellow. I wouldn't mind now being taken to Korle Bu if I were ill.'

Grace did not respond. When she rang up Vida Sese in the evening and narrated what happened in minute detail lasting forty-five minutes, she told her, 'When he prattled about the doctor being pleasant, I snubbed him and thought: you wicked, irresponsible, worthless, common driver, how dare you!'

Danso tried twice or thrice over again to say a few words, as he thought, to cheer up his mistress. When on each occasion there was no answer, he turned his head quickly to see if she was unwell, but she looked grim and hostile. He wondered why but, 'Who am I to bother her if she doesn't want to talk?' he thought to himself. So in silence they drove home. That evening Kafu dismissed him.

And that evening Kafu went to Odofo. Odofo was preparing the dinner which he had asked for. Odofo was not happy about the way he looked. 'What is it, darling?'

'H-mm, I don't know,' and he slumped into a chair and unknotted his tie. Odofo left the cooking to her maid and came to him. Kafu found her presence alone cheering; yes, cheering, or was it? Well, what he relished was that in her company he was protected; how or why, he couldn't tell. And need he? It was so nice and warm and he did not have to think it over. That evening Odofo looked more like his mother, his sister, his everything, maybe his original womb. She said maternally, 'You're not happy, why?'

'The problems are mounting.' He took the day's *Liberator* to re-read but it fell from his hand.

'What problems can there be, money?'

Kafu brightened up a bit and asked, childlike, 'Are you giving me some?'

'But that can't be what you call problems? I know how you look when it's money you want. What's on your mind, really?'

'Gloria Opoku, my maid, collapsed this morning. Grace took her to the hospital and it was found to be an induced abortion.'

'The fool! That is criminal!' Odofo cried.

'I'd even forgotten about that,' Kafu ran both hands over his hair thoughtfully. 'I might as well get in touch with Dr Ayitiah when he returns from Kumasi to intervene.'

'And who's the wicked man?'

'Grace says it's Kofi Danso, so I've sacked him.'

'Why, did Gloria tell her?'

'I don't know.'

'Did you ask him?'

'To sack a driver is not much trouble. Grace will nag if I don't. The problems are many and weighty. I've begun to solve them!'

'Solve them? Getting rid of them? Sweeping them under the carpet? Which, Kofi? I'm so very sorry for Danso. Why not recall him until the girl is discharged?'

'Grace won't let me, I tell you,' Kafu said helplessly.

'And what's the next problem?' she asked, kneeling affectionately before him and holding his knees with both hands.

'This coup that is rumoured, Odofo, do you believe in it?'

'It's hard to say, Kofi, but it's happened before. Why not assume it can happen again?'

'But what do they want? We've asked them to dinner, fed them well and promised them lucrative civilian jobs in addition to fat pensions, haven't we?'

'And you fired their imagination. Now they will dish out the jobs. So, granted it's going to happen, how are you prepared against it? What are you going to do?'

'Money.'

'Money?'

'Yes, money. I must garner a lot of it before the blow falls.'

'How much?'

'As much as possible. Just any amount, Odofo.'

'Galore? From Salamatu? Be reasonable, Kofi. What money

166

haven't I given you? Now Amega is pressing for his money. Amega is a tough smuggler. He doesn't take ordinary decisions. Have you no money at all to pay him, at least some of the amount?'

'I think I have.'

'Are you sure?'

'Of course, I am, dear. At least half the amount.'

'Where did you get it? Two thousand cedis? Where is it?'

'Mercy gave it to me for safe-keeping. It's in the house in my steel cabinet.'

'Casino winnings?'

'No! No, no! I swear! I tell you, I've stopped gambling.'

'All right, all right! I believe you, but why not let me keep it for you to be sure Amega gets it? I don't want him to trouble you. We'll give him this half and persuade him to drop the rest!'

'To hell with Amega! He can't do a damn thing. I should probably have him rounded up. Don't you think so? It'll cut a long story short, hei?'

'It will be pretty bad if you do. It'll be a debt that will be on your conscience. You'll give back his money to him, won't you?' And she gave him a kiss. Kafu sighed with relief. He felt happy and said, 'Don't worry, dear, I will.'

'And tell me, Kofi, what about your building? It could become state property, you know.'

'Ah, yes, that reminds me. Nee Otu has given me some advice, but I haven't had time to act on it!'

'Good old Ataa Nee, what did he advise?'

'You're still fond of him, why?'

'Kofi, you don't have to say such things. You still owe him a good deal of money and yet he didn't grudge you the advice. Tell me from your heart of hearts, which of us loves you more, me or your Sala? And mind you, I haven't said anything about Mercy!' She kissed him warmly and Kafu smiled. She knew he was appeased and asked, 'Did he ask you to transfer it to Mercy for safekeeping?'

'No.'

'Sala?'

'No.'

'To him?'

'No,' and Kafu smiled, held her hand affectionately and said, 'I'll tell you when the time comes.'

She withdrew her hand and asked, 'Which time, Kofi? Think of your wife and children. You must have somewhere to lay your head when you're old.'

'I understand. We'll talk it over again. At the moment so many things impinge on my mind.'

'Such as?' She took his hand now and squeezed it gently and caressed it.

'Some graduate teachers have sent a long memorandum written in intemperate language asking for salary hikes and promotion. It's their coarse language that annoys me.'

'Softly, Kofi, softly. A politician never gets angry. You can make me laugh, why not make them laugh? Just call them and make them laugh. You need not promise anything. Let them feel you care. That's all.'

'I love you. That's the difference. I hate pretence. When Baisi tried to play the fool with me, I hit him hard. Oh yes, I did. And he'll never be the same again. Odofo, I won't provoke them, I'll talk to them, politely but firmly, but I'll give no quarter, I don't want any crazy questions. The opposition may be behind it. To deepen the crisis, just that, I know. Beer, please!'

The beer was brought. He guzzled down half a glass in one go and smacked his lips. He belched before he could put his hand to his mouth, stretched his legs out, folded his arms and resumed, 'They know jolly well there is no money. We've spent heavily on the rural areas, we've over-imported goods and raised too many international loans. We've got to stop somewhere and husband whatever we have. You see, these people are always laying traps. They'll always be baiting you with requests. Government should do this, government should do that. Everything government must do. You offend one or two of them and they want to see you fall, never to rise again. One or two members of government misbehave and all the members of government must go to the gallows. It's all some sort of reckless political mischief that helps to preserve the instability of our political institutions. Some people thoroughly dislike a man for being a minister of state. Just that. Cowards! They don't want to try. When others win they think it's easy and want to pull the carpet from under them.' He took another big draught and emptied the glass. He put it down with a crash and asked, 'When is dinner?'

'It's ready, darling,' Odofo assured him, 'but have another beer while I wash. I had to listen to you, dear, to help you unburden yourself. Kofi, when you take a risk, you don't need to talk much about it, do you? In business, we don't approach problems by talking a lot. Why not give me ten minutes? The food is good, dear. I suppose you learned men are trained to talk. I like your voice, Kofi. Make sure you eat well tonight or don't expect me to cook specially for you.'

'Ah, the food smells good, I know.' He poured himself another glass and watched the table being laid.

The graduates whom Kafu invited to come and defend their memorandum on salary and promotion were three in number. They called themselves the 'Sacrificial Trio', since they were fighting not only in the name of all graduate teachers but for themselves, and hopefully for the benefit of all if they succeeded. They were Asare Antoban of Mayera Secondary School, a physics teacher; Bawa Apea of Kona Secondary School, a chemistry teacher; and Emilia Hansen of Elmina Girls' Secondary, a new ultra-modern school where each girl had a cubicle to herself, a modern mathematics teacher.

Bawa Apea, a thin, wiry man, bushy-headed but balding, with a penchant for championing cantankerous causes was the leader and spokesman. Asare Antoban was a gentle-looking fellow full of frustrations against the Church, the education administration and recently the state itself. He spoke so gently that one could not easily detect that he was in fact a man permanently angry against all constituted authority. Emilia, a tall, unmarried girl aged twenty-seven and a first-rate teacher, was famed for her short temper and brilliance in mathematics. She hated long explanations in argument and so restricted herself to cold essentials that her best admirers thought she lacked warmth. She was interested only in boys of her age who could help her get whatever she wanted for the moment, a government loan to buy a car or a fellowship to tour an overseas country for a couple of months. Otherwise she could not abide emotional attachments. Indeed, she found giving the body away uninspiring. And no man could stand her for more than a year and a half. Both Bawa Apea and

Asare Antoban had tried and withdrawn. There was no apparent ill feeling after the separations, though Antoban had lingering regrets, for he had computed the size of their joint income if they had married. He wondered whether he had not tried hard enough.

Kafu looked them closely in the face and asked, 'Who advised you to appeal to me? I'm not the person you should appeal to in the first instance.'

Bawa Apea: 'We advised ourselves. We got to know you were once a teacher and thought you could easily help us.'

Kafu: 'Easily? I'm not the only past teacher in government. Anyhow, your memo is full of cliché. It's coarse and turgid. Take this sentence – "Our salaries are so low that we have come to the conclusion that the government still believes in the idea that if you are a teacher you must be exploited on earth in order that God may reward you in heaven. The ministry must answer this question: how about those teachers who may not be fortunate enough to squeeze into heaven?" Now, Mr Bawa Apea, nowhere in your petition have you provided, for example, a comparative analysis of other emoluments in the public services to back up your case. This business of heaven and medals is calculated to insult, am I right?'

Emilia Hansen: 'We are not sure you are right. The people look down upon teachers, so the government does too; and this is reflected in our salaries. The government pays lip service only to science and maths. If they are easy, why don't we have many students taking them? Business is wiser; once you are a scientist or a mathematician they pay you well!'

Asare Antoban: 'And when the deceivers go round the universities towards the end of the academic year to recruit us to teach science or maths in the institutions, they promise glorious amenities. But when we get there, there is nothing. And then we hear the same sing-song every day – the department hasn't done this, the department won't do that, the department must be overhauled. Meanwhile these heads themselves aren't doing badly at all. When we threaten to quit, they tell us we can't leave teaching. We are tied.'

Kafu: 'Lady and gentlemen, you must have seen several people waiting in the lobby. I'm a busy man. Tell me, what do you want me, Kafu, to do?'

Bawa Apea: 'To intervene on our behalf.'

Kafu: 'Intervene in what?'

Bawa Apea: 'We want an additional fifteen cedis added to our monthly salary.'

Kafu: 'Impossible. The money isn't there. If you were the only three perhaps one would try but you are many. No, I won't. What's your next point?'

Bawa Apea: 'If we can't get the salary increase, can we be promoted earlier to make up for it?'

Kafu: 'How many years have you people done?'

Bawa Apea: 'We all finished university the same year and we've done four and a half years. Our contemporaries in the army, police service and business have been promoted once already.'

Kafu: 'So what? Lady and gentlemen, discipline. What is most needed in this country is discipline, especially self-discipline. Nobody forced you to be teachers. You knew you would have to do five years before you would be promoted. Now you've come here whining about not being pushed up before it's time. Look here, let me tell you. If you're here on your own volition, then both your style of request and demand for promotion are irresponsible. If someone advised you to come, then you're misguided. I was a teacher before, yes, I admit. But here I am today. Go and advise yourselves! Good morning and don't let me hear from you again. Silly bums!'

The 'Sacrificial Trio' rose dispiritedly and left Kafu's office. When they got outside and were about to enter their cars a bitter quarrel arose over Bawa Apea's performance, which Asare Antoban insisted fell below expectation. Finally, as they were going to part, Emilia Hansen said, 'I advised against our coming to him. Did you watch the way he looked at us? Did you note what he said? He said we were bums. I've never been so insulted since I grew up! Have I worked hard for nothing?'

'I feel sorry for this government,' Asare Antoban said, his face looking extremely calm. 'It must be overthrown.'

'I agree entirely with you. The army is always ready,' Apea Bawa said with a broad smile.

That evening when Kafu went home, he saw Gloria chatting playfully with Kafu Junior. She had been discharged in the after-

171

noon and looked good. Grace was in the kitchen with Afua Cudzoe, supervising the preparation of the evening meal. She had noticed that Kafu had somehow become fussy about the type and quality of his food. He would often use this as an excuse and refuse to eat at home for days. Whenever, therefore, he rang to say he was coming home for lunch or dinner, it was an event that required the personal attention of Grace.

Though he passed close to Gloria and Junior rushed to take his hand, he pretended he hadn't seen her and went to the kitchen and called Grace. They had hardly reached the lounge when he asked, 'What did she say? Who did it?'

'She said the pills were sent to her by Osofo.'

'Which Osofo is this? We've no Osofo in this area.'

'I mean Opia.'

'Which Opia, Grace? Can't you give a man's name or are you in league with her?'

'Kofi, I mean Opia Dan Sese.'

'Dan Sese? Ridiculous!' and he sat in a chair and held its arms with both hands. 'All right, assuming it was Dan Sese who gave her the pills, did she say he was responsible for the pregnancy? Didn't you say it was Kofi Danso? What did she say to that?'

'Kofi, for a long time she would not talk, except to insist it wasn't Kofi Danso; so I asked Afua to coax it out of her. I'm sorry; she says it's Opia.'

'Wh-a-a-t!' Kafu said, full-throated. 'How did Opia get at her and when did he bring her the pills? I can't see how.'

'I didn't ask about the first, but the other was when he attended the funeral of Dr Mills Blankson.'

'And she waited for so long before taking them?'

'She says that was Opia's inst uctions. Kofi,' Grace continued in an agitated voice, 'please recall Danso. I'm sorry. Let's have him back, shall we, Kofi?'

'Wh-a-a-t?' Kafu said again, as if someone would assure him that Opia had nothing to do with it. 'Opia? An elderly man? All the way from Cape Coast? Are you quite sure she said it was Opia?'

'Oh yes. She must know. Opia is too respectable to be mentioned lightly. You can ask her yourself.'

'Me? Never! Opia? Too bad! Grace, I've been thinking deeply

these days; why, I don't know but the thoughts just come and go. It occurred to me, you know, it just did, that one can never have friends. I suppose I've never known what friendship means. Now take Opia. Has he really been my friend or has he just found me useful? I believe all friendships are fragile arrangements founded on convenience and self-interest. I believe the same thing applies to marriage. Opia? I just don't know! Shall I ring him and damn him? Shall I have him removed? What do I do with Opia? Gracious Lord!' He threw back his head on the backrest of the chair and was lost in his thoughts; he would not talk.

Grace would not talk either and waited for some fifteen minutes as if she was watching the TV. She asked him, 'Kofi, we're taking back Kofi Danso, aren't we?'

'Of course not,' Kafu said with a sweep of the hand to indicate finality. 'Employment is not an electric lamp to be switched on and off just like that. We didn't tell him why he was dismissed. So he goes his way, we go ours. But Opia!' and he lapsed into thinking again.

Grace was unhappy with this answer so she waited again and then switched on to a different subject, hoping to use it as a softening preamble to resume her pleading for the driver's reinstatement. She said, 'Kofi, before you became a minister you promised to improve the facilities at Korle Bu. It's getting on to three years now.'

'There's a Minister for Health. That's his business. If those ailing fools don't want to pay economic fees for the treatment they receive there they mustn't blame anybody if they have to sit in the pathogenic and sun-drenched corridors of the consulting rooms. These things cost money and take time to provide. If you fall sick you'll have to go to 37. Why bother?' And he got up to go and wash.

Grace went to the study, sadly, to phone Vida, but when the call came through the first thing Vida told her was that her house was virtually complete and she must now find the resources to furnish it and let it. She had not been talking to her about it because she was determined to give her a pleasant surprise. Grace was so excited, she was so grateful, that she could not muster the courage to talk about Opia.

In fact Kafu had wanted to ask Gloria to leave the house. But

Salamatu and Odofo advised against it. He insisted to them however that the whole pregnancy affair and the dismissal of Kofi Danso rankled in his mind. He spent very little time in the house therefore, except during those days when he had to work at dawn on the accumulated files.

Kofi Danso had after his dismissal joined the Road Haulage Union when he became a driver of a petrol tanker. He had also become a full member of the NUP and he began to explain to his colleagues the way of ministers as he had seen and experienced them. So when the Union decided to go on strike unless the tanker yearly road-licence fee was reduced, he gave the strike action wholehearted support.

And in view of what happened to the *Morning Herald*, its editor and Mensah Quartey, and also because of the general state of disaffection among the people, the NUP gave the Union clandestine but powerful support. Indeed the strategy of the NUP was to use the strike to paralyse fuel distribution in the entire country. This would trigger off food shortages in the cities and other urban centres, cut off the rural areas, unhinge the economy and generate an instant national crisis. A catchy song was composed about Adjin Yeboah as a great national hero who had died mysteriously. Actually the NUP had let loose the rumour that he had in fact been poisoned by Odoi Hammond, but this was hushed by the Liberation Party Government.

It was arranged then that the strike would start in Sekondi where the huge petrol storage tanks were. Kumasi would easily pick it up, as usual, and Accra would collapse in no time. Sunyani and Ho would, instead of joining, be writing petitions in the hope of delaying the strike but that would be no great matter.

Somehow Nee Otu Lartey got to know about the plan, as he told Salamatu years later, through a contractor friend whose building scheudule would be disrupted if the strike succeeded. Nee Otu went straight to see Kafu in his office. Kafu was busy studying confidential intelligence reports on the potency of the planned strike. He had ordered that no one should be allowed to see him, but when Nee Otu Lartey insisted that his call was urgent and pressed that he should at least be allowed to speak to Kafu on the phone, Kafu caved in and Nee Otu appeared in his office. 'Nee Otu, why this insistence?' Kafu asked with a frown.

'Kofi, just be patient and listen. The impending strike is no joke.'

'I know. Anything else?'

'It is calculated to paralyse the whole country.'

'I'm aware of that.'

'And it will be a prelude to a coup.'

'Nonsense. I don't have this report. Don't come here and dabble in state security. Who will stage the coup? Do you know the group?'

'What I've been told is that it will be done by army officers. Some colonels, I hear.'

'This part sounds plausible. It's always the colonels who upset the apple-cart. What reasons will they give for intervening? Has anyone mentioned them?'

'I understand there are three: to restore law and order, to patch up the economy which is a shambles now, and to set up a national service corps to train civilians in the art of the sound management of lasting elective democratic institutions.'

'What's that? Repeat the third one!' Kafu cupped his ears; his face was taut with a mixture of anger, curiosity, anxiety and eagerness.

'Haven't I said it clearly and slowly enough? Here it goes: to set up a national service corps to train civilians in the art of the sound management of lasting elective democratic institutions. Clear?'

'This is the most high-sounding, highfalutin rubbishy idea I've heard in all my life! Nee Otu, it's all a red herring.' He paused, smiled bitterly and said, 'A farrago of empty words.' He paused, again, looked at the ceiling and said, 'Nee Otu, let me tell you something. Politics is like friendship. It's rooted in self-interest, which can be stated bluntly as the hankering after power, glory and maybe wealth. Damn it! It's about self-fulfilment in the grand style through the manipulation of men and institutions. The rest is nothing but pious declarations to conceal from the people this crazy overdose of ambition in the individual. You see what I mean? All they want is power, power, power! Nee Otu, you remember you told me about power being a prize to be won? You were right, except that power is not boring. Everybody wants to be a hero! We will stop them. We will frustrate

175

them. We will crush them! Whoever upsets the democratic process will never restore it firmly. How can it be stopped and restored at the same time? This is my country, I cannot watch it go astray! I will forestall this danger, Ataa Otu. I don't mind perishing in the process!' Kafu said. His fist crashed on the table to emphasise his determination. His eyes were bulging out and he looked dead earnest.

'Kafu, gently. Gently, please,' Nee Otu counselled. 'The Party executive is in full agreement with the government that what is happening is serious and must be contained at once. We agree that if you go to Sekondi, as was announced this morning, you must promise them free and frank discussions to resolve the issue. After all, it's a simple matter; you reduce the fee and put the difference on something else, say a pesewa more on cigarettes and ask the manufacturers to absorb it. But please talk to them like equals. These drivers have a wonderful sense of humour. Why not quote one of the aphorisms they write on their vehicles to explain the point: "One man, no chop". Government needs their contribution as well as everybody else's to provide for the country.'

'Boring, boring! Nee Otu, that's boring! These are tough times. Some graduates came here the other day. One of them, a woman, looked like smoked mudfish. I told them they were silly bums and they got up from their seats like people who had just risen from a drunken sleep. I see your point. If they're well behaved, it will be music all along; but if they're rude I'll give them a shake-up. Are you coming with me?'

'I can't. This is official.'

'Ah, well,' Kafu sighed, disappointed by Nee Otu's refusal. 'I'll take Mr Vuga then.'

'Mr Vuga? I don't advise it.'

'Why? He won't be doing the talking, will he?'

'I know, but he's bitter, disloyal and would like to see this government fall. Haven't you got a single loyal man here?'

'Vuga is bitter and disloyal, I know; but he'll never be loyal to any government, be it civilian or military. There are others here who are good. I think ... er ... W. W. Mensah, for example. He's sometimes uncomfortably frank but he's dedicated.'

'Then take him.'

'No, I can't. I think I was telling you something about this the other day. Vuga is the boss here. He sits tight on all of them. If I use Mensah where he thinks I should use him, he'll write in the confidential report on Mensah that Mensah curries favour with politicians, and that alone will label Mensah as unreliable for the rest of his career. This is the problem, Nee Otu.'

'But you're the government, and you can't even make full use of the manpower you have. Kafu, you're being inept. That's what you are. I wouldn't have this in my business.'

'Ataa Otu, be patient. We're looking into it.'

'Another way of saying you've shelved it. Heaven help us! All right, you take Vuga, but don't provoke the drivers. Petrol, gas oil, kerosene – all these are at stake. If they strike, you are out! The paralysis will finish you!'

'Not just yet, Ataa Nee, not just yet. Your pessimism is not the sign of a great soul. I've been wanting to talk to you about my house. Come and see me when I return.'

'I'll come on two conditions. You must give me definite instructions as to whose name should go on the plan, and the cash for furnishing it. Why do you find these difficult?'

'Be patient. I've made up my mind and I've got the money. There's no time now. You come on my return.'

Mr Vuga sat behind Kafu in a slightly oversized coat hastily put on at the last minute in the best tradition of permanent secretaries and department heads. His mouth was shut tight – to show he was noncommittal; his ears were highly cocked – to catch it all for the records. The Gyandu Park, Sekondi, was fully packed. It overflowed, not only with drivers but with landlords, market women, junior civil servants, middle-senior civil servants (the top, as usual, were afraid to be there) taxi drivers, private business employees, and a surprisingly balanced proportion of Liberation Party and NUP supporters, all of whom were disappointed with the government. Even the Methodist Primary School park was overflowing with an assortment of diverse people.

Kafu had charisma still and spoke forcefully. The crowd applauded unexpectedly when he said, 'Governments make mistakes but governments also correct mistakes. Tell us what you want and we will do it for you!' Then, continuing with verve, he said suddenly with a contemptuous broad sweep of the arm, 'You are all being misled by the opposition, and you will end up by making fools of yourselves!'

Driver one: 'What did he say? Foolish people?'

Driver two: 'Yes, he says we are fools.'

Driver three: 'What? We are fools? I hear he takes bribes.'

Driver one, shouting hard: 'How about the bribe money you've kept?'

There was an uproar. Kafu hadn't heard him well, so he asked Mr Vuga, with his hand covering the microphone, 'What did he say?'

'He says you've taken bribes and stashed them away in Swiss banks, sir,' Mr Vuga whispered with a charming smile into Kafu's ear, and Kafu's reaction was instantaneous. He cried into the microphone, 'Who is corrupt, me, or you who give money to policemen before they have time to check your licences? Liars! Unthinking rats!'

Driver one: 'Hei, what do I hear?'

Driver three: 'He says we stink like rats!'

Driver four: 'We do?'

Driver two, yelling: 'Kafu, your mother!'

Kafu: 'Silly idiots! If you play the fool, I'll order the police to use tear gas. Anyone who destroys property will be shot! Go home and talk this over with your wives!'

Driver one: 'We will strike. We are on strike!'

The crowd, roaring: 'Yes, we will all go on strike!'

Driver four, whispering to driver two: 'You see that policeman over there? Watch the way he looks at me. We clashed over a groundnut-seller.'

Driver two: 'Why? Those girls don't wash.'

Driver four: 'But this one was very good, you see. I tell you, if they are asked to shoot, he'll release bullets into my guts for nothing.'

Driver two: 'I bet he will. I don't like the way he smiles secretly at you, winks and then looks at his weapon. Let's go home. The strike is on anyway.'

Driver one to driver two: 'I beg your pardon?'

178

Driver two: 'I say we should all go home. The police will shoot. The strike is on!'

Driver one, shouting: 'Run home, everybody. The strike is on! The police will shoot!'

The crowd broke up in all directions, hurling insults and stones. The police fired warning shots into the air and threw tear-gas. As the crowd reached Essikadu, where most of them lived, they regrouped and formed a long procession, children, youth, elderly and all, chanting: 'Kafu, your mother!' 'Kafu, your father!' 'Kafu, send us to Nsawam!' 'Kafu, we will strike!' 'Kafu is a thief, Kafu is a thief!' 'Adzaa! Adzaa! Adzaa! Dzadzaa, dza! Dzadzaa! Dza, dza, dza, dza!' And the lissom teenage girls danced sinuously with the right thumb pressed against the fore-head and the left one pressed against the left buttock, the feet astride while their waists moved up and down in the hopping, lusty dance.

Meanwhile Amega and Ofori Nortey were working out the details. 'Are you sure the watchman is asleep between five and six in the morning? What's his name, by the way?'

'I tell you, I've watched for a whole week. He gets tired by that time, expects no trouble and sleeps heavily. Odofo once said his name was Bukari.'

'Very well,' Amega decided. 'We'll climb over the wall by the road and tiptoe quickly into the office. We'll only frighten him. We'll get the money.'

'How much will you give me?'

'Five cedis.'

'Not enough.'

'Ten?'

'No, twenty.'

'Right, Ofori, considering the reconnoitring you've done; twenty, settled.'

'Je-e-sus Christ, this is my chance!' and Ofori Nortey knelt and prayed while Amega watched him, amused.

It was the first dawn after the declaration of the country-wide strike. Kafu was busy in his study at home, compiling a memor-andum on it for the consideration of his colleagues. Suddenly he saw Amega and Ofori Nortey standing before him. He had the unsafe habit of opening the door leading outside to let in the fresh, cool morning breeze, which he enjoyed as it often helped to clear his hangovers. When he saw them, he asked, 'How did you enter the house?'

'Bukari let us in,' Amega replied.

'And what does this man want here? I'll call the police,' and he rose as he said so.

'No, you won't.' Quickly and expertly Amega held his hands behind him and trussed him. Ofori Nortey then stood in front of him and drew a pocket-knife. He asked, 'Kafu, where is Amega's money?'

'Amega, I've told you I'll pay.'

'You have, but I want it right now. It's in the steel cabinet. All you have to do is to open it and give the two thousand at least to me. If I get it there'll be no trouble!'

'Good heavens, how do you know I have money there? Did the girls tell you?'

'Kafu, Mr Minister,' Ofori Nortey said with the grin Kafu hated, waving the pocket-knife close to his nose, 'we started with those girls before you did. This is my day, so says the Lord!'

'You realise the criminal enormity of your conduct?'

'Kafu, I'm prepared to go to jail so long as I get my own back on you. The army will release me anyway. They will overthrow you sooner or later. I can wait for them there. Where is Amega's money, you swine?'

Kafu so despised Ofori Nortey that he would not answer. Ofori Nortey, tired of being despised, said, 'No answer? And how did your wife enjoy reading my letter on your sexual exploits, pleasure haunts and political incompetence?'

'Wh-a-a-a-t!' Kafu cried painfully, 'so you wrote that letter, Conception Contractor?'

'*Onye s-mling* wha-a-a-t! Do you know you're a foolish man?'

'A-a-ah! When will you Gas stop being crude and vulgar?' Kafu asked. He found the insult disgusting.

'Ha-a-a! Come on! See, *hwe*!' and Ofori Nortey held Kafu's right ear and pulled it. '*Mma nnye rough kwaraa, atseaa?* When you and that whore, Mercy, went to the Hotel Continental and spent hundreds of Amega's money in one night, when you ate that excellent dinner of lobsters and whatnot while I had to sit outside on the verandah watching you, Mr Minister and Lady

Mensah, through the curtains, hungry and on a mini bottle of beer; when you went down to gamble and I had to go and sit in the park opposite the hotel shivering with cold till the small hours of the morning, that is refinement, isn't it? *Heie, kooyoo!*

Kafu was furious. He struggled to break loose but couldn't. He asked, 'Who sent you to spy on us?'

'Odofo, of course. I spy for all your women. They pay well. I tell you, you know English for nothing. Why give me the name Conception Contractor? Amega, did I conceive the plan to come here?'

'No, but why worry about that? Kafu, where is my money?'

'Amega, am I a contractor working for you?'

'Ofori, I say this is not important. Let's get the money quickly and go away.'

'Kafu, this is your first and last chance to give me a name. Have you ever been to a military camp?'

Kafu did not answer.

'They will shave your head, pull your trousers down and kick you in the arse; they'll make you hop, jump and roll on the ground. How about all that, my friend?'

Kafu did not respond. He was stunned, helpless.

'And you will see blood!' So saying, he gave Kafu a little sharp cut on the forehead with the pocket-knife.

Kafu gave a cry of fright when he felt and saw the blood trickling down. Amega was furious, but before he could reprimand his friend he saw the arrow being aimed and cried, 'Ofori, dodge!' Down went Ofori Nortey. The arrow missed him and pierced deep into the chest of Kafu. He lurched forward. Amega let go and he fell on the arrow.

When Bukari saw he had mortally wounded his master, he wailed, 'Allah, kai! Allah, kai! Wallai!' He rushed forward into the study, holding an arrow, and fell on it. As it pierced deep into him, dying, he embraced Kafu.

Just then footsteps were heard. An army officer carrying a gun shouted, 'Hold it! Hands up! Move to the wall. Drop that knife! Sergeant, search them!'

'We are not burglars, sir. We have shed no blood. The minister was our friend and...' Amega pleaded but he was cut short. 'Shut up! You may have shed no blood, but there has been blood-letting all right. Look at that knife, and the cut on the forehead. We are taking over power, but we hate bloodshed. You have been a nuisance. The people will not understand. They'll think we killed him!'

'Sergeant, ring for an ambulance. Then go to the front door, ring the bell and bring the wife.'

When Grace saw the dead bodies, she gave a piercing cry and collapsed in the arms of the officer.